Elmer E. Barton

City of Minneapolis

A review of her growing industries and commercial development,

historical and descriptive

Elmer E. Barton

City of Minneapolis
A review of her growing industries and commercial development, historical and descriptive

ISBN/EAN: 9783337293710

Printed in Europe, USA, Canada, Australia, Japan

Cover: Foto ©Andreas Hilbeck / pixelio.de

More available books at **www.hansebooks.com**

RESOURCES OF MINNESOTA

SERIES.

City of Minneapolis.

A Review of Her Growing Industries and Commercial Development,
Historical and Descriptive.
Prominent Places and People and Local Reminiscences. For use of
the Buyer, Shipper, Tourist, Investor and all others interested
in the growth and advancement of our City.

FOR POPULAR DISTRIBUTION.
ILLUSTRATED.

MINNEAPOLIS.
E. E. BARTON, PUBLISHER.
1889.

THE CITY OF MINNEAPOLIS.

A GREAT MODERN CITY.

Minneapolis stands conspicuous among the great cities of the modern world. She has grown more rapidly than Chicago and more substantially than San Francisco. Her commerce vies with her manufactures in extent and importance. The metropolis of the great Northwest, the receiving and distributing center of an empire capable of infinite development, she presents the picture of a complex modern municipality possessing all the instruments of production, all the facilities of distribution, and all the intellectual and moral agencies characteristic of American civilization. She is proud of her matchless record and conscious of her present greatness and her still greater future. She is the wonder of the continent, and the queen among American cities.

ADVANTAGES OF SITUATION.

Minneapolis is the county seat of Hennepin County, Minn. The city is situated on both sides of the Mississippi River, at the Falls of St. Anthony, and is about eight miles west of St. Paul, as the crow flies, and ten miles by water.

The Falls of St. Anthony, those stupendous engines of nature, lie in the very heart of the city, inviting man to utilize freely their gigantic power and almost limitless possibilities. These falls were discovered by Louis Hennepin and Picard du Guy, in October, 1680, and Hennepin named them in honor of his patron saint—Anthony of Padua. Lieut. Zebulon M. Pike, on his first expedition up the river, in 1805, visited the falls, and in 1817 Major Stephen L. Long, a distinguished engineer, ascended the river on another government expedition, and in his report described the falls as the most interesting and magnificent he had ever witnessed.

The present site of Minneapolis was principally within the reservation lands of Fort Snelling, which the government acquired by the treaty which Lieut. Pike made with the Sioux band of Indians, for the United States. During the time the Fort Snelling buildings were being erected, Major Russell, the quarter-master, in order to procure the necessary sawed lumber for their completion, had built a small saw-mill on the site of the great flour-milling district. After the treaty with the Indians in 1837, all the lands east of the Mississippi River were ceded to the United States, and preparations were at once made by certain parties to secure claims on the east bank of the river, so as to command the water-power. One of these was Franklin Steele, a Pennsylvanian of revolutionary ancestry, who, during the year of the treaty, visited the falls, made a careful survey of the land on the east side, and selected the spot he desired, but could not occupy or claim it, as no occupation or claim would be valid until after the ratification of the treaty.

BEGINNINGS OF CIVILIZATION.

The first real estate transfer in Minneapolis occurred in 1838. In the fall of that year there were only two houses at the falls, one being the old government house, built in 1822, on the west side, and the other Mr. Steele's log house, which stood on the east side, and for some years after this, all the real estate operations were confined to St. Anthony, on the east side of the river. In 1845, the settlement contained a scattered and mixed population of about fifty persons, but the most valuable portion of the property, including the falls, belonged to Mr. Steele. In 1847 Charles Wilson arrived and settled in St. Anthony, and in June, of the same year, came Wm. A. Cheever, and through his negotiation a sale was made by Steele to Caleb Cushing and other eastern parties, of his nine-tenths interest in the water-power of the falls, they paying him $12,000 therefor. Thus, then, was formed the nucleus of the world's great milling center.

The first sale of these lands by the government was made in 1843, when Mr. Steele perfected his title to his property by paying therefor $1.25 per acre. During this year Mr. Steele completed his little saw-mill, it being the first one erected on the east side of the river. During 1847 the settlement increased materially in population, many settlers coming and bringing their families. R. P. Russell and C. A. Tuttle laid the foundation of mercantile greatness by starting a small store in Steele's log-house. In 1848 Mr. Cheever platted his town on the tract below the University, which is still frequently referred to as "Cheevertown." The first marriage in St. Anthony was in October, 1848, being that of Mr. and Mrs. Russell, and the first death occurred during the same year.

EARLY GROWTH.

When the Territory of Minnesota was organized, in 1849, Minneapolis made a struggle to secure the capital. It failed, but through a compromise, got the State University. In the same year a school was established, also a post-office, and a social or reading society was formed, they having gathered together a library of two hundred volumes, and the survey of the town was made by ex-Governor Marshall; and the real growth of St. Anthony dates from this year. Mr. Steele, during this year, started up two more saws, and Anson Northrup began the erection of the St. Charles Hotel. Rev. E. D. Neill conducted services every other Sabbath in the school-house, and lectures were occasionally given there. The Territory of Minnesota having just been organized, Judge Meeker held the first court in the house of Mr. Bean, on the west bank of the river, opposite the falls, the old government saw-mill being utilized for the accommodation of the grand jury, of which Mr. Steele was foreman.

During the first session of the Territorial Legislature, in 1849, a bill was introduced by the St. Paul members to fix the capital permanently at St. Paul, which was strongly opposed by ex-Governor Marshall, who was then a resident of St. Anthony and a representative from that district. He strongly urged that St. Anthony should be the Capital, and urged its removal to that place. It was a drawn battle—the bill was defeated, but no place definitely settled upon.

In the spring of 1849 Willoughby and Powers commenced running the first stage ever run in Minnesota, between the villages of St. Paul and St. Anthony. In 1850 a church was built, and on May 1, 1851, the first newspaper, *The St. Anthony Express*, made its appearance, Judge Isaac Atwater being its first editor. Up to 1847, the river could not be crossed except by fording at low water on the ledge below Nicollet Island, but a ferry was established near the site of the present suspension bridge, from the island to the west bank. In 1854, a company, with Franklin Steele and H. T. Wells as principals, undertook the erection of a suspension bridge, and completed it in eight months, and on July 1, 1855, the first team was driven across it. It was a great event and a marvel of enterprise for those days. This structure was the first bridge built across the Mississippi River at any point.

ON NICOLLET AVENUE.

HOW THE NAME WAS CHOSEN.

By 1855 there had been developed a very respectable little village, though devoid of any striking features to distinguish it from scores of others scattered over the great Northwest. As has been stated, the original city was on the east side of the river, and was not Minneapolis, but St. Anthony. It was incorporated in 1860. After the building of the bridge the march of civilization began on the west bank of the river. There had been a straggling colony here for years. A school house had been opened in

8 RESOURCES OF MINNESOTA.

1852 and a church was soon established. The name first given to this new settlement was "West St. Anthony"—sometimes it was called ".All Saints"; then "Lowell" was adopted, but subsequently changed to "Albion." Finally, some one, in the *St. Anthony Express*, suggested "Minneapolis," a compound of the Sioux *Minne* (water) and the Greek *polis* (city). This name was adopted, and soon became familiar to all. In 1853 the reservation was reduced, so that what is now known as Minnehaha Creek became its northern limit. A land office was opened in 1854, and, by an act of Congress, the land was permitted to be taken by actual holders on pre-emption claims at the government price. Claims were proved up in the spring of 1855, from which time the local record titles of Minneapolis run. Minneapolis, which had been informally organized in 1856, was incorporated under a town government in 1858, and as a city in 1867. In 1872 St. Anthony was incorporated in the Minneapolis municipality, and together they have progressed with rapid strides to the proud position of the present metropolis.

To comprehend the magnitude of the growth of Minneapolis is almost beyond the power of the average imagination. Some idea of the present proportions and importance of the city may be arrived at when it is learned from the census reports that eight years ago there were but fifty-seven cities in the world with over 200,000 inhabitants, and only ten in the United States containing that population. In 1870 this country contained 107 cities larger than Minneapolis; in ten years this city outstripped seventy-two of these, and stood in a list of thirty-seven cities boasting of 46,000 inhabitants and over. This was considered a marvelous record and astonished the world. But the most wonderful epoch of the city was yet to come. During the twenty years after Minneapolis had reached 5,000—1860 to 1880—the city doubled its population once in every five years and two months. During the ensuing seven years, however, it doubled population twice, or once every three and one-half years. At the end of this period the city contained 160,000 inhabitants, and to-day, with a population of 215,000, stands fourteenth on the list of American cities, and ranges between eighth and tenth in commercial importance, according to clearing house reports. The early growth of the city was slow and ordinary; that of the decade, 1870–1880, was extraordinary; that of the last six or seven years has been simply phenomenal. The figures themselves tell the story in the briefest space:

Population in 1845,	50
Population in 1850,	2,200
Population in 1860,	5,826
Population in 1865,	8,101
Population in 1870,	13,066
Population in 1875,	32,493
Population in 1880,	46,887
Population in 1885,	129,200
Population in 1887,	170,000
Population in 1888,	200,000
Population in 1889,	215,000

But the increase of population of a city, unless attended by a proportionate increase of those branches of industry and commerce which reach out to the surrounding country and gather in the wealth, therewith enriching and solidifying it, is no true criterion of desirable growth and normal development. Have the other essentials and progress been present or wanting? The best evidence on this subject is the following compact showing of comparative figures for three years:

THREE YEARS OF PROGRESS.

Building improvements, 1886,	·	·	$11,474,402
" " 1887,		12,214,723
" " 1888,		15,033,071
Manufactured products, 1886,		$62,537,000
" " 1887,		66,836,570
" " 1888,		83,075,071
Wholesale trade, 1886,		$155,341,000
" " 1887,		156,650,000
" " 1888,		187,696,000
Bushels wheat received, 1886,		35,066,100
" " " 1887,		45,504,480
" " " 1888,		45,827,015
Bank clearings, 1886,		$164,301,748
" " 1887,		194,777,533
" " 1888,		215,995,500
Value flour output, 1886,		$24,504,922
" " " 1887,		27,211,638
" " " 1888,		36,278,889
Feet lumber sawed, 1886,		267,196,579
" " " 1887,		220,822,974
" " " 1888,		337,663,301
Assessed valuation, 1886,		$100,872,498
" " 1887,	·	107,000,000
" " 1888,		127,069,756

FOUR GREAT ADVANTAGES:

There are four things that have contributed conspicuously to the marvelous speed with which Minneapolis has attained metropolitan dimensions and influence, and that will insure her growth in the future. These are: her unequaled water-power; the marvelous richness and rapid development of her tributary territory; her admirable railway facilities, and the brightness, energy and ambition of her population.

PROTECTING THE FALLS.

The water power of St. Anthony Falls has not only been a source of wealth to the city, but an important factor in her rapid development, and the destruction of the falls and loss of their vast water power would have been a most serious calamity to the community. On several occasions there has been good cause for the great alarm experienced by the people, for the natural disintegration of the river bed—hastened by numerous mechanical enterprises intended to share the water power, such as dams, canals and the like—presaged the total destruction of the Falls in the near future, unless immediate steps were taken for their preservation. In 1868, workmen excavating a tunnel from Hennepin Island, under the island and beneath the river, to reach Nicollet Island, were driven out by a great leak. A cave in the roof followed, which let in vast quantities of debris, and threatened irreparable mischief. The rock bed of the river extends only twelve hundred feet above the Falls, and at the time of the settlement of St. Anthony had cut its way nearly through the limestone layer. The temporary expedients resorted to were continued, renewed and changed, until, by an appropriation from the National Government, municipal and private contributions, elaborate plans were carried out for the permanent preservation of the falls. The companies controlling the water power had made, in 1886, an attempt to protect the crest of the falls by a timber apron, but this was carried off in the spring following. A survey made in 1869, by Major G. K. Warren, called the attention of the general Government to the necessity of arresting the destruction that was impending. James B. Francis, of Massachusetts, was summoned to examine the falls and to report as to the best means of averting the catastrophe. He recommended, as a protection against a further recession of the crest, a substantial apron of timber, with heavy crib work at the bottom; for the dangerous tunnel—that it be filled for four hundred feet with a puddle of clay and gravel; and against the third great danger—the action of frost—that the limestone be kept flooded by low dams. No time was lost in carrying out energetic measures. The national appropriation of $550,000, was expended, beginning with 1875, and ending March, 1879. A concrete wall

EXPOSITION BUILDING.

was laid in the bed of sandstone beneath the limestone ledge, six feet in thickness at the base, four feet at the top, and forty feet in height, for the entire width of the river; thus effectually preventing further damage. The amount contributed by the citizens of Minneapolis was $334,000. The whole cost of an improvement thus buried out of sight, was nearly a million of dollars, but by it the 130,000 horse-power of the falls was preserved, and with it the hope of a great and growing community.

RICH TRIBUTARY TERRITORY.

The richness and rapid development of the tributary territory of Minneapolis were noted as the second cause of her phenomenal growth. During the last decade the population of Minnesota increased

100 per cent. and it has doubled since 1880. Dakota increased 450 per cent. from 1870 to 1880, and 500 per cent. from 1880 to 1888. Montana has increased about 600 per cent. in eighteen years. The increase of Minneapolis for the same ten years was 350 per cent. and up to 1888 about 500 per cent. One of the strongest points in favor of Minneapolis' continued growth and solidity is the vast amount of tributary country yet undeveloped and unoccupied. In the big Souix reservation in Dakota lie 13,000,-000 acres, a tract nearly as large as the states of New Jersey, Delaware and Maryland combined, and to which we have direct railway communication, simply awaiting an agreement between the government and the Sioux Indians, and outside of this tract in the same territory are 36,000,000 acres unsurveyed. Minnesota has yet 7,000,000 acres of unsurveyed land, Montana 41,000,000, and Washington Territory 44,000,000. It is estimated that at the present rate all the public lands will be occupied in twenty years.

RAILWAY FACILITIES.

The railway facilities of Minneapolis are a very marked factor in its development.

It would be almost impossible to take a map and draw a line for a new railway running out of Minneapolis which should find for itself a belt of country not already fully occupied by existing roads, so numerous are the radiating tracks of steel which center in the Flour City. To Chicago there are six competing lines, each with its own tributary territory for local traffic and each bringing a long list of towns and cities into business relations with Minneapolis. To St. Louis there are three lines. Southern and Southwestern Minnesota are penetrated by the roads of three different companies. Five lines of road stretch out to the Red River Valley. Three run to Duluth. One reaches out eastward to the Sault Ste. Marie for a new and short route to the tide-water of the Atlantic.

Minneapolis and St. Paul form a double-headed railway center. Roads that strike St. Paul first continue on to Minneapolis, and in like manner those that first enter Minneapolis end at St. Paul. For this reason it is impossible to discuss the railway interests of one of the Twin Cities separately from those of the other. No company can afford to neglect the trade of either city, whatever may be its local attachments or prejudices.

The total length of railway lines centering in Minneapolis and St. Paul is 32,756 miles. The trains of all the Eastern roads are made up at Minneapolis, that being their terminus.

While the railway facilities are the chief factor in transportation facilities furnished for the business of Minneapolis, each year increases the influence of water routes in freight tariffs.

It is but a brief period since the St. Paul & Duluth and Lake Superior, with the meager freight capacity then navigating the route from Duluth to Buffalo, was the only water route to the seaboard. The capacity of the railroad and marine was limited, and the water route by way of Duluth cut but a small figure in the commerce of the Northwest. The situation is entirely changed. The St. Paul & Duluth Railroad, under new management, is in first-class condition, with ample rolling stock and facilities for an immense traffic, which, by refusing to join in combinations with all-rail lines to the East, they have received. The Northern Pacific has a through line to Duluth. The Chicago, St. Paul & Omaha have lines to West Superior and Duluth at the head of Lake Superior and one reaching Ashland. Washburn and Bayfield, important shipping ports on the south shore of the lake.

The St. Paul, Minneapolis & Manitoba, during last year, constructed a road direct to West Superior and Duluth. The Wisconsin Central line also reaches Ashland. This gives five lines, operated by independent companies, direct to the head of Lake Superior. Early in 1888 the "Soo" road became a competitor for the lake and railroad traffic, via Gladstone near the foot of Lake Michigan, and was successful in securing a large traffic. The Lehigh Valley Company put on a line of fine iron steamers, erected flour, coal and ore docks. The shipments of flour from this city by the "Soo" road in 1888, the first year after it was completed, were 931,502 barrels, most of which went by the Gladstone route. In addition to the routes above named, quite large shipments of flour are made via Green Bay and Milwaukee, thence by lake. By these railroad and water routes forty per cent. of the flour shipped East during the year has reached its destination without traveling around the head of Lake Michigan, and this at a saving of five to ten cents per barrel in freight, and reaching its destination about as soon as by all-rail. The entire supply for the Northwest of Pennsylvania and Ohio coal comes over these lines, as does much of the merchandise for the twin cities and the Northwest.

ST. PAUL, MINNEAPOLIS & MANITOBA.

The St. Paul, Minneapolis & Manitoba Railroad is the largest wheat-carrying railroad in the world. The Company delivered at Minneapolis 21,435,800 bushels of wheat during the year 1888 of the 44,552,730 delivered in the city, besides that delivered at Minneapolis; several million bushels were delivered by this road at Duluth, Superior, and to country milling points. As a distri-

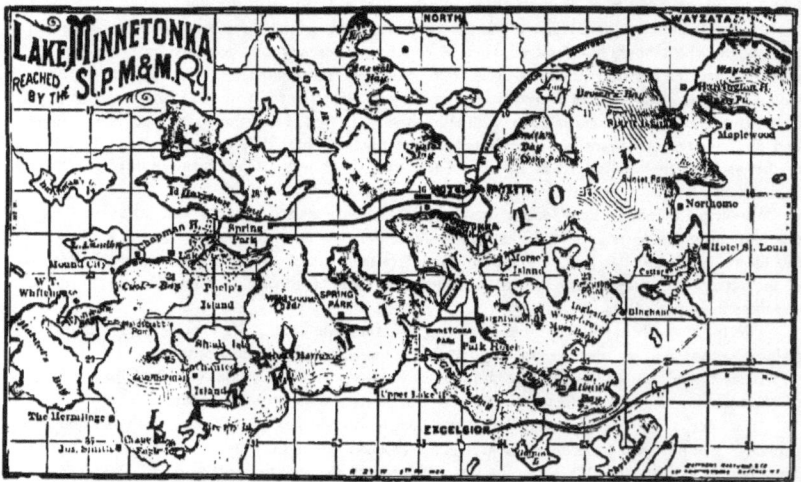

butor of merchandise, machinery and many other articles, the Manitoba stands at the head of the list of the systems entering at Minneapolis. This Company has four distinct lines penetrating all sections of Central and Northwestern Minnesota and Dakota, extending through Northern Montana to the great mining districts of Helena and Butte. The Company has a four-track line from Minneapolis to St. Paul and a double track to Lake Minnetonka. During last year the Company extended its road from Hinckley to Duluth and Superior, and is made an important factor in the flour and other carrying trade via Lake Superior. The Company have added to their mileage during 1888, 313 miles of road, and its total mileage is 3,025. The Manitoba is a competitor for the Montana and Manitoba and all Pacific Coast business, and traverses a new territory in Northern Dakota and Montana of great agricultural facilities, which will no doubt draw to it a large immigration, until it is occupied and improved, when it will have an immense local traffic as the older lines of the Company have to-day.

THE NORTHWESTERN LINE.

Among the lines centering in Minneapolis not one has contributed more largely, or is of greater importance to the commercial prosperity of the city, than "The Northwestern Line"—Chicago,

St. Paul, Minneapolis & Omaha Railway. It is the short line between Minneapolis, Chicago, Sioux City and Omaha. It reaches out to the wheat fields of Dakota and the rich corn belt of Iowa and Nebraska, and brings their products to our mills and warehouses. From the Michigan Peninsula, from the Great Lake Superior towns of Duluth, Superior, Ashland, Bayfield and Washburn; its lines reach, via the St. Paul & Minneapolis, to the many new and thriving towns of Nebraska, to the Black Hills, and the wonderful coal and oil fields of Wyoming, and through its connections to St. Joseph, Lincoln, Kansas City, Denver and the far West. "The Northwestern Line" comprises over 7,000 miles of road, and is being constantly extended.

CHICAGO, BURLINGTON & NORTHERN.

It is a little more than two years since the Chicago, Burlington & Northern Railway entered Minneapolis as a competing line for its trade and that of the Northwest. As a result of the liberal policy pursued by the management, the road has enjoyed a large patronage, its flour shipments, particularly, dwarfing those of other lines. The equipment is first-class, both passenger and freight. The Chicago, Burlington & Quincy, of which system the Chicago, Burlington & Northern is a part, is the only company running over its own tracks to Chicago, Peoria, Quincy, St. Louis, Kansas City, St. Joseph, Omaha, Cheyenne and Denver. As a passenger road it has no superiors and few equals in the country. The mileage of the Chicago, Burlington & Quincy system is 6,261.

CHICAGO, MILWAUKEE & ST. PAUL.

What is now the Chicago, Milwaukee & St. Paul was the first company to open railroad communication between Minneapolis and Lake Michigan, or any of the outside world. The company has now three distinct trunk lines entering the city from the Southwest, West and East, each of which have branches from the trunk lines, so that the entire West, Southwest and Southeast can be reached on the rails owned and operated by this company. Their lines traverse the Central and Southern portions of Minnesota and Dakota, reaching to a junction with the Northern Pacific at Fargo. The entire State of Iowa is reached by this line. The company has 5,678 miles of road under its management. This road was selected by the postoffice department as the line over which the fast mail between the Northwest and the seaboard should be transported, and on the expiration of the first contract the service had been so satisfactory that a new contract was awarded to them. The headquarters of all the lines of this company west of the Mississippi River and north of the Chicago & Council Bluffs division are located in this city, with its car and repair shops.

CHICAGO, ROCK ISLAND & PACIFIC.

The Chicago, Rock Island & Pacific, of which the Minneapolis & St. Louis forms the Minneapolis connection, is another great railway tributary to Minneapolis. The Chicago & Rock Island Company was the first to open railroad communication between Chicago and the navigable waters of the Mississippi River in 1852, when their line reached LaSalle, connecting with the streams to St. Louis, and later with the main river at Rock Island. Until the completion of the Chicago & Alton Railroad, nearly the entire travel between the Mississippi Valley and the lakes was over this route to Chicago. The bulk of the merchandise for St. Louis and the Missouri Valley was transported over this line. The Rock Island Company has from its organization been a company of progress. It was the first to construct a railroad bridge over the Mississippi River, third to connect Minnesota and the Northwest with Chicago, and has ever been in the front ranks in all reforms and improvements in its service. Its lines pass through the most thickly settled portions of Illinois, Iowa, Minnesota and other States and Territories, and it has always had a full share of the travel to and from this city. It operates 4,516 miles of road.

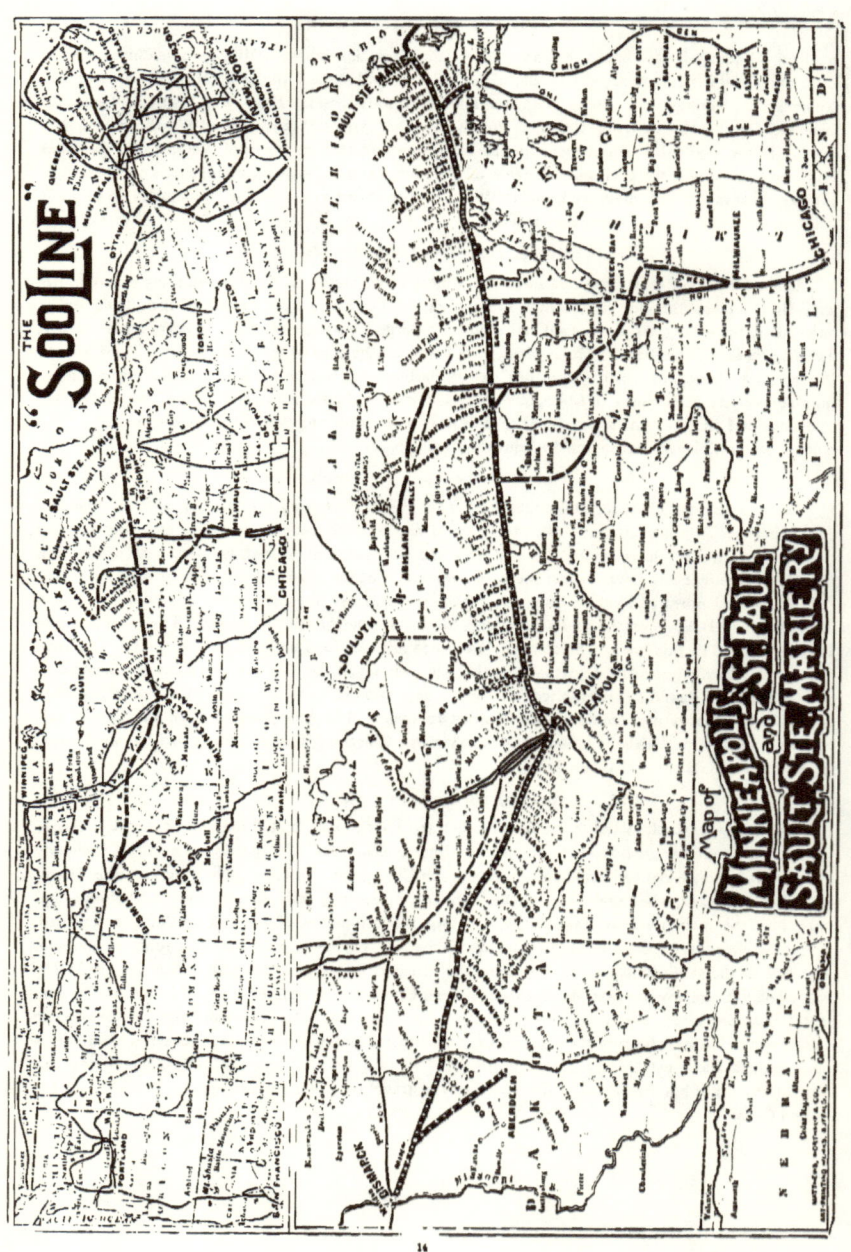

The Minneapolis, St. Paul & Sault Ste. Marie Railway, less formally known as the Soo line, has entered the field as a competitive road to the Atlantic seaboard during the past year. It has filled the gap left open by the closing of navigation each year in keeping Minneapolis freed from the domineering despotism of Chicago and her lines of railway. Since the completion of the Soo, Minneapolis has enjoyed lower freight rates to and from the Atlantic coast than ever before known for any length of time. Various schemes have been attempted to cripple its usefulness, even by congressional action, but so far without avail. The Soo will be the great route between the East and the Northwest, and the business will be done directly with Minneapolis, and not by the way of Chicago. The road is an outlet not only for Minneapolis, but for the great Northwest. The Soo Line operates about eight hundred miles of road. Its main lines run from Minneapolis and St. Paul to Sault Ste. Marie, Mich., and from Minneapolis to Boynton, D. T. It also has a line graded from Aberdeen to Bismarck, D. T. The Canadian Pacific Railway Company having completed its line from Sudbury Junction to Sault Ste. Marie, makes in connection with this line a through line from Minneapolis and St. Paul to Montreal, Boston, New York and all New England points. In addition to this, traffic arrangements have been made via the Straits of Mackinaw that open to Minneapolis and St. Paul via the Soo Line by means of the Grand Rapids & Indiana Railway all points in Michigan and on the so-called Vanderbilt system of railway. The shops of this company are in Minneapolis.

NORTHERN PACIFIC.

The Northern Pacific Railroad has within the past year constructed a road from the United States boundary to Winnipeg. This gives an independent line to Manitoba's capitol, owned and operated by this company. Previous to this construction, the Canadian Pacific controlled the railroad traffic between the British Northwest and the States. It was but natural that the Canadian company should pursue a policy that would divert trade from the States and over their own lines to the Eastern provinces and the seaboard. The Northern Pacific gives to shippers and travelers the choice of route which is beneficial to both the States and the Province of Manitoba. The country traversed by its lines is rich in agricultural and mineral values, and the scenery from the Yellowstone Park to the Pacific coast at Portland or Tacoma is grand, and full of interest at all points. The traffic on the Northern Pacific to and from this city is steadily and rapidly increasing. The total mileage owned, leased and operated, is 3,499.

CHICAGO, ST. PAUL & KANSAS CITY.

The Chicago St. Paul & Kansas City Railroad owns and leases eight hundred and fifty miles of road. The line passes through a rich and finely developed country in Minnesota, Iowa and Illinois.

WISCONSIN CENTRAL.

The Wisconsin Central is one of the six trunk lines centering Minneapolis and connecting with the trunk lines east from Chicago. It also connects with Lake Superior at Ashland, and with Lake Michigan at Green Bay and Milwaukee. It is one of the short lines to Chicago; when completed it will have the finest terminal buildings of any road entering that city, located in the business center of the city. The line runs through the best portion of the State of Wisconsin; its northern terminus is Ashland, where it connects with the Northern Pacific, with which it has recently effected close traffic relations. The northern half of the line passes through a country rich in mineral and timber resources; the remainder through a fertile and well developed agricultural country. On the line are many thriving cities and towns, furnishing a large local business. It is a successful competitor for through traffic at Minneapolis and St. Paul, obtaining a fair percentage of the business. It now operates seven hundred and seventy-five miles of road.

ST. PAUL & DULUTH.

Having been the first road to open up an outlet via Lake Superior for the products of the Minneapolis mills, and having demonstrated time and time again that it could at all times be relied upon to protect the vital interests of the "Twin Cities" in the very important matter of transportation as against combinations in other directions, it is not strange that the St. Paul & Duluth Railroad should be considered as one of the important factors in the growth and development of Minneapolis. This line has 231 miles of track, and is equipped and operated in first-class style.

THE EASTERN RAILWAY.

The Eastern Railway, of Minnesota, has this year constructed and put in operation a line of railway from Hinckley, Minn., to West Superior, Wis. At Hinckley it connects with the Manitoba Railway for St. Cloud. The Eastern also has trackage rights, by lease, over the Manitoba, so that it runs its own trains between Hinckley and Minneapolis, thus operating a through line between this city and the head of Lake Superior. The Eastern has surveyed an independent line from Hinckley to Minneapolis, which, when constructed, will save much distance and afford low grade and a curvature so light as to be most inconsiderable, there being only one curve of more than one degree. The Eastern is establishing an independent line of steamers on the lakes to run in connection with the road, thus furnishing Minneapolis with a route independent not only of the Chicago railway lines, but of the old line transit companies on the lakes as well.

A GREAT MANUFACTURING CENTER.

Minneapolis gained its first start as a manufacturing city, and its first large manufacturing industry, after that of lumber, was the production of flour. For many years it has been the greatest flour-manufacturing center in the world, and in this capacity has wrested from Milwaukee and Chicago the title of the greatest primary wheat market in the world, receiving and itself consuming in the manufacture of flour a larger quantity of wheat per day than those cities ever handled to supply their speculative and forwarding trade.

HISTORY OF MINNEAPOLIS FLOUR PRODUCTION.

The old government mill, which in 1822, with its single stone, ground out a little flour for the garrison at Fort Snelling, stood on the present site of the Sidle-Fletcher-Holmes Co.'s mill in the heart of the West Side milling district. In 1851 a small grist-mill was started on the East Side, adjoining the Steele saw-mill. In 1854 Rollins, Eastman & Upton built the Island mill, with five runs of stone. It was a three-story mill, and its size 40x60 feet, and grain for it had to be brought from Iowa, there not being sufficient for it in this section. The St. Anthony Water Power Company was incorporated in 1856, with a capital stock of $160,000, and subsequently increased to $640,000. This company controls the water power on the East Side. The Minneapolis Mill Company was also incorporated in 1856 for the improvement of the West Side power. They sell or lease the water power to the operators of the mills. In 1858 a Mr. Getchell sent some flour East on consignment, to liquidate certain claims against him, which proved so acceptable that an order for one hundred barrels of Minneapolis flour was soon received, and other orders followed. Ex-Governor C. C. Washburn, of Wisconsin, played a conspicuous part in the development of the milling industry, and introduced in his mills here all the improved machinery, and the adoption of the roller process was mainly through his instrumentality. The middlings purifiers were perfected, and the Pillsburys subsequently had them in their mills, and soon all the mills had all the improved processes. The "new process flour" raised the price of flour known as such $3 or $4 per barrel, and in 1878 it was introduced into the English markets.

In 1878 there was a fearful explosion in the Washburn "A" mill, which shook the city like the shock of an earthquake, and was felt even in St. Paul. The mill was discovered to be on fire, and fourteen men were burned with it. Five other mills caught fire and were destroyed at the same time. The property destroyed was valued at $1,000,000. The mills have since been rebuilt. There was another terrific explosion in December, 1881, when four mills and a cotton mill were destroyed by fire, and several persons lost their lives. The property destroyed was about half a million dollars in value. The mills were subsequently rebuilt.

There are now twenty-three mills in Minneapolis, which have an aggregate daily capacity of 36,150 barrels. The Pillsbury "A" is located on the East Side, and is the largest mill in the world. It has turned out 7,000 barrels of flour in twenty-four hours. The Washburn "A" mill, located on the West Side, is second in size; has a capacity of 4,000 barrels daily, and when fully equipped can turn out 6,000 barrels. The total product of the Minneapolis mills during last year was 7,056,680 barrels. The exports for the year were 2,197,640 barrels.

THE LUMBER BUSINESS.

Lumbering was the parent manufacturing industry in Minneapolis. Before the United States soldiers located on the Fort Snelling reservation (in which was then included the present site of Minne-

RESIDENCE OF E. A. MERRILL, FROM "SATURDAY SPECTATOR."

apolis) had learned to utilize the power going to waste in the Falls of St. Anthony, for grinding in a crude and unsatisfactory way the cereal products of the country, they had put it to use in sawing the white pine logs, found within two days' journey on the banks of the Mississippi. A dozen years ago no one alluded to Minneapolis as the "Flour City," and everybody—particularly in St. Paul—called her the "Sawdust City," and tinged the phrase with something of sarcastic derision. But while other manufacturing industries have since somewhat dwarfed in comparison the manufacture of lumber, until it is apt to be given a secondary position in the count of the elements of greatness possessed by Minneapolis, the fact remains that it has shown steady and rapid increase, and that more lumber is manufactured in Minneapolis than at any other point west of Lake Michigan. The total cut for 1888 was 337,663,301 feet of lumber, 106,736,150 shingles, and 74,016,479 pieces of lath.

But the future of Minneapolis as a lumbering city does not promise to rest alone upon her capacity to convert saw-logs into salable lumber. For the past five years one-third as much lumber has been shipped into Minneapolis as has been shipped out of her lumber yards. Her own enormous local consumption, and her growing importance as a lumber market, has made all this necessary and natural. The development of the railroad system centering here, which is now going on, promises to make more marked each year the growth of this purely wholesaling of lumber. Chicago, which has been for years the great distributing point for white pine, recognizes it, and has proof of it in the annually diminishing amount of lumber put forth. The railroads are rapidly revolutionizing the whole course of shipment of lumber from the pine regions of Minnesota, Wisconsin and Michigan, to the prairies of Southern Minnesota, Iowa, Missouri, Kansas, Nebraska and Dakota. The region in Northern Wisconsin, which seven years ago was an almost unbroken forest, has from year to year been penetrated by feeders and main lines of great railroad corporations. The lumber manufacturer, who, five years ago, used to find it cheaper to float his lumber down some stream to Lake Michigan, and ship it by schooner to Chicago, now loads the product of his mill on a car at the very tail of his mill, and ships it by the most direct route West and Southwest. When the Wisconsin Central first penetrated the great pine region of Wisconsin, with its line to Ashland, a saw-mill sprang up every five or six miles along the line. These mills flourished under the stimulus of the boom of 1882-3, but it did not take their owners long to find out when competition began to be sharp, and margins of profit small, that they couldn't ship lumber East, to Milwaukee and Chicago, and compete with lumber already moving West, from across the lake. Nor did it take long for the shrewd men in control of the road to discover that this chief industry along their line must pave an outlet West. This outlet has found a terminus in Minneapolis, and the lumber from the Wisconsin Central mills finds a market and a point of distribution here. The Minneapolis, Sault Ste. Marie & Atlantic Railroad is playing an even more important part in determining the movement of the product of the Wisconsin saw-mills. It is true that the supply of white pine will not last forever, but while it lasts, it will bring money into the coffers of Minneapolis.

THE PACKING INDUSTRY.

To these two great industries of Minneapolis, in which she leads the world, there is now to be added another, which will appear second in the list in point of importance—beef and pork packing. There were handled last year at the Minnesota transfer 87,000 Montana cattle alone. This year there will be many more handled. Minneapolis is the natural gateway to the seaboard for the cattle and hogs of Montana, Nebraska, Northern Iowa, Dakota and Minnesota. The Soo line is 400 miles shorter than any Chicago line, and it is but natural that it should become the great thoroughfare for the dressed beef and hog products en route to Liverpool and European ports and the East. The Minneapolis stock yards are located at the great vantage point—the junction of the Soo and the Northern Pacific, Kansas City and Manitoba railroads. As the loads of cattle arrive from the West in a direct air line, they will be unloaded, dressed and packed in refrigerator cars, sent out over the Soo road in refrigerator cars bound for Montreal; there to be packed in refrigerator steamers bound for Liverpool, or else landed in Boston and New England points by this short line of the continent. The importance of this great enterprise as pertaining to the future of Minneapolis can scarcely be estimated; for as the business develops it will carry with it increased population and be of lasting benefit to all lines of trade.

OTHER MANUFACTURING INDUSTRIES.

The manufacturing industries of Minneapolis do not end with those of flour and lumber and packing. Articles innumerable are produced in the city, in both large and small quantities. There are thirty-nine foundries and machine shops, threshing machine and agricultural implement works, woolen mills, glass factories, paper mills, knitting works, railroad car manufacturing and repair shops, and hundreds of minor industries of which the public know little. The following list of the principal articles manufactured, and the number of establishments, will give the reader an idea of the magnitude of the manufacturing interests of Minneapolis:

MANUFACTURES.	No.	MANUFACTURES.	No.
Agricultural implements and dealers	35	Meerschaum pipes	1
Architects' supplies	1	Nails	1
Artificial stone	2	Overalls	1
Ash frame and door	1	Oars	2
Antique metal workers	1	Neckyokes	1
Art furniture	3	Paper	1
Asbestine stone	1	Pop	2
Awning and tent	5	Pottery	2
Bags	2	Printing ink	1
Barrels	16	Ranges	1
Baskets	1	Sash, doors, blinds	16

SYNDICATE BLOCK " NICOLLET AVE. MINNEAPOLIS

Baking powder	3	Saw mills	15
Billiard balls	1	Shingles	8
Blank books	5	Shirts	8
Blacksmiths	91	Silver plated ware	1
Boots	1	Spring bed	3
Bolts	1	Starch	2
Boots and shoes	8	Stoves	2
Boxes	3	Suspenders	2
Breweries	6	Threshing machines	1
Brick (and dealers)	20	Tanneries	2
Brick wheelbarrows	1	Tallow	2
Brush	1	Tiling	4
Butter	4	Trunks	2
Butter tubs	1	Washboard	1
Band Cutter	1	Water tank	1
Billiard tables	3	Wine works	1

MANUFACTURES.	No.	MANUFACTURES.	No.
Boilers	7	Woolen goods	4
Books and stationery	2	Yeast cake	2
Bottles	1	Show cases	1
Brackets	8	Soap	2
Brass founders	5	Steam heat apparatus	2
Brick mold	3	Stencils	6
Brooms	3	Straw board	2
Bustles	4	Terra cotta	4
Cooking stoves	1	Tinware	2
Cork	1	Trucks	1
Crackers	3	Violins	1
Carriages (and dealers)	24	Vinegar	2
Chairs	1	Whips	1
Cigar boxes	1	Woodenware	2
Confectionery	4	Wagons	19
Cooper shops	16	Washing machines	2
Cornice	6	Wrought iron pipe	3
Corsets	2	Models	6
Caskets	4	Meat packing	4
Chemist	1	Mineral water	2
Cider	1	Monuments	6
Cigars	28	Picture frames	2
Clothing	53	Plumbers	32
Distillery	1	Preserves	4
Egg cases	1	Plated ware	3
Engines	1	Lithographing	2
Electrotyping	2	Lard	5
Flour mill mach	1	Lamps	2
Files	1	Medicine	4
Furniture	9	Mill picks	1
Gloves	4	Oil filter	1
Glue	4	Oil	1
Grain cleaners	1	Perfumery	1
Guns	1	Pipes	3
Harvesters	1	Paint	3
Hoopskirts	1	Pickles	1
Hair works	6	Plows	4
Iron works	10	Portable car	1
Fence	4	Pressed bricks	2
Flour mills	28	Radiators	2
Foundries and machine shops	16	Rye flour	1
Ginger ale	2	Sausage	2
Hard soap	2	School furniture	3
Harness (and dealers)	30	Reflectors	1
Heaters	1	Refrigerators	9
Horse collars	1	Pumps	2
Jewelry	6	Rubber goods	1
Knit goods	1	Starch	1
Optician	1		
Total			584

The small establishments are rapidly growing, and within another decade, as in the history of every growing city, the present seemingly unimportant factories will have acquired wealth and proportions which would, without the acquisition of new institutions, hold the city foremost in rank as a manufacturing center.

The demand for goods manufactured in Minneapolis is rapidly increasing, orders coming in from Michigan to the Pacific Coast, and from Southern Iowa to the Northwest Territory. Factories from all over the country are removing to Minneapolis, attracted hither by the rapidly developing contiguous country and the increasing facilities possessed by Minneapolis for distributing goods throughout the Northwest.

AN INTERESTING TABLE.

The following table, carefully compiled by the Minneapolis Tribune, shows the capital invested in Minneapolis industries, on the 1st of January, 1889, and the value of the products put out by each in the year 1888:

MANUFACTORIES.	CAPITAL.	VALUE OF PRODUCTS.	MANUFACTORIES.	CAPITAL.	VALUE OF PRODUCTS.
Agricultural implements and mill furnishing machinery............	$1,520,000	$1,787,000	Harness, trunks and belting......	130,000	285,000
Awnings, tents, etc.................	25,000	70,000	Hoopskirts, bustles, etc..........	47,000	77,000
Bags, paper boxes, etc.............	300,000	250,000	Jewelry and plating...............		64,000
Barrels............	325,000	1,149,028	Lock and gunsmithing.............		25,000
Blacksmithing...................		275,000	Millinery and hair goods,.		50,000
Boots and shoes (manufacturers)	519,000	790,000	Opticians' supplies		10,000
Boots and shoes (custom work)..	130,000	300,000	Packing meats....................	150,000	560,000
Bottling		725,000	Paints and oils...................	395,000	415,000
Breweries	700,000	385,000	Paper	50,000	50,000
Brick, stone paving and cornice..	50,000	875,000	Patterns and models..............	10,000	35,000
Brooms and brushes	15,000	50,000	Potteries and tinware.............	50,000	380,000
Carpentering and building.......		10,000,000	Picture frames...........	20,000	50,000
Cars and repairing.................		3,000,000	Planing mills.....................	1,200,000	3,750,000
Cigars..	120,000	485,000	Plumbing.........................		280,000
Clothing (tailoring)................	200,000	1,158,000	Printing and lithographing........		1,697,684
Clothing, women's................		180,000	Saw mills........................	2,500,000	4,826,000
Clothing, overalls, etc.............	300,000	500,000	Sash, door and blinds.............	1,175,000	2,585,000
Confectioners	215,000	823,000	Soda and mineral waters		65,000
Creameries...........................	30,000	154,000	Sewer pipe.......................		75,000
Electrotyping and printers' supplies		25,000	Soaps and perfumery..............	135,000	100,000
			Show cases and office fixtures...		175,000
Feed mills........................		500,000	Spices and starch................	75,000	200,000
Flouring mills	7,000,000	36,278,889	Suspenders.......................	17,000	28,000
Fence works...................	116,000	197,000	Stencils......	15,000	76,000
Foundries and machine shops...	1,143,200	2,610,500	Underwear, shirts, knit goods..	200,000	142,000
Furniture, mattresses and carpets..............................	300,000	1,317,000	Wagons and carriages..............		500,000
			Woodenware, boxes..............	75,000	380,000
Glass bottles, stained glass.......	80,000	150,000	Woolen mills.....................	250,000	600,000
Gloves, moccasins and furriers...		145,000	Wheelwrighting		75,000
Granite and marble works.......	57,000	230,000	Miscellaneous		1,500,000
Hardware, stoves and heaters...	225,000	210,000	Total		$83,075,101

The magnitude of these figures is indicated by the fact that the census of 1880 shows only seven cities with a manufacturing product in excess of this enormous output, and the smallest of these, Cincinnati, contained a population of 225,000.

AN ENCOURAGING PROSPECT.

What Minneapolis has acquired in past years in manufacturing institutions is in a fair way of being dwarfed by the achievements of the future. No particular effort has been made to attract industries to the city in the past three years, yet, as noted above, manufacturers have located here in large numbers. But the citizens of Minneapolis are aggressive, and have lately turned their attention to soliciting the

presence of reputable companies desiring to locate in the Northwest, and while they are opposed to buying a plant to get it, a well-meaning manufacturer will generally find a reasonable amount of capital ready to invest in an industry with a future before it and ability back of it.

THE JOBBING TRADE.

Like many other features of the growth of Minneapolis, that of her jobbing trade has been phenomenal. The rapidity of its development has had no parallel in any city anywhere in the Northwest, Middlewest or Southwest. This is a broad assertion, but it rests on the solid foundation of facts. Twenty years ago there were no jobbing interests here, whatever; to-day they reach far up into the millions. Quite a number of the leading jobbers in this city began their career as retail dealers, and from jobbing in a small way from their retail stocks developed into full-fledged wholesalers. The rapid development of the country tributary to this market afforded excellent opportunities and supplied an irresistable stimulus to their ambition. As a man must eat first of all, the jobbing grocery trade is usually the first to develop in a new city. Dry-goods, hardware, boots and shoes, drugs and other staple lines follow. The pioneer grocery houses were originally retail establishments. There were no railroads, and the routine of their retail trade was occasionally broken by the sale of a job lot of merchandise to a country dealer, who would drive into market, load up his wagon or ox-cart, and make his way back to some little settlement on the almost uninhabited prairie, or in the solitary depths of the backwoods. Naturally the territory was very limited, but with the building of the railroads and the opening up of the country incident thereto this was steadily extended. It was not long until the commercial traveler became a necessity, and the grocery jobbers began to send these trade scouts and skirmishers into the country. With their proverbial persistence, the gripsackers steadily pushed to the front, not only following up the new railroads, but pressing on in advance of them. At first the grip-carrier could only go a comparatively short distance by rail, and would have to complete his circuit by stage, enduring in winter, with far less glory, hardships sometimes almost as severe as those suffered by North Pole seekers. Thus, in a few years, the volume of business in this line has increased from a few thousands of dollars to millions. All of the fine wholesale grocery houses have ample capital and are in a highly prosperous condition. One firm is conceded to be the largest in this line in the Northwest. Goods are shipped in great quantities to the Manitoba line on the north, to Montana and Washington on the west, and hundreds of miles towards other points of the compass. Every year shows a material increase in the total sales.

There were no dry goods business in Minneapolis until 1874. Retail dealers now and then sold a jag of goods to a country merchant, but this was not regarded as of any consequence. The pioneer house opened up when the population of the city did not exceed 1,800. Two skirmishers were then sent out. The Manitoba line at that time extended only as far north as Alexandria. Travelers, on reaching that point, made their way by stage to Fergus Falls, Breckenridge and other towns. When the Northern Pacific line was being developed, the grip-sack men would travel by rail as far west as Moorhead, and thence up and down the Red River Valley by stage. Traveling salesmen in those days would meet fort-

traders at Bismarck, and run down the Mississippi River to Standing Rock and Yankton. The multiplicity of railroad routes has changed all this. It is safe to put the total of sales in the dry goods line for the first year at less than $100,000. But the dry goods jobbers were aggressive and pushed their trade into new territory in advance of the railroads, until now goods are sold throughout Minnesota, Da-

ARTESIAN WELL, CENTRAL PARK.

kota and Montana, in Washington, the Black Hills country, Iowa, Wisconsin and even Nebraska. The leading firms occupy mammoth buildings, and do business that mounts into the millions annually.

This city has long been the recognized headquarters in the Northwest for agricultural machinery and implements. It has held the lead for years. The only rival in the whole country has been Kansas City. While the latter place has been gradually losing ground Minneapolis has been more rapidly gaining. This has taken place in spite of adverse circumstances, which make our growth all the more surprising and gratifying. To-day Minneapolis, both in the volume of business done and in the confidence of those whose confidence is most to be valued, stands without a peer as a center for the handling of agricultural machinery.

The fruit shippers of the original markets look upon Minneapolis as a phenomenon. No place in the North or West, outside of Chicago, can compare with Minneapolis in this line. She has been a heavy consumer, and besides has been a point of distribution for a large territory.

The jobbing in dressed meat received a strong impetus during 1888. The prospect of a considerable development of the packing industry here seems to have aroused the outside concerns to aggressive efforts. Two large packing firms have established important branches and have done a fine business. There has been little if any falling off in the sales of the agencies formerly established, so that the business, as a whole, has been noticeably increased.   The North American Beef Company began business last fall.   This is a branch of the George H. Hammond Company, which has houses at Chicago, Omaha, Detroit and New York.   The Kansas City Dressed Beef Company, whose goods have hitherto been handled at this point by other parties, placed a branch here early in the year and have done a thriving business.

The popularity of the Northern-grown seeds has resulted in an increase in that line of business of from forty to fifty per cent.   There is a strength in seeds grown in this latitude that commends them to planters all over the country.   They are accordingly preferred to all others, and are rapidly attaining a reputation.   The territory covered by Minneapolis seed men is much wider than it was a year ago, and its growth is but beginning.

FIGURES WHICH SPEAK VOLUMES.

The entire jobbing business of Minneapolis is on a healthy basis, and is rapidly developing.   The following table shows the amount of business transacted in each line during last year.   The showing made is an admirable one, the more especially so if allowance be made for the fact that last year was a presidential year:

Agricultural machinery, wagons, carriages, etc....	$13,950,000
Billiard tables and barroom supplies....	76,000
Boots and shoes....	1,290,000
Cigars and tobacco....	1,230,000
Confections, crackers, biscuits, etc....	600,000
Crockery and queensware....	120,000
Curtains and draperies....	150,000
Dry goods....	3,000,000
Drugs and paints....	950,000
Fruits....	2,500,000
Fuel....	3,234,300
Furniture....	175,000
General produce....	4,000,000
Glass and glaziers' supplies....	750,000
Groceries....	10,380,000
Hay, feed and millstuffs....	765,000
Hardware, iron and stoves....	2,450,000
Hats, caps, millinery and furs....	400,000
Hides and pelts....	1,250,000
Imported woolens....	30,000
Jewelry....	300,000
Lime, cement, brick and building material....	600,000
Lumber....	1,304,500
Live stock....	500,000
Machinery, engines and machinists' supplies....	645,000
Mantles, tiles and interior decorations....	175,000
Meat and provisions....	2,285,000
Musical instruments....	450,000
Oysters, fish, etc....	500,000
Oils....	1,000,000
Paper, paper bags, etc....	715,000
Plumbers' supplies and heating apparatus....	500,000
Printing materials....	200,000
Rubber goods, belting, leather, etc....	450,000
Saddlery, harness, etc....	300,000

Sash, doors and blinds...	600,000
Seeds..	350,000
Sporting goods...	90,000
Surgical and optical instruments, barbers' and photographers' supplies.........	100,000
Trunks..	40,000
Wines and liquors...	800,000
Total..	$56,204,800
Total for 1887...	56,669,250
Increase.....................................	$2,535,550

To make a complete showing of the business, which may be properly called wholesale, but all of which cannot be strictly put in with the exclusive jobbing trade, it will be necessary to add the goods jobbed by manufacturers and the grain commission business, both of which are really jobbing. The grain commission business this year has been enormous. It was last year, according to Secretary Sturtevant, of the Chamber of Commerce, double what it was a year ago. The transactions in the Chamber for the last three months of last year averaged over $1,000,000 per day. The rest of the year the amount was also much larger than usual. The lumber, of course, has been jobbed by the manufacturers and mill men, and is as much entitled to be

AT THE SOLDIERS' HOME.

considered in the jobbing total as groceries or dry goods. The same is true of the flour business. The grand total is given in the following summary :

Exclusive jobbing...	$ 59,204,800
Manufactured goods jobbed..	21,435,000
Grain commission..	125,000,000
Flour..	38,000,000
Lumber, shingles and lath..	5,125,000
Total..	$248,704,800
Total for 1887...	193,136,682
Increase...	$ 55,628,118

FREIGHT TRAFFIC STATISTICS.

Counting the various branches, there are twenty-seven or twenty-eight railroads running into and out of Minneapolis. The amount of traffic done by them in a year is something enormous, and each year greatly swells the fast-growing figures which represent this traffic. The amount of business done at this point, however, has been very large, as will appear from the following table, showing the number of cars received and shipped from December 1, '87, to December 1, '88:

	Receipts. Cars.	Shipments. Cars.
December	15,667	11,227
January	9,152	7,411
February	13,240	10,559
March	12,532	12,109
April	13,507	13,045
May	10,972	14,535
June	11,578	13,027
July	12,331	13,750
August	11,012	15,310
September	15,977	15,056
October	21,799	16,609
November	20,734	12,953
Total	167,481	155,583

LUMBER EXCHANGE, FROM "SATURDAY SPECTATOR."

The receipts were less than the receipts for 1887, from January to January, by 4,900 cars, but the shipments are 1,700 cars larger.

The principal items which go to make business for the roads here are wheat, corn, oats, flour, lumber, millstuffs, fruit, machinery, coal, etc. It will be interesting to note that the merchandise received during the period from December, 1887, to December, 1888, weighed 339,200,696 pounds, which is 9,000,000 pounds more than the weight of the receipts for the year 1887. The shipments of merchandise for the year ending December 1, 1888, weighed 349,376,620 pounds, being an excess of 8,000,000 pounds over those for 1887. Thus, while the number of car loads was less, the amount of merchandise was greater this year than last.

The following summary shows in brief the traffic in some of the most important items for the year 1888.

	Receipts.	Shipments.
Merchandise, lbs,	339,200,696	349,376,620
Machinery, lbs,	35,755,644	37,633,510
Wheat, bu,	44,725,050	11,170,960
Corn, bu,	940,400	219,000
Oats, bu,	1,695,600	
Barley, bu,	369,000	519,000
Flax seed, bu,	464,500	124,000
Flour, bbls,	64,962	6,973,265
Millstuffs, tons,	6,991	214,009
Fruits, lbs	47,091,071	
Coal, tons,	295,304	25,815
Lumber, feet,	43,420,000	172,630,000

The most popular, best patronized, handsomest, safest, and the finest ventilated Theatre in the Northwest. Seating capacity, 2000.

THE BANKS OF MINNEAPOLIS.

Banks are the commercial barometers of the nation. When the business is good in the commercial world the banks are prosperous and bankers happy. But let a depression come and money cease circulating, then the banks, first of all, suffer from the stringency. The year 1888, generally speaking, was a bearish year throughout the country. In the East, particularly, new enterprises were scarce, and business in commercial lines dull, and in consequence the clearances fell off heavily from the previous year. But not so in Minneapolis. The commercial and manufacturing center of the most productive section of the country was very little affected by the stringency which prevailed elsewhere. While even the clearings of St. Paul showed a decrease of more than twelve per cent., Minneapolis clearings and banking business continued to grow in keeping with the development of the city and surrounding country.

There are in the city six National, fifteen State, and two savings banks. Following is a list showing the paid-in capital of each bank in 1887 and 1888:

	Paid in capital.	
	1888.	1887.
Bank of Minneapolis...	$150,000	$150,000
Citizens' Bank of Minneapolis..	250,000	250,000
City..	300,000	300,000
Commercial Bank of Minneapolis...	200,000	200,000
Farmers' and Mechanics' Savings Bank......................................	....	....
Farmers' and Merchants' State..	40,000	25,000
First National..	1,000,000	1,000,000
Flour City National..	500,000	400,000
Franklin State..	50,000	50,000
Garland Bank..	75,000	....
German-American..	100,000	....
Hennepin County Savings Bank...	100,000	100,000
Irish-American...	100,000	....
National Bank of Commerce..	750,000	750,000
Nicollet National..	500,000	500,000
Northwest National...	1,000,000	1,000,000
People's..	100,000	100,000
Scandia...	100,000	50,000
Security..	1,000,000	1,000,000
Standard...	25,000	25,000
State Bank...	75,000	75,000
Swedish-American..	100,000	....
Union National...	500,000	500,000
Total...	$7,015,000	$6,375,000

The deposits of these banks, according to their statements in October, 1888, aggregated $13,706,249, and their loans and discounts, $22,822,007.

The aggregate yearly clearings of the Minneapolis banks, since 1882, are as follows:

1883	$ 87,508,000.00
1884	110,556,619.00
1885	125,477,478.00
1886	164,301,748.00
1887	194,777,533.38
1888	215,895,359.56

With this presentation it is proper to advert briefly to the growth of the Minneapolis banking business. Snyder & McFarlane established the first bank in 1858, which was followed by one bank per year for the next twenty-four years: but they kept dropping down like pins in a bowling alley. Of the twenty-five banks established during this period only ten survived in 1881, representing an aggregate capital of **$2,550,000.** They were the First National, started in 1857 by Sidle, Wolford & Co.; Bank of Minneapolis, 1867; City Bank, 1869; Hennepin County Savings Bank, 1870; Northwestern National, 1872; Farmers' and Mechanics' Savings Bank, 1874; Citizens' Bank, 1876; Security Bank, 1878; Commercial Bank, 1880.

FINANCIAL CORPORATIONS.

Minneapolis is becoming the headquarters for heavy financial institutions in the West. During the year ending August 1, 1888, more companies were incorporated than in any three previous years, an increase in number of nearly 70 per cent. The list of new corporations organized during the past year

TURN HALL.

includes mining companies to a great extent, manufacturing institutions, commercial and railroad companies. They numbered 143, with capital approximating **$77,000,000,** while the corporations existing prior to August 31, 1887, numbered but **222.** Each of these institutions is of great benefit to the city. A large number, being composed of residents of other cities, serve to bring in outside capital and interest Eastern business in Minneapolis. The mining companies are, as a general thing, owners of new but promising mines of all classes, located as far east as the iron fields of Michigan, as far south as the gold, silver, mica and tin deposits of the Black Hills in Dakota, and as far west as the rich mineral fields of Montana. In time, they will give employment to large clerical forces at headquarters, and thus augment the population of Minneapolis.

THE RETAIL TRADE.

The Flour City has always been ambitious as a retail town. Her broad avenues, level streets, and elegant and commodious business blocks have tended to stimulate this ambition and its consequent fulfillment. Long before the city had assumed a metropolitan aspect, or presumed to compete with St. Paul in the jobbing field, she was recognized as the more promising retail mart of the twins. This is probably characteristic of industrial cities, and has been fully justified by the outcome. Nicollet Avenue is known from one end of creation to the other, and our merchants are famed for their progressiveness and enterprise. We surpass any other city in the Northwest in number and variety, as well as the dimensions and completeness of our retail establishments, and we leave all our rivals so far in the rear as to render comparisons unnecessary.

Minneapolis is the undoubted favorite with the country trade, whose "shopping" in person and by mail is a prolific source of profit to our merchants.

All lines in which the retail trade of Minneapolis has lacked first class representation in the past have long since been filled by a class of firms than whom there are no abler exponents in any city in the West. The most noticeable feature in the growth of the retail business is the evolution of the general store with its miscellaneous stocks into the numerous abodes of special and exclusive·branches of merchandise, and the resultant betterment and embellishment of these establishments with newer and brighter displays of the most modern products of the looms and workshops of the world.

This gradual advancement of trade conditions has resulted in creating a degree of competition which has had a two-fold effect; first, in stimulating the dealers to renewed energies, and second, in bestowing corresponding benefits upon the buyers or consumers.

BUSINESS MEN'S ORGANIZATIONS.

Of the numerous business men's organizations which flourish in Minneapolis, there will be room here to speak of only a few as representatives of all, beginning with the Board of Trade and the Chamber of Commerce. While there is nothing ostentatious about the actions of these two important bodies, having for their object the welfare of the city, they have, in a quiet way, accomplished a vast amount of good, substantial work for Minneapolis. The Minneapolis Board of Trade was organized in 1872, with W. D. Washburn, H. T. Welles, Richard Chute, John Potts Brown, A. B. Barton, J. S. Walker, E. W. Herrick, Jacob Stone, Jr., and W. W. McNair, as incorporators. The object, in the beginning, was to direct and control the transactions of this market, as well as to represent in public affairs the interests of the mercantile community; but since the organization of the Chamber of Commerce, the Board has been wholly devoted to the public service, influencing legislation, disseminating information, and fostering that spirit of energy and emulation which now animates all pursuits. The Board is composed of two hundred and fifty of the most energetic, yet conservative, citizens and business men of the city. It holds weekly meetings, which are well attended and very interesting. During the past year many important matters have been taken in hand and adjusted, and the Board now has under consideration a number of propositions from large manufacturing and commercial institutions which desire to locate in the city.

The articles of incorporation of the Minneapolis Chamber of Commerce bear date of October 11th, 1881. On November 15th, following, the first meeting under this charter was held. Briefly stated, the objects of the Chamber are to facilitate the buying and selling of all products, the adjustment of business disputes, the dissemination of information; in short, organized co-operation to advance the interests of its members and the community. The principal transactions of the Chamber are in grain and flour, domestic produce and commodities of that nature not being quoted on its floor. The handsome and tasteful structure occupied by the Chamber cost $180,000, and with its site, is valued at $250,000. The membership roll of the Chamber of Commerce was augmented by the addition of sixty names during the last fiscal year, which ended October 31, 1888. The new members are many of them men of wealth, who have come to the city from outside cities on account of the superior facilities for dealing in grain in

Minneapolis. Outside grain men are beginning to realize that Minneapolis controls the wheat marke of the United States, and that if they would do business to advantage they must be at the market center.

The flour millers of Minneapolis all belong to a body, which was organized in 1875, for their mutual benefit and protection. It is known as the Minneapolis Millers' Union.

The Jobbers' Association, organized in 1884, for the purposes of mutual protection and social intercourse, comprises the leading wholesale merchants of the city.

The Lumber Dealers' Association, the Real Estate Exchange, the Produce Exchange, the Underwriters' Association and the clearing House, are among the other business organizations of Minneapolis.

MINNEAPOLIS REAL ESTATE VALUES.

Minneapolis dirt is valuable. A front foot of it on a leading business street is worth $1,500 to $2,000. For the past seven or eight years there has been wonderful activity in the real estate market. Values have risen by startling leaps, the recorded transactions have piled up prodigiously, property everywhere within five miles of the business center has been platted. It has not been a ficticious "boom." The general growth and up building of the city has warranted the remarkable advance in values. Here are the figures showing the number and aggregate consideration of deeds filed in the register's office for each of the past ten years:

SWEDISH CHRISTIAN MISSION CHURCH.

	No.	Consideration.
1888	11,800	$42,679,600
1887	15,406	57,322,239
1886	14,493	36,833,778
1885	8,160	25,297,079
1884	8,872	25,008,443
1883	10,220	28,308,550
1882	1,811	19,161,291
1881	5,902	8,425,045
1880	3,161	4,608,017
1879	2,402	3,080,245

The total for 1888 was not quite up to that for 1887; still the record was an excellent one for a quiet year. These figures are quite remarkable, and indicate not only the vast increase in the volume of business, but the increase in values, for while the number of transfers have increased five-fold the considerations have increased about fourteen-fold.

The platting during the past eighteen months has gone on at a pretty lively rate, even if the times have been dull. There were fifty-one new additions offered to the Council during the year 1888, containing 3,493 lots. These new plats were for the most part a subdivision of previously platted property. There have been few additions platted away out.

THE CITY GOVERNMENT.

Minneapolis does all her voting once in two years, spring elections having been abolished by charter amendments two years ago, and all voting for Municipal, County, State and National officials concentrated at the biennial election held on the second Tuesday in November of the even numbered years. This gives the community political peace each alternate year, tends to greatly simplify the political system and political issues, avoids the expense, the confusion and the business disturbance incident to annual or semi-annual elections, encourages the average, well-meaning citizen to attend to his political duties and familiarize himself with the questions to be passed upon, and the character of the candidates to be voted for, and dwarfs the importance, diminishes the pernicious activity, and largely destroys the occupation of that superfluous patriot, the local professional politician.

The municipal legislature consists of a single body known as the City Council. Each alderman receives a salary of $60 a month, and the mayor a salary of $2,000 a year. There are four municipal boards—the Board of Park Commissioners, the Library Board, the Board of Education and the Board of Police Commissioners—the first three being elective by the people and the last-named elective by the City Council. The mayor of the city is also *ex-officio* a member and president of the police commission, and not more than two of the four elective members of the police commission can legally be members of the same political party. All three of the municipal boards named are organized on a non-partisan basis.

Saloons in Minneapolis pay an annual license of $1,000 each, and are confined to a narrow strip of territory along the river banks, in the business district. Approximately one-twelfth of the geographical extent of the city is within the saloon section, and eleven-twelfths exempt. Obviously a leading and a most beneficient result of the system is to free the entire residence portions of the city from the presence or proximity of drinking places, and their usual demoralizing annexes and environments. The system prevents the establishment of schools of vice among the homes of the people, and gives a degree of public order and safety not otherwise approachable. It is an interesting economic fact that this measure greatly reduces the aggregate of actual drinking in the city, the decrease probably reaching forty per cent.—showing that the removal of drinking facilities and temptations, even to a moderate distance, keeps thousands away from the saloons, and especially deters the young from forming the drink habit.

MUNICIPAL IMPROVEMENTS.

The city authorities have for years been bothered to keep pace with the city's growth in the matter of public improvement. Six years ago there was not a foot of pavement in the city and scarcely anything worthy the name of a sewer system. The water department was equally crude. The record sinnce then has been one of tremendous activity in the attempt to catch up and keep up. The attempt has been fairly successful, and Minneapolis is now as well equipped with public improvements as any city of its size and age in the country.

There are now twenty miles of paved streets in the city, sixteen miles of cedar block and four of granite. The total cost has been $794,208. The total length of sewers in the city is forty-six miles. These figures do not include the great central sewer tunnel, now approaching completion, or the tunnel in Northern Minneapolis.

HEALTH, POLICE AND FIRE DEPARTMENTS.

The health department is well organized and active, and the sanitary welfare of the city is carefully guarded.

The police system is capable and energetic, and Minneapolis is among the most orderly of the large cities of the United States.

The Minneapolis fire department is one of the best equipped and best organized in the United States. The equipment of the department is as follows: Six first-size fire steamers, eight second-size steamers and one in reserve. Seventeen hose carriages and two in reserve, six chemicals and one in reserve, five trucks and one in reserve, three supply wagons and one in reserve, and four buggies. The Gamewell system of fire alarm, which is the best in the world, now consists of 166 sheet boxes, ten circuit repeaters, 112 miles of wire and 470 cells of battery to run it. During 1888 there were 402 fire alarms. The loss by fire was $201,215, and the insurance on the property $778,300.

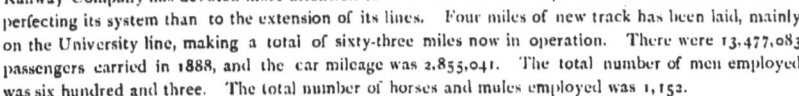

TRANSIT FACILITIES.

During the past year the Minneapolis Street Railway Company has devoted more attention to perfecting its system than to the extension of its lines. Four miles of new track has been laid, mainly on the University line, making a total of sixty-three miles now in operation. There were 13,477,083 passengers carried in 1888, and the car mileage was 2,855,041. The total number of men employed was six hundred and three. The total number of horses and mules employed was 1,152.

The improvements on the motor line property lately have been mainly confined to laying a double track between the stations at Lake Harriet and Calhoun. The grounds of the company at Lake Harriet, however, were greatly improved last year, and the new pavilion or music hall was completed at a cost of $15,000. This has undoubtedly had much to do with the decided increase in the number of passengers carried from the city to the lakes last season. The number of men employed on the motor line last season was one hundred and sixty-two; total miles in operation, twenty-five; number of passengers carried, 3,259,136.

TELEPHONE AND POST-OFFICE BUSINESS.

The Northwestern Telephone Exchange Company has 1,600 subscribers. It uses 1,200 miles of wire.

The rapidly growing business done by the Minneapolis Post-Office is an interesting index to the growth of the city. During last year there was an increase of over $15,000 in the net increase of the office. The number of pieces of mail handled in 1888 was 64,226,309. The money order transactions last year aggregated $1,965,680, and the number, 168,625. The total receipts, including stamp sales, were in 1888, 290,797.

MINNEAPOLIS HOTELS.

No city has built hotels faster than Minneapolis. There are now nine hostelries, capable of accommodating comfortably 2,300 guests, and this capacity can be largely increased upon any special demand. The finest hotel is the West, with its four hundred perfectly furnished rooms and places for one thousand guests. The West has maintained the plane of excellence with which it was started. Everything is first-class. It is one of the interesting places of the city, and its promenades and parlors are the favorite center of fashionable receptions and balls. The Nicollet is the old hostelry of the city, and one of the best. It has two hundred and fifty rooms and can accommodate five hundred people. The Windsor Hotel has been enlarged, until it now has one hundred and forty-four rooms, and is the third largest in the city. It is first-class in every respect, and is of the class ranging next to the West . and Nicollet. The St. James Hotel has been made a very attractive house. It does an entirely transient business. The number of the rooms is sixty-four, but the accommodations are ample for a larger number. The National Hotel is of about the same size as the St. James. The old Clark House, now the Brunswick, has been modernized, and is a good house of its class. The opening of family hotels has been a feature in Minneapolis in the last few years. Among these are the Ardmore, which has been in existence over two years, and the Holmes, which occupies a large brick block on Hennepin Avenue and Eighth Street. It has one hundred and forty rooms.

THE THEATERS.

Minneapolis is one of the best show towns in the United States. It has three modern ground-floor opera houses, two older amusement temples, and a large museum. The Grand Opera House is one of the finest places of amusement in the United States. It was never designed for a business specu-lation, but savored more of a public enterprise. Although a separate structure, the Grand is a part of the splendid property known as the Syndicate Block. The growth of the city in population and dramatic taste has been so rapid, however, that the Grand has not been a losing venture, and has paid a modest rate of interest on the money invested.

The oldest theater in Minneapolis is the Pence Opera House, built in 1857, by J. W. Pence, who is still its owner. The house was regarded with open-eyed wonder by the natives of that early day, and was "rented to strolling players" rather than to star combinations.

The Bijou Opera House, formerly the "People's Theatre," is ably managed by Jacob Litt. The house was finished and opened in August, 1887, and, having an elegant interior and sumptuous furnish-ings, it very naturally leaped into instantaneous popularity. The Bijou Theater was built to supply a demand for a ground-floor house with a greater seating capacity, modern comforts and popular prices. The Hennepin Avenue Opera House was a still later venture, and owing to the present manager, Mr. Harris, who came into possession of the house last spring, it is now a great success. It is a beautiful house, and one of the most popular and best patronized places of amusement in the city.

The attractions which are presented in these places of entertainment comprise the best in the various classes of amusement enterprises which the United States affords. All the noted singers and actors drawn hither by the high reputation that Minneapolis people have attained as patrons of good shows, find their way here about once a year. During the two or three years last past several dramatic organizations of national fame have opened their traveling seasons here. The standing of Minneapolis as a show town is a good thing in two ways. It brings here the best that is going in the way of travel-ing companies, thus enlivening the existence of residents who enjoy the recreation which the theater affords; and it makes the city more fascinating to people from the surrounding country who come in to purchase goods, thus helping to cement the pleasant relations between them and their favorite metropolis.

THE MINNEAPOLIS INDUSTRIAL EXPOSITION.

The Minneapolis Industrial Exposition, established in 1886, gives annual exhibitions, which are prominent among the amusement as well the educational institutions of the city. The Exposition building is one of the largest and finest of all the structures of its class in the country. It occupies a most commanding site, within less than half a mile of the business center of Minneapolis, is reached by street cars from every quarter, and is within a few minutes' walk of every railway station in the city, besides having its own station within the grounds. The Art Gallery is separated from the main building by a glass covered court (used for the exhibition of sculpture and casts) and contains fourteen rooms, perfectly lighted, which, together with four large rooms in the basement, makes a building second to none, and equal to any in the country for the purpose intended.

A CITY OF CHURCHES.

Nearly one hundred and fifty church spires rise above the din and hubbub of this big, busy city, in silent, eloquent testimony to the fact that the Minneapolitan does not worship Mammon alone and altogether. On the contrary, they have evidence to prove that he has put into his religious enterprises the same restless progressiveness that is apparent everywhere else. During the last seven or eight years there have been organized each year an average of ten new churches, and the building records have shown an annual expenditure for church improvements of from $150,000 to $300,000. The double duty has been imperative of planting young churches in newly-developed centers of population, and replacing small and old-fashioned buildings in the old centers with large and fine houses of worship.

Chief among the first concerns of a large class of people in a city, and those seeking new homes, is the church

STREET SCENES.—FROM "SATURDAY SPECTATOR."

facilities of the point to which they contemplate removing. Every man of family wishes his children to be educated under Christian influences, and desires the best church advantages for himself and family. In its churches Minneapolis is far in advance of most cities of even larger population. The church membership is growing at the rate of 30 per cent. a year, more rapidly in proportion than population, which is accounted for in the fact that as a city grows older, the increment of population is more largely composed of men of families, who are church-goers to a greater extent than those who comprise the advance stages of a city's population.

The church organizations of Minneapolis doubtless contribute more money to works of benevolence in proportion to the membership than those of any other city west of New York. As an index to the amount contributed, the Plymouth Congregational may be cited. The philanthropic work of the church is very extensive. The Bethel day nursery, where mothers leave their children while they go out to work, is an institution of the church. The church supports two kindergarten schools, with two teachers and 100 pupils, at a cost of $2,500. Three evening schools, a reading room and coffee room are among the philanthropic institutions of the church. The church alone supports five missions at home and abroad, and the benevolent gifts of its individual members rank the highest of any Congregational Church in the United States. During the past year gifts of this character amounted to $100,000. Other denominations make equally liberal contributions.

Minneapolis at present has 146 church and mission edifices. They are denominationally divided as follows:

Adventist	2	Friends	2
Baptist	18	Hebrew	2
Catholic	13	Lutheran	27
Christian	1	Methodist Episcopal	21
Congregationalist	9	Methodist, African	2
Congregationalist Branches	9	People's	1
Disciples	1	Presbyterian	16
Episcopal	10	Swedenborgian	1
Episcopal Missions	3	Unitarian	2
Evangelical Associations	2	Universalist	4

The total membership at the close of 1888 approximated 32,000. The aggregate value of Minneapolis church property approximates $5,000,000, and the number and beauty of structures entitle the city to be called the Brooklyn of the West.

Minneapolis boasts of one of the most active Young Men's Christian Associations in the United States. The association at all times keeps in the field seventeen aggressive committees, and by perseverance has been enabled to accomplish a great deal during the past year. At present the organization has headquarters in the Syndicate Block, on Nicollet Avenue, but work is progressing rapidly upon one of the finest association buildings in the country, to cost $130,000, which will be standing evidence of their activity. The total membership is 1,194. The average daily attendance at the rooms this year was 212. There are five branches and departments.

The officers of the association are: President, David C. Bell; Vice-Presidents, John T. Barnum, B. F. Nelson; Recording Secretary, Edward Savage; Treasurer, F. A. Chamberlain; Assistant, G. N. Atterbury.

The charitable institutions of Minneapolis are worthy of the wealth and Christian culture of the community.

EDUCATIONAL INSTITUTIONS.

The University of Minnesota is situated in Minneapolis, on the east bank of the Mississippi River. The grounds are about forty-five acres in extent and possess great natural beauty. The University buildings are spacious and sightly structures. The public school system of Minneapolis is among the finest in the United States.

An educational institution that deserves special mention is Stryker Seminary in St. Anthony Park, midway between St. Paul and Minneapolis. Hourly trains on the Manitoba Short Line stop at St.

Anthony Park Station, and in cold or stormy weather pupils from the two cities are conveyed to and from the depot. The new building is full of comfort. It is elegantly situated on a bluff commanding a view of Minneapolis, and all the Park region. There are two acres of ground, affording room for lawn tennis, croquet and other sports. Stryker Seminary is a select Home School for young ladies. Boarding pupils are limited to twenty. Health, morals, manners and mental training are carefully attended to. Each pupil receives special attention, and each is made happy. Motherless girls, and those who are delicate and sensitive, and young ladies who are backward in their studies are cared for as each requires. This school has had great success in cases like these, while those of strong brawn and brain have by individual treatment made rapid progress. In several instances the remark has been made "Our daughter has learned as much from your instruction in one year, as she did in three years in other schools."

THE STRYKER SEMINARY   St. Anthony Park, Minn.

Stryker Seminary commenced in the fall of 1884 with ten pupils. It has since had a steady and healthy growth. It claims to be equal in its advantages to any school in the country.

The following testimonials have been given:

From Ex-Gov. John S. Pillsbury, Minneapolis—

"I cannot but believe that with your new location and suitable buildings, which I am glad to see you are to have, that the facilities which you will offer to the young will be fully equal or superior to any offered in this State."

From Rev. T. DeWitt Talmage, D. D., Brooklyn—

"Rev. Peter Stryker, D. D., inherits from his father, who gave his life to the instruction of the young, ther equisites of mind and heart. Parents may put their children under his care, knowing they will have the best literary and moral advantages. Stryker Seminary, situated in a beautiful and healthful region, opens with the good wishes of the twin cities of Minnesota. I expect for the institution a prosperity corresponding with the wonderful growth of those cities."

Similar testimonials have been received from Gov. Merriam, Dr. Herrick Johnson of Chicago, Postmaster-General Wanamaker, and others.

A full corps of instructors is connected with the school. Rev. Peter Stryker, D. D., is President, Rev. Dr. Stryker and Miss Anna K. Stryker, are associate principals.

The Board of Advisors consists of Rev. D. J. Burrell, D. D., Rev. Chas. F. Thwing, D. D., Rev. John P. Stafford, D. D., Hon. Ell Torrance, Mr. Charles H. Pratt, Prof. Carl V. Lachmund (Music), Douglas Volk (Art), Minneapolis; Rev. R. F. Maclaren, Rev. S. G. Smith, D. D., Hon. A. R. McGill, H. Knox Taylor, A. G. Postlethwaite, B. F. Wright, J. R. McMurran, St. Paul.

Stryker Seminary reprints the following references: Hon. Alex. Ramsey, formerly Governor of Minnesota, St. Paul; Hon. D. M. Clough, Senator of Minnesota, Minneapolis; Hon. John Wanamaker, Postmaster-General, Washington, D. C.; Hon. H. L. Humphrey, Circuit Judge, Hudson, Wis.; Hon. Elliott F. Shephard, New York City, N. Y.; Rev. Cyrus Foss, D. D., LL. D., Bishop of M. E. Church, Philadelphia; Rev. Howard Crosby, D. D., LL. D., New York City, N. Y.; Rev. David R. Breed, D. D., Chicago; Isaac Staples, Stillwater, Minn.; Rev. Robert Christie, D. D., St. Paul, Minn.; Rev. M. D. Edwards, St. Paul, Minn.; Rev. E. E. Wells, Minneapolis, Minn.; Rev. R. N. Adams, D. D., Minneapolis, Minn.; Rev. George W. Merrill, Minneapolis, Minn.; Mr. Thomas Cochran, Jr., St. Paul, Minn.; Mr. James S. Lane, Minneapolis, Minn.; Mrs. J. P. Laird, Minneapolis, Minn.

GLOBE BUILDING.

THE NEWSPAPER PRESS.

The newspaper press of Minneapolis is as bright and enterprising as might be expected in a community so thoroughly representative of the best elements of American civilization. The leading journal of the city is the Minneapolis *Tribune*. A stock company, whose members were leading Republicans of the city, purchased the business of the *State Atlas* and *Daily Chronicle* in May, 1867, and merged them into a new publication, the *Tribune*. Whilst its efforts to furnish full telegraphic and other news met with a fair share of popular appreciation for some years, at length, in 1876, financial reverses compelled the relinquishment of its Associated Press franchise, which was acquired by the St. Paul *Pioneer Press*. For a time afterward that paper was conducted as the St. Paul and Minneapolis *Pioneer Press and Tribune*, rejoicing in one of the longest newspaper titles in the United States. The attempt thus to control the entire field for daily journalism in Minneapolis aroused indignation. A syndicate of twelve citizens resolved to break this monopoly; obtained for a time custody of the *Tribune* property, but their efforts to revive the paper failed of any practical result, except that for a time the *Evening Tribune* competed with the consolidated *Press*. In May, 1880, after many delays, the *Tribune* was issued as a morning eight-page daily, devoted strictly to the interests of Minneapolis and territory of which she is the center, and has since obtained recognition as an exponent of them, and as one of the leading representatives of Western journalism. Its proprietorship has undergone several changes. It is now owned by Haskell & Palmer.

The *Evening Journal* is another creditable journalistic representative of Minneapolis. The first issue of this superior publication bore date of November 2d, 1878. Started as a three-cent morning daily, it was sold soon after a fire which had destroyed its plant, April 6th, 1880, and from that time, with improved mechanical facilities, liberal expenditure and spirited business methods, has maintained its place as the principal evening paper of the city. It is owned by a stock company.

The St. Paul *Pioneer Press* and the St. Paul *Globe* maintain news and advertising bureaus in Minneapolis, and Minneapolis departments are a prominent feature of both papers.

The weekly, semi-monthly and monthly publications of Minneapolis are numerous, varied as to aim, and as a rule able and flourishing.

A WALK ABOUT THE CITY.

Minneapolis is not an un-broken plain, but the prominent parts of the town lie very level and open. It abuts itself picturesquely against the curving Mississippi. The "Eastern visitor," remarks Joel Benton, is drifted in very close sight of this stream as he closes his journey, and comes in under the roar and splendor of the Falls, or looks off at the almost canyon-like depth of the stream below them. It is an inspiring sight. The streets are wide and open, and they seem to have been waiting for your arrival. The sky is blue and broad. There is no bluff to cast a shadow or to limit your view. The city takes you to its heart at once and captivates your own. You don't need

UNION LEAGUE, FROM "SATURDAY SPECTATOR."

to defile through crooked or narrow streets to find it. Its physiognomy is tonic and bracing, and warrants high expectations, which are amply fulfilled by a visit, and confirmed the longer you remain. The city broadens out to the lakes of famous summer resorts. It is redolent of legend and poem. Over its space the wonderful exploits of Hiawatha took place. Here Longfellow's imagination wandered to work out one of its most charming creations. What other city would not give away half its present renown to have so fine a falls as those of St. Anthony, on one side, and so poetic and beautiful a feature as Minnehaha—the Falls of Laughing Water, on the other?

MINNEAPOLIS ARCHITECTURE.

That a city depends largely for its beauty upon its architecture is surely true, whether its streets are built up compactly with brick and stone or have the additional attraction of garden and foliage.

Minneapolis is exceptionally well located, naturally, for a large and beautiful city. The land is suffici-ently level for its business portion, and its compact residence portion, and there is room to grow for many years to come, without expensive grading to prepare the way. Thanks to the long-headedness of those who laid out the city, and more especially to the energy and good taste of those who have pro-jected and laid out our system of parks and boulevards, we are preparing a setting worthy of the purest gems, in the way of buildings, that architects may conceive of, or the people accept and produce. The bluffs along the western part of the city should be, and will be, the finest residence portion of the city; and what has been a wall of woods is rapidly becoming the most beautiful part of the city and the most healthy.

Our office buildings, stores, churches and dwellings compare favorably with other cities and are models of convenience in being fitted with the latest modern appliances for comfort and the despatch of business. All Minneapolis buildings of importance, if not thoroughly fireproof, are sufficiently slow burning to be safe under ordinary conditions with watchful care.

Lake Harriet Pavilion

More than one hundred churches of all denomina-tions attest the moral char-acter of the city, and places of refined amuse-ment abound. Fine streets, bordered with handsome trees, and broad avenues lined with beautiful residences, dis-tinguish the city. A system of parks and boulevards, second to none, has been inaugurated, the former accessible to all portions of the city, the latter offer-ing the finest drive, and thus the health of the city has been assured at the same time that her beauties have been preserved.

No city in the Northwest possesses more elegant public buildings than Minneapolis. The West Hotel, built at a cost of $1,500,000, is the finest hostelry in America, the Chamber of Commerce, the Masonic Temple, the Public Library Building, the Boston Block, the Loan and Trust Building, the Court House, the Guaranty Loan Building and the New York Life Building, are types of architectural beauty and lasting monuments to the solid spirit of Minneapolis enterprise. The great Industrial Exposition Building, representing half a million of money raised off-hand by the people of the city, crowns the high bluff on the east side, and by its proportions and the history of its unrivaled achieve-ments, attracts the wonder and admiration of the stranger and the citizen alike.

SOME OF THE BIG BUILDINGS.

Considering the briefness of the time since Minneapolis was the haunt of the red man, the number of massive buildings which she contains is wonderful. Structures from seven to twelve stories in height, built of granite, elaborately adorned, and furnished with steam-heating apparatus, hydraulic elevators, and other modern conveniences, they are buildings of which even New York might be proud, and their presence in Minneapolis impresses the most casual visitor, as well as the inhabitants of the city and close students of the development of American cities in general. It impresses that hard-headed and practical class of people, the investors in real estate, and gives them assurance that Minneapolis is not a mushroom metropolis, but a city with a great future, which is being builded with reference to its manifest destiny.

Following is a partial list of prominent buildings in Minneapolis which cost $100,000 each or over:

Court House	$2,000,000	Post-office	$ 700,000
West Hotel	1,600,000	Exposition	350,000
Guaranty Loan Building	1,250,000	Science Hall	125,000
Pillsbury "A" mill	1,100,000	Library building	190,000
New York Life Building	1,000,000	Soldiers' Home	100,000
Nicollet House	100,000	State University	150,000
Oneida Block	100,000	Chamber of Commerce	285,000
Globe Building	185,000	Temple Court	250,000
Wright Block	140,000	Masonic Temple	300,000
Mutual Block	160,000	City market house	225,000
Glen Block	200,000	Public Library	250,000
Langdon Block	120,000	Hennepin Avenue Theater	140,000
Central Block	150,000	Stillman Block	200,000
Syndicate Block	600,000	Orphan Asylum	125,000
Gates' tenements	125,000	House of Good Shepherd	200,000
Lowry's residence	100,000	Loan and Trust Company	125,000
Eastman & Cook's mill	100,000	Lumber Exchange	250,000
Soo shops	145,000	Builders' Exchange	100,000
North Side pump station	214,000	K. of L. building	100,000
Buel tenement	100,000	Hall Lumber Company	100,000
Washburn "A" mill	750,000	Bank of Commerce	185,000
Washburn "B" mill	500,000	Union elevator	375,000
Christian & Co.'s mill	100,000	Minneapolis & Pacific elevator	118,000
High School building	100,000	St. Anthony elevator	154,000
Church of Dominican Fathers	100,000	Boston Block	200,000
Zier tenement	100,000	Edison Electric Light	100,000
Mead tenement	100,000	Kasota Block	100,000
Y. M. C. A. building	125,000		

The most magnificent and costly of the buildings now in course of erection, and the most expensive building in the Northwest, is the new court house. Externally this building will be very elaborate and ornamental; it will be 290 feet square, with a court 130 feet square, and the principal entrances will be on Fourth and Fifth Streets. There will be an ornamental tower 300 feet in height on the Fourth Street side. The building will be four stories above the basement and surrounded by an attic story and roof of handsome design. There will be five stories on the court side, which will have a flat roof.

Next in magnitude comes the Guaranty Loan & Trust Company's office building adjoining the new post-office. The materials used in this building are iron and stone; it will be twelve stories high, with a tower and lookout rising two stories above the twelfth, the whole surmounted by a lofty staff. The lot is 132 by 135 feet and the building will occupy it entire, with the exception of a passageway on the post-office side. There will be about twenty-seven offices on each floor, or about 320 offices in all. The first floor is designed for banks and financial institutions. The finish will be very costly and elaborate.

The New York Life Insurance Company's building, on Fifth Street and Second Avenue South, will be ten stories high, fireproof, throughout, and will be finished in the finest style of modern architecture.

Next in consequence is the Masonic Temple, on Hennepin Avenue and Sixth Street. The material used is blue Ohio sand-stone, and it will be eight stories high, with a front of 88 feet on Hennepin by 155 on Sixth Street. The building will be entirely fireproof, with all the modern improvements.

The National Bank of Commerce Block, recently finished, is a beautiful, six-story brown granite building, fireproof, and containing all modern improvements. It is located on the corner of Fourth Street and First Avenue South.

The *Globe* Block on Fourth Street, is one of the most beautiful structures recently erected. It is of brick and stone, eight stories high, and fire-proof. The building is enclosed and will be used for office purposes.

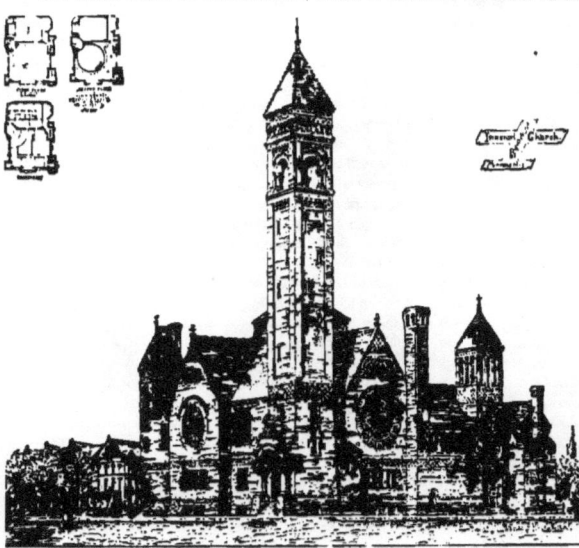

EMANUEL BAPTIST CHURCH.

The Co-Operative Block is a stately nine-story brick and granite building, adjoining the Kasota Block on Hennepin Avenue. It is fire-proof and supplied with all modern conveniences.

NATURE'S BEAUTY SPOTS.

One feature about Minneapolis worthy of more than passing mention, is the number of lakes and other pleasure resorts within the city limits. Here rest and recreation may be found in the summer, and an abundant opportunity for exhilarating sport is offered in the winter. There are three lakes of considerable size within the city limits and within four miles of the business center. There are almost innumerable ponds and other bodies of water, but the three of any considerable size—Lake Calhoun, Lake Harriet and Lake of the Isles—are all full-fledged lakes and very picturesque. The motor service brings these resorts within a very short distance of the business portion, and as the population increases and the cottages reach out into the suburbs, these charming sheets of water are rapidly losing their identity as summer resorts.

The largest of this trio is Lake Calhoun, located about three miles from the down town terminus of the motor line. Its shaded shores are rapidly becoming dotted with cottages. Its waters are deep and clear, affording excellent bathing in summer, and good skating in winter.

Lake Harriet, situated a mile beyond Calhoun, is a picturesque body of water. In days gone by, when Minneapolis people regarded the trip as an excursion, this lake was a favorite picnic ground, but now that the intervening space has become populated, it seems like going from one part of the city to another, and Minnetonka has, to a large degree, usurped Lake Harriet's place as a picnic ground. The drive around the lake is a charming feature, and in summer it is the Mecca toward which owners of speedy horses turn their faces.

The Lake of the Isles may properly be designated as in the heart of the city, for it is nearly surrounded with cottages and fine residences. In summer the avenues along its shores form delightful drives. Owing to its central location, the Lake of the Isles is resorted to by throngs of people during the skating season. The motor and horse car lines go within a few blocks of it.

Another point of interest within the city limits, and within a few minutes' ride of the business portion, is the spot made famous by Longfellow. Minnehaha Falls might never be regarded as grand, for there is seldom sufficient water to render it such, but to one standing on

SCENE IN CENTRAL PARK.

the banks below the Falls, there is something about the scene that is so picturesque that it does not seem strange that the poet found sufficient inspiration for those beautiful gems of word painting familiar to every schoolboy. On an eminence near the Falls is located the Soldiers' Home, and it is truly a beautiful place, in which the battle-scarred veterans can spend their declining years.

These are but a few of the thousand and one beautiful spots which environ the city of Minneapolis. Added to these are the numerous boulevards and pleasant drives in and about the city. It is no doubt owing to these natural attractions that Minneapolis has come to be regarded as the city of conventions. A national convention is often tedious and tiresome, but it would be a peculiar delegate who did not look forward with anticipation of a large amount of pleasure attendant upon their annual gatherings in this city. Owing to the attractions of Minneapolis in this respect, she has been particularly fortunate in securing these gatherings, and in the past five years a large number of national conventions have been held here.

LOOKING DOWN 43D ST. TO LAKE HARRIETT.

THE PARK SYSTEM.

While really far from full development, the park system of Minneapolis is a marvel, and a source of great pride. It is only six years since any move for park improvements was attempted. In April, 1883, a board of park commissioners, consisting of fifteen members, was organized, pursuant to an act of the Legislature. Hon. Chas. M. Loring was chosen president.

While the board elected at that time has accomplished wonders, yet the gradually developing beauty which nature will bestow upon the system is hardly noticeable as compared with the promised magnificence of future years.

Including the land acquired during the year, the board now controls a park area (land and lake) of about 1,045 acres, and over thirteen miles of parkways, and when the system is complete, will have more than twenty, for which it will have paid less than one-third of the present valuation, a large portion of which will be received back in the shape of park assessments, and a larger portion of which is to be so returned to the board, the assessments being distributed into ten equal parts, payable in as many years. The comptroller estimates the present market value of the lands included in the Minneapolis park system, but not including Hennepin, Lyndale and Kenwood boulevards (which are used as public streets), at upward of $1,500,000, an estimate which may be classed as conservative.

BUILDINGS, UNIVERSITY OF MINNESOTA, FROM "SATURDAY SPECTATOR."

The acreage of the various parks (including lake) is as follows: Lake of the Isles, 161.00; Lake Harriet, 415.00; Lake Calhoun, 406.33; Central, 33.50; Prospect, 20.52; Riverside, 19.78; Washburn, 10.08; Moulton, 10.00; Elliot, 4.00; Murphy, 3.33; Hawthorn, 1.13; sundry small parks, 8.50.

The length in miles of the parkways or boulevards under control of the board are as follows: Lake of the Isles, 3.57; Lake Harriet, 3.50; Hennepin Avenue, 1.33; Lyndale, 1.80; Stinson, 1.00; Kenwood, 1.75; Central Park, 0.35; Dean, 1.10.

THE STATE OF MINNESOTA.

The location of Minnesota is very nearly the center of the American continent, and equidistant from the shores of the Atlantic and the Pacific. The Canadian provinces of Ontario and Manitoba bound it on the north, the Red River and the Territory of Dakota on the west, Iowa on the south, and the Mississippi River and Lake Superior on the east. It has an area of 84,287 square miles, or about 54,760,000 acres, and is therefore larger than the six New England States and nearly equal to Indiana and Illinois combined. Its greatest length, from north to south, is 380 miles, and its greatest extension, east and west, 350 miles. It lies between latitude 43° 30' and 49° 27', and between longitude 89° 29' and 97° 12'. Except the mountain districts, it is the highest land on the continent, and the sources of the three great water courses of North America are within its borders. Its mean elevation above the ocean level is 1,200 feet. Though far from the sea, it is the best watered State in the Union, having, besides numerous rivers, upward of 700 lakes, varying from fifty yards to thirty miles in diameter. Prof. Maury, in his official report to the Government, says: "There is in this State a greater number of these lovely sheets of laughing water than in all the country besides. They give variety and beauty to the landscape; they soften the air and lend all their thousand charms and attractions to make this goodly land a lovely place of residence." The climate is one of the healthiest in the world. The natural resources are rich and varied, inviting the agriculturist, the miner and the manufacturer, and crowning their easy labors with rich reward. Within the past few years settlers have poured into the country north and west of it, and its admirable transportation facilities have made it the center of an extensive and profitable commerce.

TOPOGRAPHICAL FEATURES.

There are no mountains in Minnesota, and the height of its loftiest hills is not above 300 feet. It has none of the disadvantages of a mountainous region, though possessing most of the peculiarities of such localities that are beneficial to mankind. For instance, its elevation above the sea gives it that purity of atmosphere for which mountainous countries are esteemed, and the rapid descent of its numerous streams from the high plateaus to the beds of its great rivers affords an incalculable amount of hydraulic force, which is diffused throughout its entire extent. And, moreover, these are not only susceptible of inexpensive improvement in most cases, making them available in the fullest measure, but are easily approachable. The water courses, which form fully two-thirds of the boundary lines, except less than a fourth part of their extent, are navigable for ordinary river steamers, and so are several of the interior rivers and lakes. On the Mississippi, St. Croix and Red River, and some of the interior lakes and streams, steamers are now constantly plying during the summer seasons, while Lake Superior is coursed in every direction by steam and sail vessels of the heaviest tonnage.

The surface of the State is a high plain, sloping to the northwest north of a curved line drawn from the head of Lake Traverse, passing south of Red and Vermillion Lakes, and through the international boundary from the northwest corner of Cook County; and more gently to the southeast of that line. This surface is plowed into furrows of 200 to 800 feet in depth and several miles in width by its large rivers, and seamed in all directions by smaller streams. The only flat lands are on or near the summits of the elevations, or in the bottoms of the valleys bordering the streams. The valleys are generally so much lower than the high lands as to afford sufficient natural drainage for nearly all localities in the State. There are few rocky formations to be met with. The lakelets are mostly crowded together upon the summits of the heights, and are the sources of the innumerable streams, which meander in every

direction along the higher levels and ultimately finding paths down the slopes, afford an incalculable aggregate of water power, of which nearly every neighborhood has amply sufficient for its local needs. The Mississippi, St. Louis, Red, Rainy Lake, St. Croix and Minnesota Rivers, have, also, more or less waterfalls, those of the Mississippi, at Minneapolis, being the largest, which furnish power for great aggregations of machinery, and about which manufacturing centers are rapidly forming, as the development of the country progresses. St. Anthony Falls afford 125,000 horse-power, St. Croix River, in the vicinity of Taylor's Falls, 100,000; St. Louis River, near its mouth, 95,000; Red River, at Fergus Falls, 35,000; Minnesota River, near Granite Falls, 25,000, and a score or more of other falls and rapids upwards of 20,000 horse-power each. Most of these are susceptible of inexpensive improvement and are easy of approach for rail or wagon roads. The State Fish Commissioners have planted fresh water salmon in many of the lakes, and the experiment has so far been entirely successful.

WASHINGTON PARK.

SOME METEOROLOGICAL DATA.

The atmosphere of Minnesota is dry, clear and pure, and it is seldom that a refreshing breeze is not felt even on the stillest summer day. The nights of summer, almost without exception, are cool, so as to afford opportunity for refreshing sleep; and, although the days are frequently very warm, the heat is rarely oppressive, as is the case where humid atmospheres prevail. The winters are cold, sometimes severely so; but it is seldom, and only for short intervals, that the term "inclement" can properly be applied to Minnesota weather. The dryness of the air diminishes its capability of conducting heat from the body, and men and animals, therefore, suffer much less here from cold than where there is even a slightly greater proportion of dampness. People work at out-door employments without discomfort when the thermometer ranges from zero to ten or twelve degrees below.

MINNESOTA'S "BIG WOODS."

Fully one-third of the surface of Minnesota is covered by forests and woodlands, and as much as one-eighth more by natural groves, fringes of timber along streams, oak openings and brush lands. In the earlier settled prairie portions there are also many planted groves, the aggregate area of which is very considerable, and many of them have already become sources of fuel supply.

In the northern range of counties there are forests of white pine which cover probably one-fourth of the entire area. Interspersed among these, especially along the valleys of streams and on the margins of the larger lakes, although they are sometimes found on the higher plateaus, are belts or patches of deciduous forests hardly less in aggregate extent than the pine-covered areas. The varieties of trees found here embrace white, black and burr oak; red, rock and swamp elm; white, black and gray ash; hackberry, sugar and white maple; box-elder; linden or basswood; white and red birch; poplar; willow; cottonwood, and a few others. Wet or swamp localities occur with considerable frequency on the more northerly highlands, and are often covered with growths of red and white cedar, though more commonly with tamarack. Spruce and firs quite prevalent in still other places, and in the vicinity of openings or "burnt" districts one finds mountain ash, ironwood, mountain maple, red and choke cherry, balm of Gilead, yew, arbor vitæ, and other similar varieties. Frequent intervals occur in the lowlands where there are natural meadows, on the margins of which, the ground being higher, nearly all the varieties of shrubbery found in similar situations in Northern Indiana and Ohio grow with equal luxuriance, and in the marshes, on both high and low lands, huckleberries, blueberries, cranberries and wild rice are produced abundantly. In addition to these features, there are all through these counties, as well as in other wooded parts of the State, small, dry prairies and tracts from which the forest trees have been burned off. These sometimes contain 50,000 acres, or even more, and again are limited to less than a single section; many of them are covered with an excellent growth of blue-joint, red-top, or buffalo grass, while others are partially or wholly overgrown with various species of wild shrubbery, amongst which a variety called "jack oak" usually predominates. Again

HENNEPIN AVENUE.

there are extensive localities where only large, black or burr oak trees with wide-spreading tops and scarcely any undergrowth are found, which are known as "oak openings." Gooseberries, currants and black and red raspberries are usually abundant among the shrubbery of these openings, and wild straw berries abound everywhere except in the densest forest, swamps or low meadow lands.

Nearly all the region west of the Mississippi and north of the Minnesota River, properly belongs to the forest district. The trees which cover it are mostly of the deciduous family.

THE FERTILE PRAIRIES.

The prairie counties properly are Kittson, Marshall, Polk, Norman, Clay, Wilkin, Traverse, Grant, Stevens, Pope, Big Stone, Swift, Chippewa, Kandiyohi, Renville, McLeod, Sibley and Nicollet, on the north side of the Minnesota River; Lac qui Parle, Yellow Medicine, Lincoln, Lyon, Redwood, Brown, Pipestone, Murray, Cottonwood, Watonwan, Rock, Nobles, Jackson, Martin, Freeborn, Faribault, Mower, Dakota, Goodhue, Wabasha. Olmsted and Dodge, south of that river; and Ramsey and Washington on the east side of the Mississippi. All the others contain woodland enough to entitle them to rank rather as timbered than prairie counties, and in all of those named above there are more or less groves and fringes of timber; those farthest west and south being more nearly treeless. Owing to the undulating character of the prairies, the natural drainage is admirable. The farmer seldom has to desist from tilling his land longer than a few hours after a rainfall, because of the ground being too wet, for, between the absorbent character of the soil and the conformation of the surface, the water speedily dis-

appears. At the same time there is rarely occasion to complain of the opposite extreme, for the ground retains moisture a long time and never becomes baked and crusted.

The undulating character of the Minnesota prairie also gives them the charm of picturesqueness. Another prominent feature of their beauty and attractiveness is their verdure. Most luxuriant grasses and a great variety of beautiful flowers cover them during the entire summer season. The grasses comprise several varieties, among which are included the blue grass, so justly prized for grazing, and the blue-joint and red-top, which yield hay equal to that made from the best cultivated varieties.

PARK BOULEVARD, AT 42d STREET.

These, with the pure water that is abundant in every section, fit them pre-eminently for grazing, and, already, the herds of cattle that are pastured upon them enliven and add to the attractiveness of the country.

THE SOIL AND ITS PRODUCTS.

The soil of Minnesota ranks with the most fertile in the world. The upper layer of the drift deposit forms the soil of all parts of the State, except that in the vicinity of Lake Superior and near the Mississippi River, in the southeast corner of the State. In the latter locality the soil is a mold of similar composition with that of Ohio. The depth of the soil varies from one to five feet, and nearly everywhere the subsoil is not only similar in its elements, but equally fertile when exposed to the influence of the atmosphere. It is made up largely of alumina, silica and lime, mixed with various mineral salts, and contains considerable percentages of ammonia and phosphorous in divers combinations. It is, likewise, filled with vegetable and animal matter, and these combinations of organic remains, with the varied bases, giving it an abundant supply of fertilizing properties. In appearance the soil is of dark to grayish brown color, being darkest in the lower plains and valleys, where it occasionally approaches to blackness, and is quite viscous when wet. It is everywhere exceedingly friable, and so easily worked that a hoe is not needed in the corn or potato field.

The best test of the soil, however. is its record of averages of cultivated vegetable products. The statistical reports of crops, published by the State, which are known to be from twelve to twenty per cent. less than the actual results, give the following mean averages of the staple crops, from a term of thirteen years, ending with 1882, viz.: Wheat, 14.09 bushels; corn, 30.51 bushels; oats, 32.14 bushels; barley, 24.26 bushels; rye, 15.21 bushels; buckwheat, 11.78 bushels; potatoes, 98.29 bushels; and beans, 11.37 bushels per acre. When it is remembered that these are general averages, from a territory extending through five and a half degrees of latitude and five and a third of longitude, it must be admitted that they make a good showing. Instances might be gathered from almost every county in which farming is carried on wherein all of these averages are largely exceeded. Yields of upward of 20 bushels of wheat, 40 bushels of corn, 45 bushels of oats, 30 bushels of barley, 22 bushels of rye, 15 bushels of buckwheat, 150 bushels of potatoes, and 16 bushels of beans, are quite common, and, indeed, every careful farmer in the State would show these or greater general averages for a term of ten to twelve years.

DIVERSITY OF CROPS.

It is only within the past few years that Minnesota farmers have attempted to diversify their crops. Wheat was their great staple production, although large quantities of corn also have been grown. Until within a few years, however, wheat was about the only grain that was in constant demand for cash, and, as the latter was a commodity that the farmers stood in need of, they devoted their labor chiefly to the production of wheat, in order to be sure of speedy returns. The census gives the production of the several crops in bushels as follows, viz.:

CROPS.	1860.	1870.	1880.
Wheat	2,186,993	18,866,073	34,601,030
Rye	121,411	78,088	215,245
Oats	2,176,002	10,678,261	23,382,158
Corn	2,941,952	4,743,117	14,831,741
Buckwheat	28,052	52,438	41,756
Barley	109,668	1,032,024	2,972,955

It will be noticed that while the wheat product increased 762 per cent. in the decade from 1860 to 1870, its increase from 1870 till 1880 was only 83 per cent. In the meantime the yield of corn increased only 61 per cent. during the first and 212 per cent. during the second periods. There are several reasons for this, but the chief is, that the cultivation of wheat was the most profitable during the first period and the first four seasons of the second. About 1874, the price of wheat having declined for several years and that of corn advanced slightly, farmers were led to pay greater attention to the latter grain. And, furthermore, a disposition to diversify their farming operations and enter more largely into the growing of stock, which began to manifest itself at this time, rendered the more extensive cultivation of corn necessary. Corn is as certain a crop in Minnesota as in any other of the Northern States. Oats, rye, barley, buckwheat, potatoes, turnips, rutabagas, mangelwurzels, beets, carrots, parsnips, cabbages, pumpkins, squashes and every other field and garden crop grown anywhere north of the thirty-eighth parallel grow here as well and mature as fully. Besides the above mentioned crops, some ten or twelve thousand acres of early amber sugar-cane are grown annually in Minnesota, from which nearly a million gallons of syrup are manufactured, principally for use in the families of the producers, though there are half a score or more manufacturers in the State who place their products in market and find a ready sale for them. Several manufacture sugar of excellent quality from the syrup and have succeeded in making this a profitable branch of farming industry. Sugar-beets are grown in all parts of the State, from its southern boundary northward as far as agriculture has yet extended, except in the valley of Red River. Upward of 100,000 acres per annum are devoted to the cultivation of flax. This is raised principally for its seed, of which the yield varies from ten to sixteen bushels per acre. Upward of 100,000 pounds of tobacco are grown each year in Minnesota, and, when properly cured and cared for, the quality is good. Much of it is consumed as smoking tobacco by those who cultivate it, but it is mostly sold to resident tobacconists, who use it in the manufacture of cigars, both as wrappers and fillings. Turnips, pumpkins, squashes and beans are also important crops.

Not a few of the agricultural products of Minnesota are of superior excellence to those grown elsewhere. This is especially true of her hard Fife wheat, which makes a higher grade of flour than any grown further south, whether it be spring or winter wheat. In order to keep up their brands of flour to the highest standard, and command ready sales and good prices, the millers of other States are in the habit of purchasing this Minnesota wheat and mixing it with the softer varieties produced in their own localities.

Prospect Park Observatory

Alex Murrie, Arch
Minneapolis, July 8/

GARDENING AND FRUIT GROWING.

The soil of Minnesota is peculiarly adapted to gardening. There are no clods to interfere with the working of the ground, and vegetables of all varieties grow with great rapidity, while retaining all their excellence, or being superior in quality to those of slower growth in more humid climates. The garden vegetables cultivated here embrace nearly all the ordinary varieties of the north temperate zone, and they are usually large and deliciously flavored.

Flower-gardening is also carried on quite extensively. The out-door flowers comprise the usual varieties of roses, pinks, peonies, poppies, lilies, dahlias, china asters, pansies, lady-slippers, sweet williams, phlox, larkspur, morning glories, flowering peas, bleeding hearts, tulips, lilacs, snowballs, chrysanthemums and a host of others common to the gardens of Europe and the northern United States. There is always a fair demand for pot-plants and cut flowers, and nearly every village in the State of 500 inhabitants and upward has one or more greenhouses.

A good deal of difficulty was experienced in introducing apples into the State, but now Minnesota produces as fine apples as can be found anywhere, and the annual product reaches 200,000 bushels; a number of varieties of cultivated plums and cherries are successfully cultivated, and currants, gooseberries, raspberries, blackberries and most other varieties of small fruit do as well in Minnesota as anywhere else. The fact is, most of these are found growing wild in nearly all parts of the State, and are equally large and well-flavored with the cultivated fruits. Grapes are found growing wild in all parts of the State, and several cultivated varieties have been successfully introduced.

Bee-culture is a flourishing industry, having begun with the capture and domestication of the wild bees native to the State by the early settlers. The abundance of wild flowers and of cultivated blooming plants affords the bees ample resources to draw from, and the long winters induce them to lay up greater stores of sweets. Moreover, the blooming plants of this country, being of quick growth, do not acquire those strong, pungent qualities of flowers of slower growth, and the flavor of honey made from them is of corresponding delicacy.

STOCK-RAISING IN MINNESOTA.

Stock-growing offers great inducements to the Minnesota farmer, and more are going into it every year, as there is no branch of agricultural industry for which the State is better adapted. It is a mistake to suppose that either the length or severity of the winters are objectionable in this respect. The greater degree of cold leads to the animals being clothed with thicker coatings of hair, Nature herself making this additional provision for their protection; and as intervals of chilling rains and sleet are of extremely rare occurrence at any season, and wholly unknown during the winters, they have no to contend with this prolific cause of colds, catarrhs and pneumonia. The dry air is conducive to the preservation of their health, as to that of the human family, and they not only endure the severity of the season, but thrive during the coldest winters, if properly fed and sheltered. That they require shelter at all has sometimes been urged as an objection, but it is coming to be understood that shelter is equally needed in other States, and that the losses of cattle and sheep through exposure to the inclemency of winter weather, even in Texas, amount in dollars and cents to many times the cost of all

.NICOLLET AVENUE.

the necessary shelter these animals require in Minnesota. Minnesota cattle are free from pleuro-pneumonia and other epizootic diseases, and the rich grasses of the State make their meat firm and juicy, causing them to command higher prices than cattle from further south. An experienced cattle-raiser says that notwithstanding their higher value marketable cattle can be produced at less expense in Minnesota than further south. The wild grasses of the Minnesota prairies are not only abundant, but highly nutritious. Hay made from the blue joint variety is of excellent quality, and that from the wild red-top fully equals tame grass hay; while the blue grass, which abounds in many localities, cannot be excelled for pastures. With plenty of such provender and uniform good health, cattle mature rapidly, and are fit for market at three years of age. Shorthorns and high-graded stock will weigh from 1,600 to 1,800 pounds per head at that age, and, as they bring better prices than older cattle, there is opportunity for realizing larger profits. To this must be added the advantage arising from the minimum percentage of losses by deaths from all causes.

Sheep, hogs and horses also benefit by the pure air, bracing climate and abundant and good food which Minnesota affords. Convincing evidence that the stock-growers of Minnesota have faith in the adaptability of the climate and grasses to their business is found in the fact that they have made and are continuing to make heavy outlays of money to obtain full-blooded and high-graded animals of the best breeds. A large number of the bulls, stallions and rams owned in the State are imported, and many of them are thoroughbred. There are also a good many imported cows, mares and ewes owned here. Most of these are high-priced animals, and their aggregate cost counts well up into the hundreds of thousands of dollars.

THE DAIRY INTEREST, WOOL GROWING, ETC.

The dairy interest in Minnesota has rapidly grown to imposing proportions. The creameries make butter equal to the best product of Western New York, and cheese which has no superior.

Wool and poultry form important sources of revenue to the Minnesota farmer. Besides the opportunities already enumerated for deriving profit from his labor, he also has his garden. If he lives near enough to a large city to send fresh vegetables and berries to market by wagon or railway, he can find

ready sale for them; and the canning factories, which are being constantly established in different parts of the State, add largely to the chances of disposing of these products profitably. Tons of vegetables are marketed every year already, and the demand is not nearly supplied. In addition to these are the strawberries, raspberries, currrants, blackberries, etc., which may be inexpensively cultivated, yield abundantly and sell readily. If he is in a timbered locality he may have the further resource of cranberries, blueberries, etc., that grow wild, and of ginseng and other medicinal roots and plants that are found in most of the wooded districts.

DOUBLE ROADWAY, PARK BOULEVARD.

INEXHAUSTIBLE MANUFACTURING RESOURCES.

While the development of the agricultural resources of Minnesota have so far chiefly engrossed the attention of her inhabitants, the conditions are now arising which will cause more attention to be paid to turning some of her vast manufacturing and mineral resources to account. Minnesota is destined to, in time, become one of the busiest hives of varied industry on the continent. Her unequaled natural water powers have already been referred to. She not only possesses the motive power to operate machinery to work up material, but either does or can produce the material to be operated upon. Her forests supply abundance of pine, cedar, birch, oak, ash, maple, walnut, etc.; her quarries yield granites, syenites, quartzites, limestones, sandstones, slates, etc., which cannot be excelled for bridge and general building purposes, monuments, ornaments, etc. She has the clays for brick, pottery, delftware, and probably porcelain, and superior white sand for glass, stone yielding the best of lime and cement, and extensive beds of lime and kaolin. Her agricultural products afford cheap and excellent material for the manufacture of bread-stuffs, starch, malt, sugar, syrups, linen, cordage, paper, etc. Her flocks of sheep, herds of cattle and droves of swine can furnish ample supplies of wool and hides for making cloth, flannels, blankets, leather, etc., while the packing and curing of their flesh might also be made to afford employment to people within the limits of the State. The mines in the northeastern counties afford iron, copper, silver and other minerals.

THE DEVELOPMENT OF MANUFACTURES.

The earliest manufactories in the State were those of lumber, and this was the only manufactured product shipped hence until within the past twenty-five years. The industry was the natural consequence of the existence of pine forests and boundless water power. The next great manufacturing industry, in the order of its development, was flour manufacturing. Minnesota now has within her borders as many as 500 flouring mills, some of which are the largest in the world. Minneapolis, on account of the purchases of wheat to meet the requirements of her enormous mills, as long ago as 1884 took rank as the leading primary wheat market in the world, her receipts of that cereal exceeding those of Chicago by 2,000,000 bushels. The flour production of the State in that year reached 8,000,000 barrels.

INTERIOR OF 1ST BAPTIST CHURCH. FROM "SATURDAY SPECTATOR."

Besides saw-mills and grist-mills there are in the State, planing mills, door and sash factories, wagon, carriage and sleigh factories, cooper shops, railroad car manufactories and repair shops, threshing and other agricultural machine shops, paper mills, printing offices, lithographic establishments, wood and metal engravers, map publishers, book publishers, foundries and finishing shops, engine and boiler factories, plow and harrow factories, butter-tub factories, fruit-canning establishments, furniture factories, potteries, brick-yards, three cutting and polishing establishments, a terra cotta lumber factory and a factory of terra cotta ornaments and house trimmings, a hydraulic cement factory, windmill, chair and moulding factories, fanning mill and school furniture factories, several fence factories, factories of iron architectural ornaments and galvanized iron cornices and window and door trimmings, boot and shoe factories, fire-brick and drain-tile factories, and all the usual minor factories that are found in other States of the Union.

THE DEVELOPMENT OF MINERAL WEALTH.

The development of the mining industry in the Lake Superior region of Minnesota, although still in its infancy, promises results which the wildest range of the imagination can hardly grasp. The rocks in every part of what is known as the Burnt District, east of Vermillion Lake, and extending across the northern parts of Lake and Cook Counties, are seamed with thread-like veins of copper and silver; and, extending from Vermillion Lake seventy-five miles eastward, with a width of from twenty to thirty miles, is what is called the "Iron Range," being a vast deposit of a superior quality of iron ore, of the hematite specular variety, assaying from sixty-five to seventy-two per cent. of metallic iron. This ore is everywhere easily accessible, its upper surface being frequently exposed and nowhere concealed beneath more than a shallow covering. There is probably no other iron deposit in the world that can be so inexpensively mined, and none that is so convenient to facilities for cheap transportation. Railways, already partly built, have been projected, which will fully open up this district to the world. The iron mines of Minnesota are already beginning to compete with those of Michigan, Pennsylvania and Ohio. The City of Duluth bids fair to, in time, become the seat of smelting works as extensive as any in the Union.

Successful efforts have also been made at copper mining at several points along the north shore of Lake Superior; and near the north boundary line, from Pigeon Point to Loon Lake, fine specimens of silver ore have been obtained. Gold is found in the same vicinity, and some good specimens of plumbago have been taken from Pigeon Point. An important mineral resource of Minnesota lies in the splendid quarries of slate, granite, sandstone and limestone that abound in the State. On the St. Louis River the slate quarries are large and of good quality. From the same region comes the Fond du Lac stone—purple sandstone which is acknowledged to be one of the most beautiful building stones ever

utilized; Minnesota granite is already famous for its beauty and excellence, and is found in inexhaustible quarries of various colors, composition, etc., at Sauk Rapids. From Kasota is brought an orange tinted sandstone of great durability. At St. Paul are vast quarries of limestone; clays suitable for brick making are found in several portions of the State.

TRANSPORTATION FACILITIES.

The earliest civilized travelers who put their opinions about Minnesota on record were deeply impressed with the importance of its natural facilities for commerce. Although located in the very heart of the continent, they found it provided with two navigable water courses connecting it with the Atlantic seaboard at points widely distinct from each other. In the era preceding the introduction of railways, channels for transportation by water were almost essential to commercial intercourse, and they are still of moment, for the country that possesses them is able, through its opportunity to resort to competitive methods of transportation which they afford, to avoid submission to the oppressive policy sometimes practiced by railway companies toward communities wholly dependent upon them for facilities of commerce.

The natural advantages of Minnesota are not confined, either, to these two great outlets for conveying her products to the markets of the world, but the Red River and its navigable tributaries afford her communication with the vast, fertile region still farther distant in the Northwest, and which is now being rapidly peopled. In the not very distant future these will, no doubt, become useful as commercial highways and contribute materially to the prosperity of the State. Then there is the St. Croix and Minnesota Rivers, and the Mississippi above St. Anthony Falls, which are navigable for small steamers, and could, with slight improvement, be made to afford some four hundred miles of increased channels for commercial intercourse by water in the interior of the State. These rivers, too, are connected with navigable lakes that may readily be added to this system of interior communication and extend it still farther.

A NETWORK OF RAILWAYS.

Besides these natural thoroughfares, Minnesota is richly provided with railway facilities. Six great trunk lines connect her with Milwaukee, Chicago, St. Louis, New Orleans, and all the grand railroad systems of the United States and Canada. She has direct communication now with the Pacific coast at San Francisco and, by means of the great Northern Pacific line, at Puget Sound; and with the Atlantic *via* the newly completed "Soo" route. In the more distant future the Manitoba and Canadian Pacific roads will connect her with the vast and fertile region the latter traverses, and open still another avenue to the Western ocean. Two other great railway corporations are operating lines across Dakota. These roads place it beyond question that Minnesota affords cheap and ample facilities not only for supplying the Eastern markets with her agricultural and manufactured products, but also the nearest and most direct routes of communication with the markets of both Europe and Asia.

By their means she has become a general thoroughfare of commerce and travel. In winter whatever transportation flows eastward from Central British America, or by way of the Northern Pacific Railroad, including through freight and travel from China and Japan, is diverted from its direct course, because of the suspension of lake navigation, and seeks the continuation of its journey overland by railroad lines running from St. Paul eastward. And in summer seasons much of the travel eastward by the Union Pacific and its auxiliary lines bends northward through Minnesota to enjoy the luxury of lake voyages from Duluth. All this passing freight and travel augments the commercial importance of the

NEW COURT HOUSE.

State, and many thousands of tourists, attracted by the delightful climate, beautiful scenery and excellent opportunities for hunting and fishing, stop here every summer for recreation. Thus the peculiarities of the situation of the State not only tend to add to her commerce, but indirectly contribute to enhance the prices of her products generally in her home markets and increase the value of her real estate. The interior railway facilities of Minnesota are second to those of no other State in the Union. There is no locality in the State south of the Northern Pacific Railroad that is twenty-five miles distant from a line of railway.

MINNESOTA'S PROSPEROUS POPULATION.

Minnesota has within the memory of every adult man and woman now living been largely wrested from the grasp of savages and become the happy home of over a million and a quarter of civilized and intelligent people. The population represents all civilized nationalities, and all religious denominations, classes and vocations. They have come hither to build permanent homes for themselves and families, and are, therefore, vitally interested in the welfare and reputation of the country of their adoption. They have enacted good laws to secure the peace and safety of society and promote general happiness and prosperity, and such laws are rigidly enforced in every part of the State. Each organized county has its local officers and courts, and offenders against good order rarely escape prompt arrest and punishment, even in the frontier settlements. It may, indeed, be justly claimed for the people of Minnesota that they are peaceful and law-abiding and that the tone of moral sentiment is fully equal to that of communities generally.

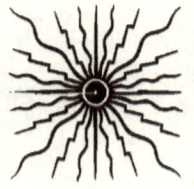

MINNEAPOLIS.

An Exposition of Her Mercantile, Manufacturing and Jobbing Interests.

MILLERS' AND MANUFACTURERS' MUTUAL INSURANCE CO., 300 Oneida Block —This company, which is a local one, was established in 1881. The officers are: E. R. Barber, President; C. McC. Reeve, Vice-President; O. C. Merriman, Treasurer; C. B. Shove, Secretary; F. S. Danforth, Assistant Secretary; J. D. Sheahan, Gen'l Agent. There is an Executive Committee and a very influential Board of Directors. The special features of this Fire Insurance Company are, that it is a mutual company, that it is the oldest mutual institution in the Northwest. It was organized to afford the same advantages that stock companies offer and at a minimum rate. The semi-annual statement of the secretary shows that the company is in a most exceptionally flourishing condition.

MINNESOTA FIRE ASSOCIATION, 300 Oneida Block—This association was organized in 1865, as the Minnesota Farmers' Mutual Fire Insurance Association. About the year 1887 it was re-organized and put up $100,000 guarantee capital, under the State law. It is now enabled to do any and all kinds of work. The following are the officers : E. R. Barber, President; O. C. Merriman, Vice-President; C. B. Shove, Secretary; F. S. Danforth, Assistant Secretary and C. K. Sidle, Treasurer. There is a Farm Department and a specialty is made of farm work and detached dwellings, also a Mercantile Department, which makes a specialty of sprinkled risks. The association has paid since its organization the sum of $265,000 on account of losses. The question of the advisability of insuring against fire is one to which there can be but one answer, and it only behooves those who avail themselves of the indemnity to see that the corporation upon which they rely is one that can bear the risk. An inquiry of this nature into the stability of the Minnesota Fire Association would surely lead to a satisfactory result.

THE WEST HOTEL, Hennepin Avenue and Fifth Street—One of the most important features of a city, at least to the traveling public, is its hotel accommodation. America is one of the most fortunate countries in the world in this respect; and if there is one city in which the hotel accommodation is better than another—all other things considered—it is Minneapolis. The West Hotel is known throughout the civilized world, and is admitted on all hands to have few, if any, equals, and certainly no superior. It was built by Col. John T. West, who had for some time been proprietor of the Nicollet House, where he was eminently successful. The cost of the West was $1,500,000, and it is one of the most thoroughly well-built structures in the United States. Everything relating to its erection and decoration was done on a grand and most liberal scale. Wherever a question arose as to whether an additional outlay should be incurred in order to make the hotel more complete, it was always decided on the side of liberality. The consequence of this is that Minneapolis can boast of the possession of a hotel which is one of the most beautiful, and at the same time one of the best appointed hotels for comfort, that has ever been built. The architecture is original, being a happy combination of the Queen Anne and Colonial styles. It is built of red pressed brick and marble, with terra cotta trimmings. The

THE WEST HOTEL.

ground plan is 196x174 feet, and the total height 200 feet. There are eight stories. The rotunda or lobby is 70x90 feet. Leading from the floor is the grand stairway, which is wholly built of white marble. There are on the same floor as the rotunda the reading, reception, news, telegraph, billiard, coat and wash rooms, which are all designed for the accommodation of 1,000 guests. The second floor is divided into the grand dining room, three private dining rooms, ladies' ordinary, kitchen, serving room, guests' parlors, gentlemen's club room, and suites of private parlors for wedding parties and distinguished guests.

All the flooring is of marble, except in the parlors and private suites, carpets of the richest kind being used there. The walls are wainscotted with marble and mahogany, with the ceilings of carved mahogany in panels. The grand dining room is the finest, beyond all possible question, in America. The floor is of mottled marble, with the finishing in mahogany, in Moorish style. Every bedroom in the house, of which there are 407. is large and well lighted, thoroughly ventilated, and supplied with an abundant flow of hot and cold water, pumped pure from an artesian well 700 feet deep. There are no dark rooms. The furniture of the house throughout is most rich and elegant, having been made expressly for the West, as were also the carpets, table linen, silverware, etc. The billiard room is 50x80 feet, and contains sixteen handsomely carved mahogany billiard and pool tables, especially designed for this hotel. One of the most important features of the hotel is the fact that it is absolutely fire proof. To point out half the advantages and beauties possessed by the West Hotel would require the space of a large volume, and only a few of them can be sketched here; but this short account would be altogether lacking in a prominent feature if it did not refer to the management of the house. This was entrusted, while the building was yet incomplete, to the care of Mr. Charles W. Shepherd. This gentleman had been connected with some of the principal hotels in New York, Coney Island, St. Louis and Washington. The great success of his management has amply proved the wisdom of the selection, and he still continues to fill his responsible position with credit to himself and to the entire satisfaction of the swarms of visitors to the house.

HAXTUN STEAM HEATER CO., 215 Second Avenue South—Haxtun Steam Heater Co. are manufacturers of steam heating apparatus and supplies, iron pipe, steam fittings, brass goods, boilers, radiators, etc., and contractors for steam and hot water heating and ventilating. The company succeeded the Anderson Steam Heater Co. in 1872. W. E. Haxtun is President, J. H. Pierce, Secretary; E. E. Baker, Treasurer; C. S. Wentworth, Manager of the Northwestern business. They have a working capital of $500,000, and the annual sales amount to over $1,000,000. The manufactory is at Kewaunee, Ill., with branch houses at Minneapolis and Duluth, Minn., and St. Joseph, Mo. They have furnished heating apparatus for thirty or more large business blocks, including Temple Court, Lumber Exchange, Syndicate Block, Loan and Trust Building, Edison Electric Light and Power Building, Kasota Block, etc. The heating and ventilating apparatus of twenty-six school buildings and that of very many residences within the city has been put up by them, and among others at St. Paul the Albion Flats, Moore Building, W. J. Dyer & Bro. Building, and throughout the State many more, including the Hotel Brunswick at Faribault, Shattuck Schools and State Normal School at Moorhead.

FARMERS' AND MECHANICS' SAVINGS BANK, of Minneapolis, Temple Court, corner Hennepin and Washington Avenues—In presenting a sketch of this bank to the thousands of readers of this work the following article from the Minneapolis Annual of the *Pioneer-Press*, published Dec. 25th, 1888, answers every purpose so well that we reproduce it complete and invite special attention to its contents: "There is not in the City of Minneapolis, nor anywhere else in the entire Northwest, an institution of more sterling merit than the Farmers' and Mechanics' Savings Bank, doing business in the Temple Court Block, corner Washington and Hennepin Avenues. It is the only real savings bank in the city, and transacts no commercial business whatever. In adopting this course it is enabled to offer its customers the most perfect guarantee against loss, thus affording the most absolute security to its depositors. Its history the past fifteen years has been one of continual advancement, and its sphere of usefulness is ever extending, as is shown most conclusively by the fact that its deposits now exceed $3,000,000. The year 1888 has been the most successful and remarkable in its career, 5,000 names having been added to its list of depositors, which now number 37,000, and $25,000 added to its surplus, after paying a five per cent. dividend to its patrons, while its deposits show an increase of $700,000. The officers of the bank are Clinton Morrison, President; Thomas Lowry, Vice-President, and E. H. Moulton, Treasurer; and these, with Messrs. John De Laittre, J. W. Johnson, William Chandler, M. B. Koon, R. B. Langdon, John S. Pillsbury and J. C. Oswald, compose the directorate. To any one at all familiar with Minneapolis and her material and wonderful progress, these names furnish a guarantee of the most substantial character, as they comprise some of the most successful, best known and most trustworthy of her business, professional and public men. The management of the bank has always been characterized by the most conservative and business-like methods, and so thoroughly perfect have the precautions taken to guard the interests of its patrons proven that not one cent has ever been lost since its doors were first opened to the uses of the public. More than this need not be said to convince any one desirous of availing himself of a safe, sure and profitable means of protecting and accumulating his savings that this bank offers most encouraging inducements to that end; and we are only too glad to say to such persons that we most heartily commend the institution to their fullest confidence and consideration." Mr. Moulton, the treasurer of the bank, to whose efforts are chiefly due its most remarkable success, is also City Treasurer of Minneapolis, and one of her most public-spirited and influential citizens.

NORTH STAR BOOT AND SHOE. CO., Manufacturers and Jobbers of Boots and Shoes, 18, 20 and 22 Third Street North—The North Star Boot and Shoe Company first began operations in the month of July, 1873. The capital stock of the company is $200,000.00. The present board of the company's officers consists of the following gentlemen : President, C. B. Heffelfinger; Vice-President, Wm. S. King; Secretary, John A. Lucy; Treasurer, Preston King. The company's building is an imposing structure, six stories high and about 57 x 157 feet square. In this they have their factory, store rooms and offices. They occupy the entire building. In their manufacturing department one hundred and twenty-five men and women are employed and kept busy during every working day of the year. This fact of itself goes far to show the magnitude, enterprise and commercial stability of the house. Twelve salesmen are constantly kept on the road, representing the interests of the company in country towns and smaller cities, and taking the orders which are always so promptly and satisfactorily filled by their house. If anything, the company seems to have throve upon Eastern competition, and have always invited instead of striving to dodge it in any particular. From a trade which at first was forced to rely for support and life upon the country immediately adjacent to Minneapolis, they have reached out into the trade marts of Iowa, Michigan, Wisconsin, Nebraska, Colorado, North and South Dakota, Montana, Oregon and Washington Territory (or State). They have spared neither time nor money to place on the market a class of goods the merits of which will bear the closest comparison with any or all Eastern or foreign manufacturers. This is distinctively a Minneapolis institution, a fact in which the proprietors take the same pardonable pride the city at large has always felt in it. The members of the company are all old residents of Minneapolis, some of them being prominently identified with other valuable business interests in the city. Major C. B. Heffelfinger is the only member of the firm who claims a war record, he having served in the First Minnesota Regiment, which rendered such valiant service in the country's hour of need. Wm. S. King, too, by his open-handed philanthropy, political and financial prominence and unbounded faith in the glorious future of the State of Minnesota and its metropolis, Minneapolis, has acquired a popularity and circle of acquaintanceship not confined to the State.

EUSTIS BROTHERS, Watches, Diamonds and Jewelry, 328 Nicollet Avenue—This is one of the pioneer jewelry stores of the city, it having been established so long ago as 1872 by the present proprietors. The business was at that time very small, and has gradually grown up with the city until it has attained its present large proportions. But not alone to the increased size of the city does the concern owe its success. It was principally the business talent of the two brothers, combined with push and energy and a thorough knowledge of the business, that brought the establishment to the prominent position it now enjoys. The beautiful stock, much of which is displayed in most elegant show-cases, is valued at $70,000. It consists of the most varied selection of jewelry, solid silverware, diamonds, watches, clocks and some beautiful cut glass of the very choicest description. The store, with its fine mirrors at the back and beautiful display, is a sight worth seeing. The Brothers Eustis are New England men. They manufacture jewelry, so that parties wishing to have jewelry produced from their designs can get it executed by this firm. They have six experienced assistants. The amount of business done by the firm ranges from $75,000 to $100,000 per annum.

R. L. PRATT, Real Estate, 323 Hennepin Avenue. Mr. Pratt is one of the oldest residents of the city, having been here for thirty-nine years. At the time of the war he was in California on business which did not admit of his leaving, and he thus missed any direct participation in the stirring events

STONE ARCH BRIDGE, MINNEAPOLIS—ST. P., M. & M. R'Y.

incident thereto. This he fretted about a good deal at the time, but he has since come to the conclusion that his being prevented from joining in the important events then happening was not the worst evil that could have befallen him. He conducts a general real estate business, but he is particularly interested in Hazel Dell Addition, in the Third Ward, corner of Nineteenth and Upton Avenues; also in thirty-five acres adjoining Hazel Dell. He negotiates loans to some extent, principally for Eastern capitalists. He also collects rents, rents buildings, and manages for non-residents.

WOLVERTON & LEWIS, Real Estate, Loans and Insurance, 251 Nicollet Avenue, Room 2 —This firm was established in 1883, but both the members of the firm had been in the real estate business for a number of years prior to that date. Mr. Wolverton has been in Minneapolis for thirty years, and Mr. Lewis for eighteen years. The property handled by them is principally their own. Among other valuable properties of theirs may be mentioned Wolverton's Addition, platted in 1882,

Thirty-second and Thirty-fourth Streets, and Portland and Third Avenues South, a very fine tract of forty acres, with two lines of street cars, city water, and dwellings of from two to five thousand dollars, in Eighth Ward; Wolverton's Second Addition, Thirty-eighth Street and Third Avenue South; Wolverton & Lewis' Addition, Portland Avenue and Fortieth Street South, very desirable additions, in which there are cheap lots of from $600 to $1,500 each, very suitable for dwellings. They have lately put up seven dwellings on Wolverton & Lewis' Addition. They do a great deal of loaning, as they have, through their long experience in the business and their excellent business standing, good facilities for placing loans. They have the highest references—Northwestern National Bank, the Security Bank, Citizens' Bank, the Hon. A. R. McGill, and C. A. Pillsbury & Co., among others.

C. F. JACKSON, Exclusively Black Dress Goods and Silks, Underwear, Gloves, Hosiery, White Goods, Trimmings and Notions, 525 Nicollet Avenue—A popular house with the ladies of the Northwest is the dry goods house of C. F. Jackson. It is the only dry goods house in the Northwest that makes a specialty of black dress goods. Mr. Jackson is a native of Ohio. He was for fifteen years a member of the dry goods firm of Marsh & Jackson, of Norwalk, Ohio. Recognizing the opening for an exclusively dry goods specialty house in the Northwestern metropolis, he sold his interest in Norwalk and came to this city in 1887. The growth of his business has been steady, and has exceeded his expectations. His store is divided into four general departments, viz.: Black dress goods, underwear, hosiery, white goods; gloves, and trimmings and notions. The main feature of his business is, however, black dress goods and silks. Eventually he intends to handle no other line but this. His business now gives employment to eight clerks. He occupies two stores, and carries a stock of $25,000. He advertises extensively and is reaping a large mail-order business therefrom.

JAMES H. BISHOP & CO., Paper Manufacturers and Wholesale Dealers, 21, 23 and 25 Third Street North—James H. Bishop & Co., paper manufacturers and wholesale dealers, operate one of the largest houses in the West in their line. The firm comprise the following named persons: James H. Bishop, Minneapolis; C. M. Smith and T. F. Rice, Chicago. Capital stock of the firm, $50,000.00. The affairs of the firm are under the immediate supervision of Mr. Bishop, who gives his time and personal attention to the details of the business, he being the President and Treasurer of the company. Their establishment is a thorough paper emporium, and is one of the principal sources from which is drawn the supply for the ever-increasing demands of the growing West for paper in its many useful and marketable forms. The area of their trade is not confined to the Northwest States and Territories, but has extended its limits back into the States of Illinois and Missouri, heretofore considered the sole market property of Eastern concerns. By their course in business they have done much to prove true the assertion that Minneapolis is the trade center of the great West. This house is represented on the road and to the outside trade by five traveling salesmen, who apparently find but little leisure in their occupation, if the amount of trade secured through that channel alone be a proper basis of an opinion. The force employed in the house, clerical and mechanical, consists of twenty-seven men and women, and a visit to the establishment will show there is plenty for each to do. James H. Bishop is a regular war veteran, having served as a member of the 4th New York Heavy Artillery, and also 140th New York Infantry. He saw all of the war, and all he ever wishes to.

JOSHUA WILLIAMS, Wholesale and Retail Dealer in General Hardware, No. 102 Hennepin Avenue—The history of this house is so intimately associated with the story of the development and growth of Minneapolis, that a word as to its career could nowhere be more appropriately inserted than in a work of this character. It is the oldest hardware store in Minneapolis proper, being in existence since 1856, and the present proprietor has been associated with the business since 1861. The trade is both a wholesale and retail one, and the stock carried is a very complete and varied one, as it includes not alone everything in the general hardware line, but also bar iron and steel, nails and carriage and wagon woods, blacksmiths' stock and supplies, etc. Mr. Williams lived in Minneapolis since he was thirteen years of age, and has witnessed the city of his adoption grow from a small hamlet to her present vast and metropolitan proportions. He is conservative and careful in his business methods, a man highly esteemed and widely known as a citizen, and stands well up in financial and trade circles.

THE MENDENHALL GREENHOUSES, City Store 15 Fourth Street South—Mr. Mendenhall, the proprietor of these greenhouses, was born in Guildford County, North Carolina, and came here in 1856, bringing a basket of flowers with him. In 1866 he commenced the business of a florist in a small way and has gradually increased his business until at the present time it is quite large, but is still

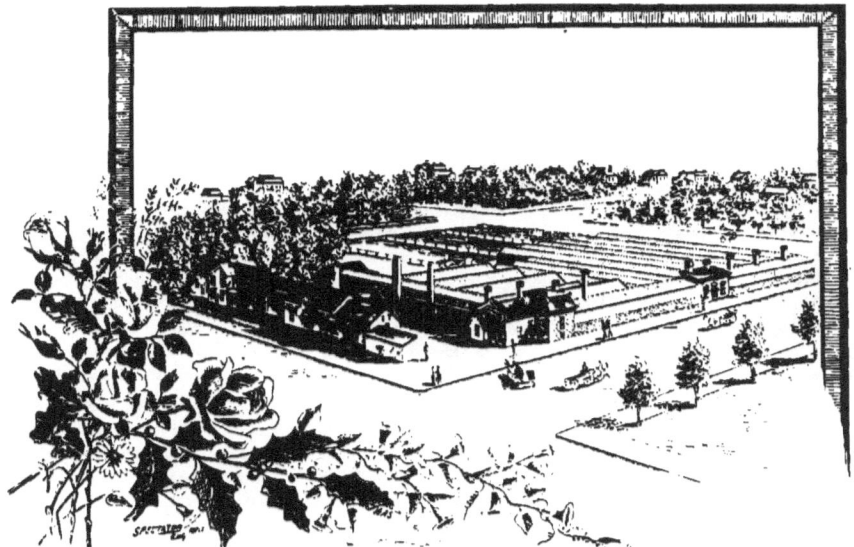

THE MENDENHALL GREENHOUSES.

steadily on the increase. The way in which Mr. Mendenhall commenced his business is unique. He began the cultivation of flowers simply as a matter of taste, and found so many eager applicants for them that he was induced to make a charge for his surplus plants. This, however, did not by any means stop the demand and, without intending to foster a trade in that line, Mr. Mendenhall found himself at the head of a flourishing business. It is unnecessary to say that he must have been well qualified for the conduct of such a concern as he now possesses. He has now very extensive greenhouses, the aggregate surface of glass being no less than 45,000 square feet. His trade extends all over the Northwest, even as far as the State of Washington, and its volume amounts to many thousands of dollars annually. He cultivates all kinds of flowers and bedding plants. His greenhouses, twenty-one in number, are at the corner of Eighteenth Street and First Avenue South.

F. S. MARTIN, Steam and Hot Water Heating and Ventilating Apparatus, No. 304 First Avenne South—The business over which Mr. Martin presides was first started in 1883. Mr. Martin was born in New York State and has been here just six years. Since he began here he has greatly extended his business, which now reaches all over the Northwest. He employs a number of hands, varying from twenty-five to fifty. Mr. Martin thoroughly understands the business in which he is engaged, and no matter whether the apparatus be required for a residence or a public building, he is equally capable of seeing that every satisfaction is secured. Nearly all his work is done by contract. The volume of his business varies from $40,000 to $60,000 annually. The great advance that has been made in the methods of heating and ventilating has greatly increased the demand for apparatus such as Mr. Martin supplies. The following are a few of the more prominent buildings in which Mr. Martin has placed his work: The Tribune Building, the new Library Building on Hennepin Avenue, the First Baptist Church, the State Experimental Farm buildings, the Brunswick and National Hotels, the Medical College, the Scandia, Citizens and other banks. Also the residences of H. Alden Smith, S. T. McKnight, Dr. S. H. Chute and many others. Mr. Martin makes a specialty of hot water heating, in which line he has a wide-spread reputation. Those building or about to build will do well to consult Mr. Martin on his special system of hot water heating.

W. B. DUNNELL, Architect, Bank of Commerce Building—Mr. Dunnell was educated for his profession at the Institute of Technology, Boston, Mass., and in Paris. For six years prior to his coming here he was a Superintendent of Construction on Government Buildings at Memphis, Tenn., and Kansas City, Mo. In the fall of 1882, he located in this city, and has practiced his profession here since that time. His general work is of a public character, and among the many buildings for which he is the architect are the following: Pillsbury College, the State Public School for Dependent Children, at Owatonna, in this State, the State Soldiers' Home, at Minnehaha, the Bloomington Avenue Presbyterian Church in this city, the third Minnesota Hospital for Insane, at Fergus Falls, and the new Reform School at Red Wing. He is a man of undoubted ability and has attained a high position among his professional brethren. The demand for buildings of a high order is on the increase in the Northwest, and the future career of a professional man like Mr. Dunnell, who has already made his mark, is pretty well assured.

CITIZENS' FUEL CO., Van Dusen & Jacoby, Proprietors, Wood and Coal, Office No. 430 Nicollet Avenue—Messrs. F. L. Van Dusen and F. G. Jacoby started in Minneapolis in July, 1888, in the fuel and supply business, and have since that time steadily become favorably known by consumers in all parts of the city. Their yards are at Sixth Avenue S. E. and Main Street, at corner Twelfth Avenue South and Washington and at Seventh and Cedar. Their business has trebled, the outlook is good and their venture has in all respects been satisfactory. Coal, wood and coke are dealt in. Business for the winter aggregated $20,000 worth of wood and $30,000 of coal. Their principal office is centrally located and the future is promising. F. G. Jacoby bought in March all the interest of F. L. Van Dusen and is continuing under same firm, with Mr. Geo. G. Jacoby as active manager.

MINNESOTA TITLE INSURANCE & TRUST CO., Oneida Block—This company was established in 1885. The officers of the company are Joseph U. Barnes, President; Putnam D. McMillan, 1st Vice-President; Austin F. Kelly, 2d Vice-President; Daniel Fish, Counsel; J. W. Mauck, Secretary and Treasurer; J. M. W. Pratt, Superintendent of Abstracts. The subscribed capital is $500,000, of which $350,000 is paid up. The guaranty fund deposited with the State Auditor is $200,000. The primary object of the Association is the insurance of real estate titles for the benefit of mortgagees and owners, and transfer of real estate. They have also a regular mortgage loan business, and they receive deposits, the same as a savings bank. They also have a trust department, and sell bonds, such as State bonds or school bonds. The officers are all men of the very highest standing. Mr. Barnes was formerly president of the Douglas County Bank of Alexandria; Mr. McMillan is a large real estate dealer here; Mr. Kelly is one of the oldest mortgage loan men in the city; Judge Fish is a well-known attorney; Mr. Pratt was abstracter and attorney in Milwaukee for a number of years, and Mr. Mauck has all the ins and outs of the title insurance business at his fingers' ends. The company has an abstract plant that has cost over $70,000 to accumulate. Every instrument filed in the Record Office is copied and the copy carefully lodged in the record department of this company. Experts are employed for this purpose—a person of two years' experience being allotted a certain grade of work, a person of three years' experience a grade higher, and so on, until the very highest grade of work is reached. The whole system is very complete, and is the result of many years' experience. It would be almost, if not quite, impossible without long experience to formulate a set of rules that would be equal to those in use in the offices of this company. About thirty people are employed by this institution.

CEDAR LAKE ICE COMPANY, Office, 4 Washington Avenue South—This is an old ice company, having been formed about twelve or fifteen years ago. The present officers are E. C. Babb, President (President of the Home Building and Loan Association), Emerson Cole, Vice-President (President

People's Bank), and D. M. Chute, Secretary and Treasurer. It will thus be seen that the concern is an important one, but a glance at its business operations will confirm and strengthen this impression. The store-houses are at Lake Calhoun, Blaisdell Avenue and Twenty-ninth and one-half Street, Dufont and Franklin Avenue, Lyndale Avenue, opposite Central Park, Twenty-second Street South and C., M. & St. P. R. R. and Nicollet Island. The quantity stored this year was about 60,000 tons. The ice for family trade is all cut from Cedar Lake and Lake Calhoun. A comparatively small quantity of river ice is cut, and that is used for cooling

CEDAR LAKE ICE COMPANY'S ICE-HOUSE.

purposes only. The annual trade amounts to about a quarter of a million dollars. Seventy-five hands and twenty-five wagons are employed by the company in their business.

COLTON'S JAPANESE AND CHINESE CURIO STORE, 606 Nicollet Avenue—This is a wholesale and retail business. It was established by Mr. G. W. Colton in 1885. This house deals in Japanese and Chinese goods exclusively, importing some of these goods direct from Japan and China, others coming through a large importing house in New York. This connection gives them a better chance of getting these goods than any one else in the trade. There is something very attractive in this class of goods. The quaintness and absence of vulgarity in the designs render them acceptable to almost all classes of purchasers, and the vast assortment and varied character of the goods present an almost bewildering choice from which to make a selection. The stock is valued at from eight to ten thousand dollars, and is, without doubt, the best selected to be found this side of New York, and every novelty is to be found in it. Seven men are employed at this establishment, and there is an extensive mail-order business done all over the Northwest. The annual sales are large for an entirely new business.

THE LEONARD & IZARD CO., Consulting and Contracting Electrical Engineers, Room 908, Lumber Exchange—This enterprising and important company of consulting and contracting electrical engineers came to do business in Minneapolis, and to identify themselves with her interests to the extent of a branch establishment here, in October, 1888. Their principal office is in "The

Rookery," Chicago, and they also have a branch office at Milwaukee, in the New Insurance Building. The business of the firm is the erection or construction of electric railroads and the putting in of all classes of electric plants and apparatus, such as incandescent electric light plants, arc light plants, electrical power transmission plants, storage battery plants, electric light wiring, etc., also the erection of high economy steam plants and the installation of apparatus for the utilization of water power; in fact, the doing any engineering and construction work where a high degree of mechanical skill and proficiency in electrical science is requisite. The electric railroad at St. Joseph, Mo., was built by this firm; also the electric street railway in Atlantic City, N. J., and many others. Mr. W. S. Andrews, who is a member of the company, has present charge of the management of its Northwestern business. A specialty is made of large electrical engineering jobs, such as incandescent and arc light central stations, large power transmission plants, etc. The firm also handle and deal in a full line of commercial electrical apparatus and supplies.

M. LARA & CO., 512 Nicollet Avenue, Carpets, Window Shades, Draperies, Lace Curtains—One of the largest carpet and drapery establishments in the city is that of M. Lara & Co., 512 Nicollet Avenue. The concern was formerly run under the firm name of Kenyon & Lara, but has been for many years doing business under its present style. Since 1882 it has increased its volume of business about four-fold. Formerly the stock carried by the firm amounted to $12,000 or $15,000; it now reaches as high as $50,000 at least. Besides a very large retail business in the city, the firm do a considerable mail-order business. Their stock of draperies and carpets is very fine. Almost every description of carpet may be found in their immense show rooms, the floor space of which exceeds 12,000 square feet. They are now doing a business of about $100,000 annually, but do not intend to stop at those figures, every year making the showing more important. They have at the back of their premises, up-stairs, a fine work-room, where carpets and draperies are made to fill the orders of customers. A carpet cleaning works, operated by steam and located at the corner of Fourth Avenue and Eleventh Street, is connected with the establishment.

BRUNSWICK CIGAR STORE, Frank J. Jungen, Proprietor, Fine Imported and Domestic Cigars, corner Hennepin and Fourth—One of the handsomest stores to be found in the Northwest is the Brunswick Cigar Store, situated on the corner of Hennepin and Fourth Street, of which Mr. Frank J. Jungen is the proprietor. Mr. Jungen came from his native State, Wisconsin, in 1881, and traveled for H. G. Harrison & Co., and their successors, Harrison, Farrington & Co., continuously from that time until January, 1st, of this year, when he embarked into business for himself. As a salesman on the road Mr. Jungen was eminently successful, a fact demonstrated by the number of years he remained with one firm, and throughout his career a great specialty of cigars and tobacco was made, giving that branch a careful study and attention. It was therefore natural that his start in business should be in this line. The location of the store is one of best business points in the city, and with its immense double fronts of large plate glass on Hennepin Avenue and Fourth Street respectively, together with the magnificent interior finish, presents an imposing appearance. No pains or expense has been spared in fitting up the store, as Mr. Jungen is not the man to do things by halves, and, being a man of exquisite taste, has certainly succeeded in fitting up one of the best arranged and finest equipped stores in the Northwest. He carries a large and well-assorted stock of the choicest imported Key West and domestic cigars, among which may be mentioned such as V. Martinez, Ybor & Co.'s, Wachelbergs & Co.'s, Lozano, Peudas & Co.'s, Celestino, Palacio & Co.'s, Manuel Garcias', Pedro Murios', Villar de Villars', and numerous other celebrated manufacturers' lines, which space will not permit of mentioning. Besides these he has a large assortment of plug, fine-cut and smoking tobacco, cigarettes, snuffs, pipes and fancy smokers' articles—in fact, everything to be found in a first-class cigar and tobacco store.

Mr. Jungen is a married man with a family, though only twenty-eight years of age, so that he has, probably, a long career before him. He is precisely of the right make-up for a successful business man, with a large acquaintance throughout the city and the State, obtained while traveling. He has started in in the front ranks and if he does not succeed, not only in keeping that position, but in getting ahead of all competitors, it will not be through lack of push, ability and business integrity and tact, or for the well wishes of his thousands of friends.

J. BRIGGS. Real Estate and Loans, Tribune Building, Room 14—Mr. Briggs commenced business here in 1881, in general real estate. He was born in Connecticut. He has city property for sale or exchange, lots in Brainerd, 200,000 acres of wheat lands, improved farms and pine lands.

OSAKIS—ST. P., M. & M. R'Y.

The pine lands are principally in this State, and the wheat lands in Dakota. He has discovered that when the demand for city property is dull everybody wants to get a farm, and the demand for such property is active. His list includes such a great variety of properties that he can scarcely ever be at a loss to meet the wishes of any would-be purchaser.

KAYSER & CO., Importers, Jobbers and Retailers of Wall Papers and Interior Decorations, 612 Nicollet Avenue—This is a branch establishment of M. M. Kayser & Co., 406, 408 and 410 Arch Street, Philadelphia, in which city Mr. Kayser was born. He has been in Minneapolis sixteen years, and established the present business about three years ago. It is increasing at such a rapid rate that it is 60 per cent. larger this year than it was last, and the operations literally extend from one end of the continent to the other. As a specimen of one day's orders it may be stated that no less than twelve different States each contributed their quota—Kansas, Montana, Dakota, Iowa, Missouri and Illinois being represented. Their place in Philadelphia has been established for the past eighteen years, and it is remarkable that people in the States contiguous will frequently send their orders to Minneapolis, while those near here will send to Philadelphia. It would seem that the first place that catches the eye in the advertisement is the one to which they send the order. The premises occupied by the concern here comprise a large and handsome store and a basement. The stock is large, but varies much on account of this being a distributing point for the Northwest.

I. C. SEELEY & CO., Real Estate and Loans, 9 and 10 Tribune Building—This business was established in 1872 by Mr. Seeley. Mr. W. J. Bishopp, the other member of the firm, joined about four years ago. Mr. Seeley was born in Michigan and Mr. Bishopp in New York. They are now interested in and part owners of Kenwood, between Lake of the Isles and Cedar Lake. Some very fine improvements are being made in this property, which is one of the best additions to the city. The firm control property aggregating about half a million dollars in value. They negotiate loans for private Eastern capitalists. Their experience is such that in seventeen years they never lost a dollar

for a mortgagee. On two occasions only has it been necessary to foreclose. At the time the two pieces of property brought $5,000 each. They are now each worth $50,000. At the time the business was first established, there were about 20,000 people in the city. Mr. Seeley erected the second stone front block in the city. It is still known as the Domestic Block. At the time it was erected it was thought to be an extravagant piece of architecture, but is now thrown in the shade by many other more ornate structures. He has also erected about

RESIDENCE OF I. C. SEELEY.

a hundred dwellings and business houses since he has been here. Mr. Seeley has been identified with the Y. M. C. A., and secured the completion of their rooms over the city market in 1876. He is now chairman of the Building Committee, which has in charge the building now in course of erection for the association, which will be one of the most complete buildings for the purpose in the United States, as soon as the citizens respond in their own liberal manner to the requests of the committee.

PARDRIDGE & COMPANY, Wholesale and Retail Dealers in Dry Goods, Carpets, Boots and Shoes, Nicollet Avenue and Eighth Street—The growing importance of Minneapolis has caused the establishment of many branches of Eastern houses. Among recent acquisitions may be mentioned the dry goods house of Pardridge & Co., whose main interests are in Chicago, where they maintain four houses. They also have branches in Buffalo, Detroit, Cleveland, Rockford, Ill., and Kansas City. Their Minneapolis branch was established October 15, 1888. Here they occupy a building 80x125 feet and two stories high. Fifty clerks and two delivery wagons are employed. Mr. F. R. Pardridge is the manager of this branch. Their store is divided into twenty-eight departments, each presided over by competent clerks. Among their leading departments may be mentioned those devoted to dress goods, millinery, flannels, fancy goods, hosiery, gloves, boots and shoes. They make a special feature of notions and fancy goods. They have a stock of $125,000, and every inch of space is utilized in their large store. It is a typical bazaar and its shelves are replete with goods to attract the feminine eye. The aggregate business done by the main house and branches exceeded in 1888 $13,000,000. With immense facilities, and handling such quantities of goods, they command the lowest prices, and can sell accordingly.

DR. CHAS. S. TALBERT, Dentist, 326 Nicollet Avenue—Dr. Talbert is justly considered one of the leading men in his profession in this city. He studied dentistry in Indianapolis, Indiana, and practiced there for ten years prior to his coming here. This he did in 1882, and his practice has been steadily on the increase since that time, until to-day he has one of the largest in the city. He performs all kinds of dental work, including bridge work and painless dentistry, the latter being another name for the administration to the patients of nitrous-oxide gas. Dr. Talbert has always kept himself well abreast with the times in all matters pertaining to his profession, and now occupies a high position in it. In fact, his practice here has been eminently satisfactory.

CITY MILLS, J. W. Shadewald, Proprietor, 514 Central Avenue—These mills are now so far advanced in the matter of making high grade corn meals, rye, graham, buckwheat and entire wheat flours, hominy, grits, etc., which constitute the specialties manufactured, that their products cannot be excelled by those of any other mills on earth, not even excepting those of world-wide fame at Akron, Ohio. The quarters occupied are also deserving of special mention, being an ornamentally constructed brick block, three stories high, with basement and engine room. The front of the building is of pressed brick, with cut brown stone and terra cotta trimmings and of elegant design. The block was built last year especially for this use, and the machinery put in is of the newest and best anywhere obtainable. The business was established in 1880, and is the property of Mr. J. W. Shadewald, who founded the enterprise. The special brands of corn meal made are, "Hiawatha," "Amber," "Oriental" and "Sun Flower;" of buckwheat flour, "Honey Comb," and of rye flour, "Best White Rye." All these goods are fully warranted to be as good as any on the market no matter where produced. St. Louis winter wheat flour is also handled in large quantities, as are also hay, corn, oats and feed. Mr. Shadewald is quite a young man and came to this city from Wisconsin about ten years ago. He employs ten men in connection with his business, and is one of that class of industrious and thrifty citizens to whom Minneapolis is in a large measure indebted for much of her phenomenal growth and prosperity.

A. L. MARTIN, Real Estate Dealer and Manufacturer of Brick, 10 South Fourth Street—Mr. Martin has been here since 1879. He was born at Pipersville, Wisconsin, in May, 1858. In 1882 he established his business as a real estate dealer. He now simply sells his own property, of which he has considerable in different parts. He is also an extensive manufacturer of common white brick. His yards are at Thirty-fifth Avenue North and Marshall Street, on the East Side, and at Coon Creek, about eight miles this side of Anoka. He employs between eighty and one hundred men in the two yards, and from five to twenty teams. He will turn out about six millions of brick this season. This sounds like a large number, but the great demand for building materials of all kinds will probably secure their sale as quickly as they are fit for removal.

GETZ, SUMMERL & CO., 305 Second Avenue South, Commission Merchants in Grain, Provisions, Stocks, Oils, Etc.—This firm was established in 1884, and first carried on business at 254 First Avenue South. They have now removed to a splendid office on Second Avenue South, which is fitted up with every convenience for the conduct of their large and increasing business. Their blackboard, loaded with figures, covers almost an entire side, and is the best that could be devised for the purpose. They have connections with the Western Union Telegraph, and have their own private wire;

also, direct private wires between this city and Chicago and New York. They have their own opera
tors. Sometimes they have as many as one hundred messages in a day between this city and Chicago
and New York. Besides, they have grain and stock tickers. They make a specialty of attending to
country orders. At the end of their extensive office are private rooms, lavatory, toilet, etc., and the
building is well ventilated and fitted with steam heating apparatus. The members of the firm are Mr.
H. S. Getz, who came to this country from Germany many years ago; Mr. E. Summerl and Mr. C. F.
Getz, both of whom are American born. They are three enterprising, wide-awake business men, who
are bound to bring their enterprise to a successful issue.

E. P. CROOKER & CO., Real Estate and Loans, 200 Temple Court — Mr. E. P.
Crooker and Mr. J. F. Travis, the members of this firm, have both been in business in the city for a
long time separately. This year they became associated under the firm name given above. They are
doing a large trade in city and su-
burban property. They do quite a
commission business, but make a
specialty of handling their own
property. At present they have
the control of several important
additions: one at Lake Harriet, one
at Minnehaha, one at Lake Crystal,
and one at Lake Calhoun. They
were both born in this State, and
are consequently well known. They
pay particular attention to the property of non-residents, both as to selling and renting. This forms a considerable part of their business.
Another feature of their trade is the
exchange of properties. Thus a
farmer, for instance, wishes to exchange his farm for city or suburban
property. By placing the matter
in the hands of this firm it is ten
chances to one he could be suited
right away. Or it might be the other

APOSTLE ISLANDS, LAKE SUPERIOR—C., ST. P., M. & O. R'Y.

way — a city man wanting to exchange for a farm. Another department of their business is loaning
money on real estate, and in this department also they have done a considerable amount. Both members of the firm are young business men of known ability, and have no doubt a bright future before them.

H. S. SMITH & CO., General Commission Merchants, 12 Bridge Square—The commission
house of H. S. Smith & Co., general commission merchants of No. 12 Bridge Square, is doing a healthy
trade. The concern was established about two years ago, but as an indication of the push and energy
of the two members of the firm it may be noted that the volume of trade (which was large in the first
year for a new concern) was more than doubled in the second year. In fact, it would be hard to find
a more complete team of business men than Mr. H. S. Smith and his partner, Mr. McLean. Mr. Smith
comes from Michigan, and has been connected with general merchandise all his life. He looks after the
internal business of the office and the finances. Mr. McLean came from Wisconsin, having been in

the business for many years previously, and he gives his attention principally to the outside business. He is an expert in the butter trade, and it may be said that in that branch of the business he has no equal. Their trade is mostly in the city, and they receive their farm produce from different parts of this State and from Dakota, Wisconsin and Iowa. Their apples come from New York, Michigan and Missouri. Their oranges, bananas, etc., are shipped direct, in car lots, from Florida and California. They employ about ten hands, and their trade is ever on the increase. One of the great secrets of their success is the personal supervision which their business receives in all its details. They will shortly move to more commodious premises on First Avenue North.

MOORE BROS., Real Estate, Loans and Insurance, 11 South Fourth Street—This business was established three years ago as Spear & Moore. Mr. Spear retired about two years ago, and Mr. J. F. Moore, who is an attorney, was admitted as a partner. Both these gentlemen were born in Ohio, and are both graduates of Dartmouth College. Mr. H. L. Moore has been in Minneapolis for over seven years and was formerly Assistant Superintendent of Schools here. The firm do a general real estate busi- ness, handling both their own property and property on commission. They have a very extensive list, and deal, to a great extent, in inside city property. They also conduct a large loaning business, mainly for Eastern capitalists. They do quite a large business in renting and collecting rents, taking charge of property and caring for it. In addition to the real estate business, they are agents for the New Hampshire Fire Insurance Company and the Northern Assurance Company, of London, and Aberdeen, England. They give some very excellent references, among others Judge E. S. Jones, President Hen- nepin Co. Savings Bank, First National Bank, Hon. George A. Pillsbury, E. A. Merrill, President Minnesota Loan & Trust Co., and Merchants' Bank, Lake City, Minn., and S. C. Bartlett, President Dartmouth College.

CHAS. L. JACOBY, Portrait and Landscape Photographer, 250 and 252 Nicollet Avenue— Ever since 1866 the name Jacoby has meant for the people of Minneapolis what it does to-day, name- ly, in designating one of the leading art photographers of the Flour City. The gallery is located on the principal retail thoroughfare, Nicollet Avenue, at Nos. 250 and 252, second floor, and commands every advantage requisite to the execution of the highest standard of artistic work. The range of sub- jects comprises everything in the line of reproductive art, such as photographs, bromides, India ink, pas- tel, crayon and water-color work and portraits in oil. The force of artists employed is the largest of any in the city, being from ten to twenty, and a vast amount of commercial work is performed. Mr. Chas. L. Jacoby, the present owner of the gallery, is a son of W. H. Jacoby, the first proprietor. He has had entire control of the business the past two years and was, prior to that time, a member of the firm of W. H. Jacoby & Son, whom he succeeds.

NATIONAL HOTEL, 205 Washington Avenue South, C. A. Merrill, Proprietor—The National Hotel, 205 Washington Avenue, is now one of the most complete of the smaller hotels of the city. The old National Hotel was built a great many years ago and will be remembered by most of those who have visited Minneapolis in earlier days. It was succeeded by the present building, which was erected by Mr. Ames, who opened it about three years ago. A little more than two years from its being opened, the fire occurred in the big Boston Building, and a good deal of damage was done to the National. After this, Mr. C. A. Merrill, the present proprietor, re-opened the building. A great deal of re-fitting and re-furnishing was required, and to this Mr. Merrill gave a liberal and tasteful attention. The building is a handsome five-story structure of Ohio sandstone, and is furnished with a passenger elevator and hot and cold water bath rooms. Mr. Merrill is one of the most pleasant gentlemen to be found in any hotel in the State. He is a veteran hotel man, as he opened the Cook House, of Rochester, in this State, so long ago as 1874, and at the present time is the proprietor of the Duncombe

House, Fort Dodge, Indiana. He is ably assisted by Mr. W. N. Merrill, who acts as clerk. The office and dining rooms of the National are peculiarly neat and attractive, and the charges are such as to make it agreeable to all who want a select and quiet stopping place.

S. E. OLSON & CO., Cash Jobbers of Dry Goods, Notions, Gents' Furnishing and Duck Goods, 213 and 215 Nicollet Avenue--One of the most striking business successes of the Northwest

is that furnished by the enterprising dry goods house of S. E. Olson & Co. At the date of its establishment, in 1882, the firm occupied but a small portion of the first floor at their present location. They began business with but three clerks. Now they give employment to two hundred clerks, require seven delivery wagons, and occupy the entire four stories and basement of the building at 213 and 215 Nicollet Avenue. They have several travel ing men constantly on the road, which is an evidence of their extensive business out side of the city. The location of their build ing is very prominent, being located at the junction of Hennepin and Nicollet Avenues, the two main thoroughfares of the city. The space of this house would, if extended over one floor, cover 33,000 square feet. The five floors are divided into twenty-seven depart ments. In the basement bazaar is found cut lery, crockery, glassware, wooden ware, toys, etc. On the first floor, some of the most important departments are silks, dress goods, hosiery, gloves and laces. On the second floor are found the departments for cloaks, millinery and fancy work material. On the third floor are departments devoted to car pets, curtains and blankets. On the fourth floor is the wholesale department. They have a very large mail-order business, which is attended to by a department especially adapted to that feature. They are also sole selling agents for the celebrated McCaul paper pat terns. They maintain an Eastern office at 56 South Street, New York City, where two regu lar buyers are constantly employed. The business of this house will exceed one million dollars this year. The house is less than two blocks from the Union depot, and is within a short distance of all the hotels. Mr. Olson is the sole proprietor of the business, the "Co." being nominal. Mr. Olson is one of Minneapolis' most live business men, and an enthusiastic believer in her future growth. He is a native of

Norway. In addition to the supervision of his business, he is President of the State Bank of Minneapolis, one of the Directors of the Exposition, and a member of Governor Merriam's staff.

LAUDERDALE & CO., Real Estate and Loans, Room 355 Temple Court—Lauderdale & Co. W. H. Lauderdale. J. W. and F. W. Lauderdale. This firm was organized in 1879 by Mr. W. H. Lauderdale, resident of Minneapolis since 1854, and his son, F. W., and nephew, J. W., resident since '81. They have since been closely identified with the growth and prosperity of Minneapolis, especially of that part called North Minneapolis. They have at various times handled almost every piece of property in this section of the city. In 1886, when the limits of the city were extended to the north, Lauderdale & Co. sold many acre pieces which are now platted and improved. When the business portion of the city was first developing this enterprising firm were instrumental in bringing a number of investments to the city from abroad, thus helping to build up the many beautiful business blocks. A few years ago the entire quarter block cornering with Temple Court, and in same block, was sold by them for $33,000. Quite a number of subdivisions have been platted and put on the market by them, as Lauderdale & Vander Horck's subdivision, Lauderdales' subdivision of Babbet's subdivision, and several small subdivisions. They still have twenty acres unplatted in the city and fifty acres on the East Side. As Minneapolis increases these acres will be judiciously put upon the market and sold for homes and business buildings. It is to such old and reliable firms as this that Minneapolis owes in part its fabulous growth.

DURNAM & BARNS, Livery Stable, 1405 Washington Avenue North—This firm is composed of Geo. A. Durnam and I. C. Barns. Mr. Durnam started this stable in 1884, occupying for a year a location directly opposite his present stable. The stable they now occupy was built expressly for Mr. Durnam. The stable occupies an area of 54x150 feet, and is one story high. The main business of this stable is buying and selling horses, although they do considerable livery business. The sale business includes the handling of all kinds of horses. They sell about two hundred horses per year. In the livery department is found a good stock of driving horses, two hacks, six single rigs and one two-seated carriage. Fifteen horses are boarded. Five men are given employment. Both gentlemen are progressive citizens. Mr. Durnam takes quite an interest in politics and enjoys the distinction of having been elected as a Republican to the position of alderman from the Third, a Democratic ward. Mr. Durnam has lived here all his life. Mr. Barns is a New Yorker by birth and came here from Dakota.

EAGLE FOUNDRIES, George M. Bryant, Proprietor, Office, Fifth Avenue South, near Second Street—Mr. George M. Bryant, the proprietor of these foundries, is a manufacturer of all kinds of castings, columns, pulleys, machinery, sled shoes, mauls, hitching and sash weights, and everything in his line from one ounce to ten tons. Mr. Bryant was born in England, and commenced business in this city eleven years ago. He commenced without capital, and by his persevering industry worked his business up to quite large proportions. It extends over the whole Northwest. He now employs from forty to sixty hands, and his business is steadily on the increase. Only those who have had the same experience can tell what courage and perseverance are required in order to build up a large business, such as Mr. Bryant now controls, from small beginnings; and the amount of credit due to him is in exact proportion to the difficulties which he has had to overcome.

PEASLEE & COMPANY, Cigars, 12 South Fourth Street—One of the most prominent cigar firms in the city is that of Peaslee & Company. The concern was really established so far back as 1866. The members of the firm are Mr. E. C. Peaslee, who was born in Dubuque, Iowa, and has been identified with that city for many years, and Mr. P. S. Preston, who was born in New York State, but was also associated with Mr. Peaslee in Dubuque for a number of years. They carry on a very extensive brewing business there, and their ales and porters are widely known and justly appreciated. Mr. Preston came here to conduct an agency for the products of the brewery, and also to open up the cigar business which is now carried on at No. 12 South Fourth Street. They handle domestic and imported cigars exclusively, and carry a stock of about $5,000 value. Their business is extending far and near, and has already reached a volume of from forty to fifty thousand dollars annually. They are, of course, more generally known on account of their ales and porters, but the business of cigars works in with the other branch of their trade in a very convenient manner.

M. ROELLER, Manufacturer and Dealer in Fine Carriages, Buggies and Road Wagons, 246, 248 and 252 Second Avenue South—Mr. Roeller established his business so far back as 1873, and has the satisfaction of knowing that his are the oldest surviving carriage works in the city. He came here from New Haven, Connecticut. He has extensive premises fronting on Second Avenue South, consisting of offices, warehouses and factory. His business, which is principally city trade, is now quite extensive, but is still steadily increasing. His sales amount to something over $75,000 per annum. He carries a large and valuable stock (usually about $30,000) and has some remarkably handsome carriages on sale. Mr. Roeller employs, on an average, twenty hands, and makes all kinds of carriages. He also does an extensive repairing business. His undertaking has been a success from the commencement, and he has so conducted his business that he now has a host of friends.

J. E. EGAN, Civil Engineer and Surveyor, 255 Hennepin Avenue and 101 Central Avenue— Mr. Egan was born in Wisconsin, and came to Minneapolis in 1880. He had previously practiced for about two years in Wisconsin, and was therefore considerably experienced when he came here. He worked for Baker & Gilmore, on the East Side, for three years, and then came over to the West Side and commenced business for himself. Last year he bought out the office on the East Side, and now has two establishments. This is a bona fide case of success through perseverance and talent, as Mr. Egan owes his success entirely to his own exertions. In 1887 his office platted no less than 2,000 acres of land in the suburbs, which is a pretty good showing for one office to make. The East Side office is one of the oldest in the city, and is a very valuable addition to Mr. Egan's other business. Mr. Egan does about two-thirds of all the lithographing done in the city for real estate maps. Mr. Egan has some very influential references. Among them are Mr. H. G. Sidle, Marsh & Bartlett, P. D. McMillan, A. Y. Davidson, L. F. Menage, Willis Baker, Anderson & Douglas, and a host of others.

J. B. TABOUR & CO., Real Estate and Loans, 325 Hennepin Avenue—This firm was established in 1882, Mr. Tabour being an old resident of the city, having lived here for thirty-three years. They are therefore perfectly posted in all Minneapolis real estate matters and superior judges of both present and future values. The reputation of Tabour & Co. is first-class. no real estate firm standing higher as good, square business men. They have platted Tabour's First, Second and Third Additions to Minneapolis, and deal largely in Eighth Ward and Lowry Hill property. They are agents for the well-known addition of Bryn Mahr. Bryn Mahr starts with a prospect of being one of the finest parts of the city. Already a number of fine residences have been erected, and more are going up. Over $100,000 have been put into improvements on the ground besides the original cost of the land. Fine, wide streets, shade trees, artesian wells for water supply, bridges—nothing is lacking to make the place desirable as a residence. Houses built there must be a certain distance back from the street, and must be of some pretentions to taste and elegance. Forty to fifty thousand dollars will be put into improvements this year. The whole region will get its water supply from artesian wells which the Bryn Mahr Company have sunk on the addition—it is the only region in Minneapolis supplied with perfectly pure, safe water. One well flows 1,000,000 gallons of pure, cold water per day, throwing it five feet above the surface. Bryn Mahr is close to the business part of the city, and convenient for business men. It is near the lakes and country, and healthy for their families. It can be reached by railway, by Hawthorne Avenue street railway and by carriage drives, a bridge over the railway tracks doing away with the necessity of driving across said tracks. Tabour & Co. control capital to any amount, and do a large loan business on a conservative and safe basis.

W. D. VAN NORMAN, Railroad Contractor—Mr. Van Norman was born in Buffalo, New York. He came here from Illinois. He was in the practice of law until the war broke out. After serving as a commissioned officer he began, at the close of the war, to go into the contracting business, and has continued in it since. His taking to this business was what may be called an accident. Mr. R. B. Lewis, the chief engineer on the Vandalia Road, wanted him to furnish the road with some cross ties. After this was done he wanted him to take a contract for putting up some bridges for him. Mr. Van Norman was with Mr. Lewis for two years and a half, and during that time saw that he could succeed as a contractor and bridge builder, and accordingly adopted the business. He has been all over the country and the greater part of Canada West. He has been in Minneapolis about nine years. His specialty is heavy work, particularly bridge building, both iron combination and wooden structures. He con-

structed bridges in Galveston, Harrisburg and San Antonio, Texas, where he was engaged for a year and a half. He was engaged for two years and a half on the Burlington & Quincy and four years on the Northern Pacific, and put in all their wooden structures in Minnesota and Dakota. About the last work done by him was on the Winona Southwestern, with which he has a contract of about one hundred thousand dollars. He has been for two years and a half latterly doing some work for the Chicago & Northwestern and the

LAKE CARLOS ST. P., M. & M. R'Y.

Chicago, Milwaukee & St. Paul, under Langdon & Co. He has proved himself throughout to be a clear-headed business man, besides being a bridge builder of the highest ability. He has some beautiful photographs of some of the wooden structures put in by himself.

MINNEAPOLIS ASPHALT PAVEMENT CO., 309 National Bank of Commerce Building —The officers of this company are Mr. A. S. Sampson, President, and Mr. C. M. Carpenter, Secretary and Treasurer. They manufacture a pavement for driveways, sidewalks, alleys, crossings, washways, floors for stables, mills, elevators, warehouses, stores, depots, laundries, steamer and engine houses, dwelling house yards, areas and cellars, from asphalt, which it is claimed is more durable than any kind of stone. There is one thing quite certain about this kind of pavement, viz.: That it makes the smoothest and most compact roadway of any known material. There is another very important feature in it: Being elastic, it reduces the jar on horses hoofs and legs, and they are enabled to travel over it without any of the bad results that follow from continued travel over a stone road. It is also the quietest material that can be used; this is partly owing to its elasticity and partly to the smoothness of the surface, and is a great advantage, as it does away with the distressing rattle that is observable more or less in every other kind of pavement. The material from which the pavement is made comes from the celebrated pitch lake in the Island of Trinidad, and is a formation from vegetable matter similar to that which, in a temperate climate, would result in the formation of coal. This kind of pavement has only lately been introduced here, but in every case it has given entire satisfaction, as the testimonials of those who have tried it abundantly testify. One prominent citizen testifies that he knows of asphalt walks and driveways in Milford, Mass., that were laid sixteen years ago, and which seemed better last fall than when they were laid. It would not be very extravagant to prophesy that this kind of pavement will be largely used in this city in the near future.

W. H. DENNIS, Architect and Superintendent, Rooms 417–421, Rochester Building—One of our most noted architects and superintendents is Mr. W. H. Dennis, whose offices are in Rooms Nos. 417 to 421, Rochester Block. He came here from New York State, where he had previously been practicing his profession, in the year 1879. Things were beginning to look lively in Minneapolis in that year, and Mr. Dennis' ability as an architect was quickly recognized. He has since practiced here with an ever-increasing business, and some of the most beautiful and grandest of our buildings were erected from his designs. Among others may be mentioned the Rochester Block, in which his offices are situated; Citizens' Bank, Collom Block, Oneida Building, Mackey-Legg Building, G. R. Newell & Co.'s wholesale house, which has justly been pronounced by competent judges to be the best of its kind in all America; F. W. Foreman's dwelling on Park Avenue, our County Court House, and the Zier apartment residences; but to name one-half of the important structures designed by him would of itself fill a large volume and far exceed the limits of the present work.

A. F. & L. E. KELLEY, Mortgage Loans, 115 Temple Court—This firm occupies large, sumptuous apartments upon the first floor of Temple Court, one of the finest business blocks in the city. Ten clerks are kept busy recording and transacting its large business. During business hours the scene is one of quiet and orderly but intense work. In this office are negotiated loans which bring Westward much of that value which is redundant in the East but scarce in the West. Messrs. Kelley control a large amount of New England capital, and negotiate mortgage loans on Minneapolis property for New England capitalists. The firm began the transaction of business in 1874, and have been closely identified with the growth and prosperity of Minneapolis throughout its phenomenal period. During this time they have, by conducting their business on straightforward business principles, established a reputation which put them right up in front. They have, at the same time, contributed not a little to make Minneapolis what it is. Dealing with these gentlemen cannot fail to be satisfactory to those wishing for money on good security.

E. I. RUGG, Artistic Photographer, No. 625 Hennepin Avenue—Mr. Rugg is making himself a name for fine work, which is bound to lay the foundation of a successful career. From 1879, when he came here from Massachusetts, until 1887, he was working on a salary. In the latter year he determined to strike out for himself. One very serious obstacle lay in his way, viz., he had no capital. With a courage that does him credit he resolved to set this consideration aside, and accordingly started his gallery. Notwithstanding some ups and downs, he has more than held his own, and at the present time is doing a nice little business, which promises to develop into a big one before long. He enlarges pictures in crayon, India ink, water colors and permanent bromides, and executes all sizes and styles of work, but makes theatrical work a specialty. His premises are neat, and, though not palatial, are sufficiently commodious for his present moderate practice. Some very excellent specimens of his art may be seen on the walls as well as in many a home in the city and suburbs.

ASBESTINE STONE COMPANY, City Office, 323 Hennepin Avenue.—The Asbestine Stone Company of Minneapolis have an office at No. 323 Hennepin Avenue. Their works are situated on Lyndale Avenue, corner of Lincoln, just beyond Lowry Hill. The company is the oldest and largest in the Northwest. It was established in 1874, and is composed of E. H. and F. E. Barrett and D. Elliot, with A. B. Merriam, special partner. They are all practical men, who, by long experience and experiment, have succeeded in making an artificial stone entirely different in its combination and enduring qualities from any other stone manufactured, being more like natural stone in its color and formation.

HOTEL ST. LOUIS, LAKE MINNETONKA—ST. P., M. & M. RY.

It has a reputation in this country from East to West for beauty and durability equaled by no other artificial stone. It is used in almost every department for building purposes, and can be seen on and about thousands of buildings in Minneapolis and elsewhere—as on churches, colleges, school buildings, residences, blocks, etc. They have invented much of the machinery used in manufacturing their stone, such as screening the sand, crushing and pulverizing the granite (the St. Cloud granite is used largely in the manufacture of their stone and walks), in sifting the cement—of which only the best grade of Portland is used, no American or common cement being used in the manufacture of their stone—in the mixing and wetting the material, giving a far better and more perfect mixture than is possible by hand process. Their works are heated by steam. In the winter their stone is stored in warerooms especially prepared and kept warm and moist by steam until the cement has perfected a through combination with the other materials, thus securing the full strength of the cement. The company also manufacture a superior kind of floor tiling in all colors, as handsome, more durable, and much cheaper than either slate or marble. Many of the finest buildings, both public and private, are constructed in whole or in part of the product of this company. It is more generally used for floors, steps, walks, pavements, curbing, flower vases, yard ornaments, etc. They also pave walks and driveways with the celebrated Stuart granolithic compound, pronounced superior to anything else used for the purpose in this country or in Europe. Prices of granolithic are far less than that of natural stone, with which it competes successfully. In fact, it leads as *the best*, and is being largely used where great strength and durability is necessary in walks and pavements. To manufacture a good article of stone it is necessary to use the right kind of sand as well as cement, the right proportion of silica and other scientific ingredients. Without all these you have a concrete not much better than the lime and sand mixture. The company makes sidewalks a specialty, and are the pioneers in that business in this city and the West. They have laid the greater part of the stone walks in this city. They make their paving stone in the winter, so they may be old and well cured when laid. No stone is fit to use until it has age and has become hard. The company employs from fifty to seventy-five men in the works and in putting down walks, etc. They use from 10,000 to 15,000 barrels of Portland cement annually, and have about $75,000 invested in the business. This company has purchased cement for the last fifteen years of the celebrated and world-renowned Empire Warehouse Company, of Chicago, who ship the cement direct from the manufactories in Germany and England to this company. A visit to the works of this company will repay any one, and they will be surprised at the perfection to which this company has brought their art and methods of manufacture. The Asbestine Stone Company have reason to be proud of the part they have had in furnishing such a fine class of *artificial stone sidewalks* as our city rightly boasts of—it being a fact that no city in the country can show so many miles of fine sidewalks as Minneapolis.

B. W. FISK, Architect and Superintendent, 56 Tribune Building—Burnham W. Fisk, architect and superintendent. Mr. Fisk is a thoroughly competent architect and has enjoyed many advantages in his early training, having studied under Mr. G. B. Croff, well-known as the architect of many heavy commercial buildings in Saratoga, and considered one of the finest architects of his day. Mr. Fisk came here in 1872 and commenced practice for himself ten years later. During part of his career he was in partnership with Mr. Kees. Among their first work here was the Syndicate Block, one of the greatest ornaments of the city. The First Baptist Church, J. W. Johnson's Bank Building and his residence were also designed by him. He found at one time that he ran a great deal into church work, but he prefers residence work, and indeed makes a specialty of it. He is now engaged in designing some fine buildings which will ere long grace the city and suburbs. He has in charge the Universities of Northern Dakota, in itself quite an important work.

GERMANIA BREWING COMPANY, Office, Boston Block—This brewery was established three years ago as the Germania Brewing Association. In 1888 it was organized as it stands at present. John Vander-Horck, President; H. A. Westphal, Vice-President; John B. Mneller, Secretary, and Jacob Barge, Treasurer. The brewery is situated at Golden Valley, adjoining the city limits, and has a capacity of 200 barrels a day. It is fitted up with an entirely new plant of the very best description, in this respect comparing favorably with any brewery in the State. The brewing is on the Bavarian principle. Two kinds of beer are brewed—the Muenchener beer, made expressly for family use, from selected hops and malt, and another and paler beer. Both are strictly pure. The hops used in the manufacture of the beer are imported from Bavaria and the malt is selected from the best brands. In Bavaria the adulteration of beer is made a criminal offense; any person found guilty forfeits the whole of his plant and is imprisoned. The Germania Brewing Company has started with the determination that whatever else may happen they will produce a beer absolutely pure. Physicians are daily recommending the use of the beer to their patients. The aim of the company is to get the private trade as much as possible, and the beer is for the most part sold bottled. This trade has increased more than 500 fold since January 1st. The general trade has also increased; it extends all over Dakota and this State, besides that in and around the city. There can be no doubt that the adulteration of beer has done much to increase intemperance, and an institution like the Germania Brewing Company, whose primary aim is to produce a strictly pure beverage, should receive abundant support. It is gratifying to see that this support they are evidently receiving in an increasing degree.

J. D. BLAKE, Real Estate, Rooms 45 and 46 Tribune Building—Mr. Blake is a native of Vermont. In 1860 he came to Rochester, this State, and in 1882 to Minneapolis. He is the father, so to speak, of New Boston, Northeast Minneapolis. At the time he first came here, one red farm house represented the place; it is now a city in itself. In this part Mr. Blake has large investments. He has built one hundred houses and sold them out at one or two hundred dollars down, and four to six dollars a week without interest. These weekly payments are peculiar to himself. There is no direct profit

CENTRAL PARK TERRACE.

in this scheme of Mr. Blake's, but profit accrues indirectly by reason of the enhanced value of the neighboring property. Mr. Blake had one-half interest in Third Avenue Addition, all now improved, and one-half of Baker's Addition. Mr. Blake is owner of Central Park Terrace, a very valuable and unique property on Spruce Place, West Grant Street and Willow Street, fronting on Central Park, a few minutes' walk from the business center of the city, with motor and horse cars passing near it. It comprises eighteen elegant residences, which he has constructed regardless of expense and has had elaborately finished. Its system, sanitary arrangements and accommodations exceed anything heretofore attempted. It is supplied with its own plant and boiler house in a separate building with light, water and heat. Altogether it is a most complete arrangement and reflects great credit upon Mr. Blake. The rents in this terrace are exceedingly moderate, and considering the many advantages, lower than any others in the city.

J. R. CLARK & CO., Boxes and Wooden Specialties—This industry stands as a monument to the energy and unceasing efforts of its founder, J. R. Clark, who is now a resident of the Pacific Slope. The works are managed at present by his son, who is a member of the partnership and familiar in every way with the duties of the position, being also a native-born Minnesotian. Everything in the line of boxes, ladders and wooden specialties are made, and the trade, which is chiefly in Minnesota, is an exclusively wholesale one. The factory employs thirty hands, and the plant, which is one of the finest and most complete anywhere in the Northwest, is owned and controlled exclusively by the firm. As affording an illustration of the growth of the business, it may not be amiss to mention in this connection that Mr. Clark's only aid when he started the industry was a force consisting of only one boy.

BIG BOSTON CLOTHING STORE, Whitten, Burdett & Young, Proprietors, Corner Washington and Second Avenues South—Messrs. Whitten, Burdett & Young, the proprietors of the mammoth clothing house known as the "Big Boston," are Eastern gentlemen, and have similar establishments in Boston, Providence, Hartford, New Haven and Worcester. They purchased the interest in the establishment here in July, 1888, from Mr. E. H. Steele, who had successfully carried on the business since 1874. The premises consist of a fine six-story brick building at the corner of Washington and Second Avenues South, the whole of which is devoted to the business. Here may be found every description of men's and boys' clothing, including hats, caps, furs and furnishing goods, all manufactured by the proprietors. The stock carried is valued at $125,000, and any one who is unable to find what he wants, either in style, material or manufacture, must indeed be hard to please. The retail sales alone foot up to the large sum of $350,000 per annum, and are steadily on the increase. A large staff of clerks, numbering about fifty, is employed in this department alone. In the wholesale department there are two experienced traveling salesmen, who make Minneapolis their headquarters.

J. W. WHITTIER & CO., Contractors and Builders, Rear 415 Nicollet Avenue—This firm is composed of Mr. J. W. Whittier and Mr. W. E. W. Whittier, both American born. They furnish estimates on all kinds of buildings, and make a specialty of store-fitting and jobbing, and their work is always good, as they employ none but experienced and skillful workmen. Both the members of the firm are energetic and painstaking in all they do, and the result is they have built up a good trade, which is increasing each year. Among the works in which they have been engaged are the Plymouth Clothing Houses, both here and in St. Paul, both of which they built and fitted up. They also put up two blocks for Lyman Bros., but the greater part of their business consists of interior work. They employ about twenty hands, and the value of trade done in a year is $35,000.

DEMPSIE'S NEW PHOTOGRAPH ROOMS, 316 Nicollet Avenue—Mr. Dempsie succeeded to this business about a year ago. It was originally established about ten years ago, when it was conducted on a small scale. Mr. Dempsie had previously been carrying on business in other parts of the city, and is a practical photographer in every sense of the word. His aim has been to produce good pictures at as low a price as possible, and he has certainly succeeded in meeting with a large success, for at his studio four pictures by the tintype process may be obtained for the small sum of twenty-five cents. He has five rooms devoted to the business, which are conveniently fitted up for the purposes for which they are required. He executes every desciption of photographic work, transparencies, copying and enlarging, and has some very fine specimens on view.

CHAS. A. PILLSBURY & CO., Manufacturers of Choicest Grades Patent Roller Flour—Chas. A. Pillsbury & Co. are the largest millers in the world, and it is a remarkable fact that no one member of the firm was ever in the milling business prior to their commencing in that line here in 1869. In that year Charles A. Pillsbury, senior member of the present firm, came here from New Hampshire and purchased an interest in a mill of about 200 barrels capacity on the west side of the Mississippi River. This was destroyed by fire, and the mill now known as the "B" mill was built on the site. The firm operated several mills on the West Side before they built the great "A" mill on the East Side. In 1879 this mill was commenced and it was completed in 1881. A canal was specially cut, at a great cost, to supply it with power. Every modern invention to save labor and insure perfection in the production of the flour was applied, and the result is that "Pillsbury's Best" is known throughout the world as a brand without an equal. This mill is equipped with two Victor Turbine water-wheels of 1,450 horse-power each, so placed that they can either be operated singly or together, besides a 1,400 horse-power engine. The milling machinery in it consists of 400 pairs of rollers, 200 middlings purifiers, 20 run of stone, and 200 bolting reels. The daily capacity is 7,200 barrels, which is more than is made by any other two mills on the face of the globe. It takes 9,500,000 bushels of wheat yearly to supply its demands. A system is in vogue of allowing the employes of a certain standing to participate in the profits, which has been found to operate most satisfactorily to both employers and employed, and at the same time may be regarded as an evidence of the kindly feeling of generosity which actuates the firm in all its dealings towards its employes. Besides this gigantic mill the firm operate mill "B," already referred to, which has a capacity of 2,000 barrels, and "Anchor" mill, with a capacity of 1,500 barrels, both of which are also fitted with the best machinery known in the milling trade. The firm employ at least 500 men, besides those engaged in cooperage and other matters dependent upon the milling business.

CITY MARKET FISH STALL, M. Leisses, Proprietor—Mr. M. Leisses, of the City Market Fish Stall, does an excellent trade in fish and oysters, in which he makes a specialty. His business is both that of a dealer and a commission merchant, and a good many tons of fish pass through his hands annually. The goods are principally obtained from Green Bay, Bayfield, Ashland, Duluth, South Perham and Brainerd. These supplies are supplemented by the produce of the different lakes in the vicinity of the city. In addition to the business in fish and oysters, a considerable trade is done in game in season and poultry, also in early vegetables. The stall where the business is carried on is conveniently situated in the City Market, and at all times the seeker after fish may find what is desired, from the lordly salmon to the smallest fry ever used for food, each in its proper season. Mr. Leisses was born in Wisconsin.

THE PABST BREWING COMPANY, 112 South Third Street—The bottling department here of the Pabst Brewing Company, formerly Philip Best Brewing Company, is a large concern, and one which is fast growing to something very big. Mr. R. Steinmetz is the manager of the concern, and is a man of very fine business ability, pushing, energetic and at the same time courteous and affable. The merits of the Philip Best beers have been established so firmly and for so many years that it is unnecessary to dwell upon them here. The different brands handled at this place are chiefly the Export, which is a fine beer, possessing great body; the Bohemian, somewhat lighter; the Bavarian, a dark colored and easily digested beer, and the Select, a very fine quality of pale beer. Besides these there is the Best Tonic, which is a concentrated liquid extract of malt and hops, and is strongly recommended by the medical faculty as a useful and harmless restorative in cases of debility, whether from over-work, over-study, or any other cause. There are about ten hands employed in the bottling, and all the best labor-saving appliances are in use, so that a large amount of work is done by them. There are also four teams employed.

S. J. SHERMAN, Dispensing Pharmacist, 424 Nicollet Avenue—One of our most prominent self-made men is Mr. S. J. Sherman, Dispensing Pharmacist, of No. 424 Nicollet Avenue. Mr. Sherman was born and brought up near Boston, Mass. At the age of sixteen he conceived the idea of coming West to push his fortunes, and most ably has he carried that idea into practice. After going from place to place, without losing sight of his original intention, he finally settled upon this city as the most promising field for his labors. Eleven years ago he commenced business in his present stand. At that time the property now worth two thousand dollars per front foot, was only worth as many hundreds.

People laughed at him for selecting such a location—there were probably less passers-by in a whole day than there now are in any five minutes. However, with the strong belief in the future of the place, which in some few men appears to amount almost to an instinct, he persevered in his business ; and, although at first he sometimes only took in three dollars a day—his predictions have been more than realized; for the spot in which he is located is one of the best business centers in the whole city, and he has now a large and flourishing business, requiring, besides his own supervision, the aid of two competent assistants. His immense and varied stock is ever fresh, so quickly does his large trade keep it moving. Nor is this all, for in addition to his business he owns real estate worth at least fifty thousand dollars in the city, besides a large stock ranch in McPherson County, Dakota.

HOLMES & BROWN, Proprietors of Fair Ground Addition, Real Estate, 329 Boston Block— Mr. E. G. Holmes and Mr. O. D. Brown, the members of this firm, are two of the most substantial real estate operators in the city. They are doing a general real estate business, but principally handle their own property. It is only by way of exchange that they ever go outside of this in their dealings.

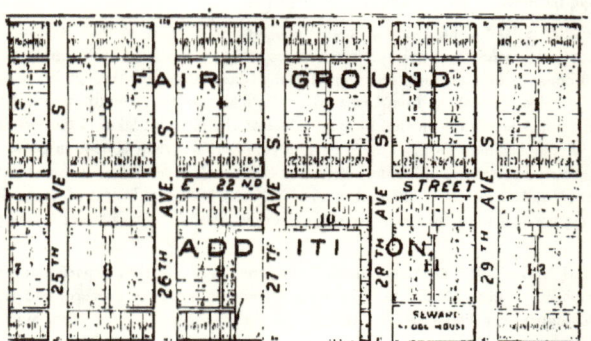

Nevertheless they have at the present time upwards of $100,000 worth of improved property in the city which has come into their hands in this way. Their principal interest lies in the Fair Ground Addition, 65 acres of beautiful land platted in 1887. There are now seventy nice houses built and a $35,000 school house. There have been more buildings put up on this property in the last twelve months than on any other addition in the city. In exchanging lots in this addition for other property, the proprietors have made it a condition that no residence of less than $1,800 value shall be erected thereon. This property possesses many valuable features. It is no isolated addition, standing by itself without any convenient means of access, but it is directly on the public highway between the two cities, has two lines of street cars, and is just two blocks from the Short Line depot. There are contemplated improvements in the immediate neighborhood which will greatly enhance the value of the property. In addition to the large interests in real estate here possessed by this firm, they are owners of the First National Bank of Detroit, Minnesota.

H. C. PETERSON, Wholesale and Retail Grocer, Produce Commission Merchant, 116 Hennepin Avenue—Mr. Peterson commenced business on his own account in 1873, when he bought out the proprietor of the store where he had been working. In 1875 he started a wholesale and retail grocery at 119 Washington Avenue South. In 1876 he opened six other stores in different parts of the city, retaining the old stand. In 1883 he sold all out and went to California. He soon after came back and bought a shoe store, 403 Washington Avenue South. This he sold to his brother and again started a grocery business. In 1886 he bought out Z. DeMeules' grocery and removed to his present quarters in 1888.

This year he again started a business at his old stand, 127 Washington Avenue South. It has been said that a rolling stone gathers no moss. This may be the rule, but Mr. Peterson is certainly a brilliant exception, for he has always managed to gather more and more moss every time he has rolled from one place to another. He is now doing a fine trade, employing fifteen hands and sending goods to all parts.

DANZ'S BAND, 509 and 511 Syndicate Block—This is the chief band in the city, and was organized many years ago by Frank Danz, Sr., father of the present leader. Mr. Frank Danz, Jr., the present leader of the band, is a musician of many years' experience, having been for a long time one of the leading violinists in Theodore Thomas' orchestra, one of the finest on the continent. The full strength of the Danz Band is fifty pieces. To those who were privileged to listen to their charming music at the Exposition and State Fair during the last two seasons it is unnecessary to say one word of praise. Suffice it to say that the thousands who visited the above named institutions were unanimous in praising the efforts of the band. Every winter a weekly concert is given at Harmonia Hall here by this band. It is, in fact, the only full band in the city, and the quality of the music is grand, aside from the renditions of the the leading soloists, places it in the front rank of musical organizations in this country.

SEXTON & RAFTERY, Sixth Avenue Creamery, 616 Sixth Avenue South—A recent addition to the dairy interests of Minneapolis is the Sixth Avenue Creamery, located at 616 Sixth Avenue South. This creamery was established January 20, 1889, by Messrs. Sexton & Raftery. This young firm is composed of practical men, who understand the creamery business in all its details. Their trade is almost entirely wholesale. Their special production is that of butter, which they sell to the grocers of Minneapolis and St. Paul. The daily output is now about 600 pounds, and rapidly increasing. Their special makes are the "Daisy" and "Creamery." They have also commenced the wholesaling of milk and other dairy products. About seventy-five gallons of milk are now received daily from Prescott, Wisconsin, and Dundas, Minnesota. Four hands are constantly employed, which number will be shortly increased.

THE MINNESOTA STONE COMPANY, General Contractors, Wm. F. Van Voris, General Agent, Office, Room 14, 408 Nicollet Avenue—Mr. William F. Van Voris, is the President, Secretary and General Manager of this company. They deal in almost all kinds of natural stone, particularly Kasota, Bayfield brown stone, Lamont limestone, Ohio sandstone, Mankato stone, New York blue stone (of which they are the only parties who handle it in the city), granites from St. Cloud and Orton-ville. Many of the buildings in the city are constructed of stone supplied by them, among others the Wolf and McCormick Block of Mankato stone; Wright Block, Hennepin Avenue, of brown stone; the Post-office basement of St. Cloud granite. Their business is steadily on the increase, the demand for good building stones getting greater every year. They make a specialty of heavy bridge masonry and cut stone, flagging for sidewalks, Lamont vault covers and flagging of every description. All their work is promptly and efficiently executed. Their business has already reached a volume from $50,000 to $60,000 a year.

J. H. DAVIS & BRO., Meat Market, 250 First Avenue South—This popular market was established in 1882, by Mr. J. S. Davis, who came to this city from Mankato, where he had been estab-lished in the meat business for many years. He first located at 300 First Avenue South, where he employed three men. October 1st of the same year he removed to his present location. In 1886 his brother, Mr. J. H. Davis, came to this city and entered into partnership with him. Their business has shown a constant increase, and they now occupy the entire three-story building at 250 First Avenue South. Mr. Davis and his brother are Vermont men. They came to Wisconsin in 1848, and in 1861 came to Minnesota. In 1867 they commenced business in Mankato. Their business in Minneapolis has kept pace with the growth of the city; to accommodate their increasing trade they established in

1886 a branch market at 1214 and 1216 Washington Avenue South. They employ eighteen men and run four delivery wagons for their retail trade. Their business now aggregates $135,000 yearly, and is constantly increasing. They do all their own packing and cure all the hams and bacon used by their trade. They also have a complete equipment for the making of all kinds of sausage. They also have a large refrigerator on Nicollet Island.

FLOUR CITY NATIONAL BANK, Lumber Exchange, Corner Hennepin Avenue and Fifth Street—This is comparatively a young bank in Minneapolis, its origin only dating from September 1st, 1887, but its flourishing condition, and the volume of business to which it has already attained, entitles

it to a leading place among the most progressive and substantially reliable financial institutions of the city. It has an authorized capital, under the Minnesota banking law, of $2,-000,000, one-fifth of which was paid in before the commencement of business, and on January 1st following another $100,000 was added, making the actual capital $500,000. At the close of its first year's business it had accumulated in surplus funds and undivided profits about $50,000, and its deposits had passed the half-million mark. The offices of the bank in the Lumber Exchange building,

LAKE PEPIN, ON LINE OF C., M. & ST. P. R'Y.

on Hennepin Avenue, opposite the famous West Hotel, are unsurpassed in the city, and the facilties controlled for the efficient transaction of all legitimate banking business are of the very best, as it has correspondence with prominent banks all over the world. The directors of the bank are all men of more than usual prominence in Northwestern affairs, as will readily be seen by glancing over the list of those who comprise that body, as follows: T. B. Walker (the president), George A. Pillsbury, C. L. Waldo, A. C. Ackeley, S. G. Cook, John Vonder Horck, Henry Hill, C. P. Jones, John Edwards, H. E. Selden, J. H. Thompson, W. A. Barnes and C. H. Chadbourne. The officers of the bank, in addition to Mr. Walker, are George E. Maxwell, Cashier, and J. D. Williamson, Assistant Cashier.

C. W. KERRICK & CO., Contractors, 22 Stillman Block—Mr. Kerrick himself is the principal of this concern. He was formerly superintendent of bridges and buildings for the Manitoba Road in this city and has been here for eight years. He was born in Greensburg, Indiana. He prefers working by contract to working as a paid employe, and has therefore severed his connection with the Manitoba Road, but still continues to execute work for them. He now has a contract with them for $3,000 worth of work. He constructed all the bridging on the Eastern Railway of Minnesota. Last year his contracts with them amounted $150,000. He has now a great many contracts on hand in various parts: Grand Forks, Dakota, $25,000, $3,000 for the Manitoba Railway, already mentioned; the Court House, Granite Falls, $10,000. He makes a specialty of heavy contracts, bridges and buildings. He employs about 300 men, and last year his work amounted to about $125,000. In addition to his business as a bridge builder, Mr. Kerrick has a lumber mill at Holyoke, in this State, on the East Minneapolis Railway.

MERCER & TOWLER, Minneapolis Steam Laundry, 109 South Second Street—This laundry was established about fifteen years ago by Meagher Brothers. The concern came into the hands of the present head of the firm, T. E. Mercer, about five years ago, and he was joined by Mr. S. H. Towler in June of this year. All the work is done by steam, for which every modern appliance and improvement is in use. First-class work is guaranteed and goods are called for and delivered free to all parts of the city. Three delivery wagons are thus kept busy all the time. The trade is principally in the city and is very extensive and constantly on the increase. About twenty hands are employed and it is in all respects one of the principal laundries in the city.

SCANDIA BANK OF MINNESOTA, Corner Cedar—The organization of this bank, in 1883, supplied a want long felt by the merchants and business men of South Minneapolis, and that they readily showed their appreciation of the same is evidenced by the fact that a good and increasing custom has been enjoyed by the bank from the very start. It has a paid up capital of $60,000, and the surplus and undivided profits, after paying fair dividends to its stockholders, are in amount equal to half as much more. It has a good deposit account and its loans and discounts are equal to its capacity to supply such demands, which indicates a most healthy condition. The bank does, also, quite a business in the sale of ocean steamship tickets, having some 500 different agencies throughout the Northwest in this line, and handling thousands of tickets each year. The officers of the corporation are R. Lunde, President; Mons Grinager, Vice-President, and A. C. Haugan, Cashier, the latter being one of the prominent public men of Minneapolis and a conspicuous member of the present city council.

DORSETT & COMPANY, Fashionable Caterers, 418 Nicollet Avenue—This is one of the best known houses in the city in its line. They are manufacturers of May's celebrated frozen creams, fruit ices, cake, trifles, jellies, etc. There are four stories in the building devoted to this business, and in them are private banquet parlors for opera suppers, wedding and other ceremonies. Any one desiring a banquet served at his own home with all the requisites of Dresden china, silver, damask, servants, lunch tables, chairs, etc., has only to write to Dorsett & Co. and lo and behold! at the moment appointed the whole thing will make its appearance like a fairy scene. A very large business is done in ice cream of the best quality, but everything in the place is of the best quality. Dorsett & Company make cake without either soda or baking powder, justly claiming that it is impossible to make them as good with either of those articles. The members of the firm are Mr. C. W. Dorsett, Mrs. M. A. Dorsett and A. Blodgett, all Americans.

LINDSAY BROTHERS, Manufacturers' Agents and Jobbers in Agricultural Implements, 104 and 106 Third Avenue North—The members of this firm are Mr. William Lindsay, who is a native of Scotland, and Mr. T. B. Lindsay, who was born New York City. They have been in Minneapolis since

1881. The business was established in 1886. They deal in all kinds of agricultural implements, bug-gies and carriages. Among the different manufacturers with whom they have dealings are John Dodds, of Dayton, O., sulky hay-rake; Scandia Plow Company. Rockford, Ill., plows, harrows and corn-cultivators; the Janesville Machine Co., Janesville, Wis., seeders and disc harrows; Joseph Dick Agri-cultural Works, Canton, O., feed-cutters; Hocking Valley Manufacturing Co., Lancaster, O., corn-shellers and feed-cutters; Seckler & Co., Ohio, buggies and carriages; also, S. L. Allen & Co., known as the Planet, Jr., farm and garden implements. They also handle binding twine of leading manufact-urers. Their trade is quite extensive, averaging from $200,000 to $300,000 per annum.

COLUMBIA MILL CO., Manufacturers of Flour—The flour mill is worked by both steam and water-power. It is fitted with all the modern labor-saving appliances and improvements, and has a very fine location on the Minneapolis Eastern Railroad tracks. It has a daily capacity of 1,600 barrels. The officers of the corporation are Mr. J. B. Bassett, President; Mr. Horace S. Wade, Vice-President; Mr. E. Zeidler, General Manager and Treasurer, and Mr. F. D. Zimmerman, Superintendent. The brands of flour manufactured are the Columbia, Golden Rod and Superlative, for patent brands; Ceres and American, for bakers' use; the Dakota, for second bakers', and Varna, for low grade. The pro-ducts are shipped to the Eastern States and to the United Kingdom, Holland and Germany, and the ports on the Continent of Europe. There are about thirty-five hands employed at this mill. Mr. Bas-sett has a saw mill, run under the firm name of J. B. Bassett & Co.

N. P. CLARKE & COMPANY, Wholesale Lumber, Office Lumber Exchange—Twenty-five years ago saw the start of the immense business done by N. P. Clarke & Co. Since that time the firm has grown to proportions second to none of its competitors. Their mills in Minneapolis are well known, situated on the East Side, by the falls. They have also mills at St. Cloud, Little Falls and Winnipeg, Manitoba, and their reputation is co-extensive with the territory covered by Northwest lumbermen. The total capacity of their mills is 75,000,000 feet per year, and these, with their camps and whole equipment, give employment to about fifteen hundred men. Their trade extends to every product of white pine, and they are one of the bulwarks of this city of lumber and flour. The members of the firm are N. P. Clarke and F. H. Clarke.

J. M. HOWES, Dealer in Staple and Fancy Groceries, Confectionery, Etc., 41 Eleventh Street South—This grocery is located in the heart of one of the best residence districts in Minneapolis, be-tween Hennepin and Nicollet Avenues, and it controls a class of trade of as desirable a character as can be found anywhere in the city. The business was established in 1887, by Mr. Howes himself, and the progress which has been made in the way of advancing its interests speaks most flatteringly of the enterprise and business tact of the proprietor, as his trade is constantly and steadily on the increase. The stock of goods kept is in every way fully in keeping with the character of the locality and the class of custom which it is intended to supply, being first-class in every respect. A good cigar and tobacco trade is also done in connection with the business, and a specialty is made of fine table luxuries, fancy groceries and choice brands of family flour.

UNION RAILWAY STORAGE COMPANY, Wholesale and Retail Dealers in Building Material, Storage and Forwarding, No. 50 Third Street South—This company, besides its storage busi-ness, does a large trade in building material, both wholesale and retail. It was incorporated in 1883, and the officers are H. M. Carpenter, President, who has been here for about thirty-five years, and who came from Providence, R. I.; H. E. Carpenter, Secretary, who has been here for fifteen years, and hails from North Vermont, and J. S. Homan, General Manager, who hails from Quincy, Ill., and came here in 1883. They are all pushing business men, and it would be strange if any concern which had their experience, commercial ability and industry at its head did not turn out a great success. The company are sole agents for Milwaukee cement, Dyckerhoff Portland cement, "Gem City" white lime, two and three-ply prepared roofing; special agents Louisville cement, importers of Portland cement, dealers in lime, cement, plaster, hair, common brick, fire brick, pressed brick, mortar color, terra cotta, sewer pipe, drain tile, etc. They obtain pressed brick from St. Louis, Mo., and La Salle, Ill. The common brick is manufactured in Minneapolis and towns adjacent. The terra cotta comes from St. Louis and Illinois. They do a business of from one hundred and fifty thousand to one hundred and seventy-five thousand dollars per annum in building materials alone, besides the storage, which is considerable.

VAL. BLATZ BOTTLING DEPARTMENT, 245 Second Avenue South, R. Mueller, Manager—Through this agency the world-renowned beer of this company is distributed through the North west. Mr. Rudolph Mueller is the manager of the concern, and has had great experience in the business. He is an energetic and live business man, who neglects no opportunity of furthering the

BAYFIELD, ON LINE OF C., ST. P., M. & O. R'Y.

interests of the company, and is pushing the trade further and further through the country. A very large bottling business is carried on here, from three to five carloads of beer in a week being handled in this way and in filling the small orders. The trade extends over the whole of Minnesota and Dakota, but the amount of beer consumed at the works here forms no indication of the volume of trade done through the agency, as a large part of the beer is shipped direct from Milwaukee to the customers, and some of them using as much as ten carloads in a week. The bookkeeper, Mr. Goebel, is very efficient in his branch of the work, and has his hands kept pretty full.

SEXTON & WELSH, Dealers in Staple and Fancy Groceries, 20 Fourth Street South—Mr. William Welsh is a native of this city and Mr. Sexton was born in this State. In 1865 they established the grocery business here in the store they now occupy. They have a very fine location, being close to the Post-Office, where thousands of people pass their doors every day. They have been doing a business of some seventy-five thousand dollars annually, but are increasing the volume of trade every week; and this year the amount will necessarily be much larger than in any of those past. Their business is all in the city. They employ about six hands and employ two delivery wagons. Both the partners are young men and have doubtless a prosperous future before them.

WINTER & LUECK, Diamonds, Watches, Jewelry, Silverware and Clocks, 243 Nicollet Avenue —This firm has one of the finest jewelry stores in the city. It is situated in about the best part of the business center, No. 243 Nicollet Avenue. Both the members of this firm, Mr. R. G. Winter and Mr. Frank Lueck, came to this country from Germany and they are both enterprising and able business men. The business was established by Mr. Winter in 1876, and Mr. Lueck joined the concern in 1886. They carry a fine stock of diamonds, watches, jewelry, silverware and clocks, and are doing a good, healthy trade, which is always on the increase. The long store, with its beautiful windows and magnificent rows of show-cases, is most attractive and well worth a visit by those who contemplate purchasing goods in the lines handled by this firm. The stock is valued at about twenty thousand dollars.

BROWN BROS., Merchant Tailors, 241 Second Avenue South and Big Boston—This business was originally established by E. H. Steele, in 1876, and the Brown Brothers succeeded to it about a year ago. Their stock of woolens is a fine and well selected one, and consists chiefly of imported goods, as they cultivate the highest class of trade. It is valued at seven thousand dollars. They have an excellent established trade, which extends outside the city, for they do quite a good deal of country trade, and their annual sales reach to about forty-five thousand dollars. Mr. E. O. Brown and Mr. Ole Brown, the two members of this firm, were born in Norway, but have been in Minneapolis since 1872, and are consequently well known and respected. Mr. O. E. Brown has been in the tailoring business since he was twelve years of age, and, of course, thoroughly understands the trade. In addition to the tailoring establishment they have an interest in two large restaurants in the city. This, however, is only a kind of side interest, for the utilizing of surplus capital.

BOSTON ICE COMPANY, 323 Hennepin Avenue—This company was established in 1885 by the present proprietors, I. J. Bartlett, E. E. Bartlett, R. L. Taylor and E. Taylor. Their crop of ice is cut from Long Lake, on the Soo Road, about seven miles from the city, and from Lake Calhoun, and is of great purity. About 20,000 tons were stored the past winter, and each year there is an increase in the demand. They employ about twenty hands and eleven wagons. The annual trade amounts to upwards of $30,000. Mr. I. Bartlett, the secretary of the concern, is an agreeable and obliging gentleman, and ever ready to attend to the wishes of those who deal with the company.

PALACE CLOTHING COMPANY, High Art Clothiers, 43 and 45 Washington Avenue South—This house opened in September, 1888, as the Minneapolis branch of the great Palace Clothing Factory, with headquarters at Chicago. The Minneapolis branch employs at present forty-six people, all of whom are engaged in retailing under the management of Maurice L. Rothschild, formerly manager of Rothschild Clothing Company. Attention is paid especially to the manufacture of high class and the better grade of ready-made clothing for men, boys and children. A stock is carried of about $128,000. Their location is pleasant and central and they enjoy a very large trade. Three men are kept on the road. The business has been very satisfactory and Minneapolis has proven a fit place for the establishment of such an enterprise as the home house has here ventured.

WHITING SHIRT COMPANY, 312 and 314 First Avenue North, Office 601 Hennepin Avenue—This concern was originally established in 1872 by Mulford & Whiting at Dubuque, Iowa. In 1881 Mr. H. C. Carlisle became associated as a partner and Mr. Mulford left the concern soon after. The business was then carried on as Whiting & Carlisle up to 1888, Mr. Whiting purchasing the interest of Mr. Carlisle. It was then incorporated as the Whiting Shirt Company, with a capital of $50,000. The officers are Nelson P. Whiting, President; Fred E. Whiting, Vice-President; H. C. Mulford, Treasurer; and Roger Charlton, Secretary. They are wholesale and retail manufacturers of shirts and underwear. They have a very extensive trade all over the whole Northwest, employing six men on the road. They have also from 75 to 100 hands at work in the factory. Their specialty is making shirts to order. Their trade amounts to about $100,000 annually and it is all the time increasing.

PEOPLE'S ICE COMPANY, Office, 6 Third Street South—Mr. J. M. Collins is the principal proprietor in this company. He has been in Minneapolis for a number of years, and was formerly with the Cedar Lake Ice Company. This company has now been established for two years, and already the demand for ice has far outstripped the amount contained in the company's stores. The plan of the company is to make monthly contracts with parties, under which they agree to supply so much ice per day. This ice is delivered in the company's wagons. The experience of this year will no doubt induce the company to increase their store next winter, so that they may be able to meet all the demands that may be made upon them. Their present success is mainly due to the popularity of the ice in which they deal, which is of great purity, and to the fact that strict attention is given to the business by the proprietors themselves, who are quite young men, and who possess all the qualities necessary to build up a good and thriving business.

NORTHWESTERN PACKING HOUSE, B. W. Frost, Proprietor, 1017 Washington Avenue South—The Northwestern Packing House was established in the fall of 1885. The firm occupies the first floor and basement of 1017 Washington Avenue South, and devote their attention exclusively to packing beef and pork. Mr. Frost brought to the business, experience and capital, and soon placed the establishment in the front rank of Washington Avenue markets. Their attention is almost exclusively devoted to the retail trade, and they make a specialty of supplying hotels and restaurants. They also make a specialty of hams, kettle-rendered lard and sausage, which are prepared in their own establishment. They have a complete equipment for the manaufacture of sausage, and their trade in this product is very large. Four men and two teams are constantly employed.

THE MOON "SPOT CASH" GROCERY, 802 Nicollet Avenue—The proprietor of this establishment is Mr. Daniel McGrigor, of Mason City, Iowa, and he is ably represented here by Mr. H. G. Roth, the manager and general superintendent of the concern, who came here from Springfield, Ohio. The business has not long been established here, but is increasing very rapidly. It is principally retail, but there is also some wholesale trade done. The terms are strictly cash, and no deviation whatever is allowed from that principle. Sometimes a lady will order a small bill of goods, and say that she will send the money in an hour or so. The answer is always a request that she will fetch the money first. Sometimes this gives offense, and customers are lost, but usually they come back again, and in many cases they have the good sense to know that the rules of the house forbid any deviation from the cash principle, and swallow their irritation. There is a stock valued at about $4,000, which is nice and clean, and the business is increasing so rapidly that it promises ere long to be a very large concern. The annual trade is already about $50,000. There are about ten hands employed and two delivery wagons. The goods are purchased here, in Chicago, New York and St. Louis. Mr. Roth, the able manager, was for some years connected with the Blue Flag Grocery, Springfield, Ohio, and attributes the success of this enterprise to the cash principle, the small margains and the quality of the goods.

WALES & CO., Pictures and Art Materials, 423 Nicollet Avenue—This is one of the pioneer houses of the place. Mr. W. W. Wales, who was born in North Carolina, came here so long ago as 1851, before there was any Minneapolis on the west side of the river. He was present at the treaty with the Indians. The whole history of the place is, of course, at his fingers' ends, and he must often pause and look with astonishment at the marvelous growth of the city. His is the leading art store of the place. He has on his walls and in his portfolios a fine collection of pictures of all kinds, oil paintings, water color drawings, photographs, engravings, etchings, etc. He is sole agent for Soule's unmounted photographs. His stock of artists' supplies is complete, comprising every kind of requisite that an artist could possibly call for; and great care is taken to add every new article that has any merit or is likely to be in demand. In addition to the art store, Mr. Wales does a large manufacturing business in picture frames, of which line he makes a specialty. Gilding and regilding frames are two of the branches of this business to which special attention is given. Mr. Wales has the good fortune to be assisted in the business by his two daughters, young ladies whose courteous and obliging manners are well known and appreciated by all who have occasion to transact business at the place.

A. B. RUGG, Photographs and Portraits, 56 South Fifth Street—Mr. A. B. Rugg, the proprietor of the only ground floor studio in Minneapolis, is one of the most successful and well-known of the photographic artists. All the success he has achieved is due, as he is fond of stating, to his close application to business and general judgment and economy—*i. e.*, not hiring hands to do work which he was capable of

doing thoroughly well himself; and, last but not least, to making a specialty of good work—offering to the public quality and not quantity, as has been too much the tendency with some members of his profession. He executes all kinds of portraits known to the art, and, in fact, carries on photography in all its branches. His premises comprise five very handsome rooms on the ground floor, which are used for waiting-rooms, office and operating rooms, and have two very handsome show windows on Fifth Street South. The printing and finishing departments are upstairs and occupy six rooms. Mr. Rugg came here in 1879, from La Crosse, where he was with Mr. Lathrop, and ran his gallery. He was born in Boston, and left that city in 1877. He bought out Mr. Brown in the old Merchants' Block, 41 Washington Avenue South, stayed there two and one-half years, moved to Nicollet Avenue, where he had a fine gallery; and finally moved to his present stand in in 1886. Business has prospered with Mr. Rugg from the start. From small beginnings he has now built it up to something like $1,200 per month. He requires the assistance of four competent photographic artists to carry out his numerous orders, but—and here lies the grand secret of his success—he never fails to exercise an active supervision over the whole concern and particularly looks after the financial part. Mr. Rugg has, in addition to his studio, some very substantial witnesses to his success in the shape of houses and lands, to purchase which, in the aggregate, would make a very large hole in $50,000.

EAGAN & CO., Retail Dealers in Staple and Fancy Groceries, 1206 Third Avenue South—This firm is composed of Mrs. Kate Eagan, of Minneapolis, and Miss M. Eagan, of New York City. Mr. John C. Eagan is the manager. The business was established in 1887. They occupy their own building, which was constructed expressly for their business. This building is three stories high and has a basement. Three men and two horses are employed. The trade is increasing rapidly. The store is one of the neatest and most attractive in Minneapolis. They carry a full stock of staple and fancy groceries, canned goods, coffees, teas, spices, fruits in season, vegetables, etc. The store is most centrally located, and in one of the most thickly populated portions of the city.

LOFGREN BROS., Merchant Tailors, 239 First Avenue South—The Messrs. Lofgren were born in Sweden, and came to America about twenty years ago. About eight years ago they came here, and commenced their present business. Their principle has been all along (and to it is probably owing much of the success that has attended their efforts) to attend to the business themselves, and they have carefully kept this principle in sight. They do all their own cutting and fitting, and their patrons may expect a square deal and satisfactory workmanship in every respect. They started in a very small way, with one or two workmen, and at the present time they employ nineteen or twenty, all experienced men, earning big wages, and their business continues to increase every year. It extends over a large territory, embracing Washington Territory and Missouri. Their stock is a good one, consisting of the finest imported and domestic woolen goods, and altogether theirs is one of the most flourishing concerns of its kind in the city—the result of industry, care, and a thorough knowledge of the trade.

ALEXANDER MURRIE, Architect and Superintendent, 608½ Nicollet Avenue—Mr. Murrie is a Scotchman by birth. He was for a number of years superintendent of special lines of buildings in Glasgow, Scotland. He was thoroughly trained in the best architectural schools in Scotland. He first went to Virginia upon leaving his native country, and thence to Mankato, and was superintendent of the Court House there. About four years ago he came to Minneapolis, and has designed many beautiful buildings. Among others, and one unique in this country on account of its hanging staircase, is the Prospect Park Observatory, with its beautiful pointed arches. Besides this there are the Spectator Office, the residence of Robert Blaisdell, Jr., and a host of others. In the competition for the Court House he took the fourth prize. He is now engaged on designs for some very extensive buildings in the business parts of the city. Mr. Murrie owes his success entirely to his own

THE LOTUS AND CITY OF ST. LOUIS—LAKE MINNETONKA.

professional merits. He has had no external aid whatever, and in an age like the present, when competition is so keen, this is no small recommendation.

ORTMAN & WOELFFER, Farmers' Wholesale Grocery House, 27 Washington Avenue North—After an existence of twenty years this house still maintains the same leading patronage which it has always controlled, as the headquarters and principal depot for the wholesale farmers' trade of the Northwest. The firm carry one of the largest and most complete stocks of groceries in the City of Minneapolis, and their retail trade here is a very large and lucrative one. Their great specialty, however, is their family wholesale trade, which they have extended all over the State and throughout Dakota. They keep several salesmen on the road selling goods in this way, and their shipments to individual consumers, country hotels, etc., are greatly increasing. The firm issues a monthly consumers' journal and price current for the benefit of their customers, in which every change in the market is accurately given.

MARVIN & CAMMACK, Proprietors of the Crescent Creameries, Minneapolis Office 31 Fifth Street South—Mr. Charles E. Marvin and Mr. E. A. Cammack are the proprietors of these creameries, which are the largest in the world. They were first started about ten years ago and the branch here has been in operation about two years. There are creameries at Rochester, Zumbrota, Kasson, Kenyon, Stanton, St. Paul, Elk River, Monticello and Cannon Falls, besides that in this city. And they have factories at Rochester, Salem, Byron, Bern and Pine Island. They employ about 200 hands. They manufacture at the rate of 15,000 pounds of butter and 5,000 pounds of cheese daily, and in this city they sell 1,500 gallons and in St. Paul 2,000 gallons of milk and cream daily. All their products are of the very finest quality. This is no doubt one of the secrets of their wonderful success.

L & C

An industry of this description is deserving of every encouragement. The amount of good done to a State by such an institution is very great. The trade in this city is chiefly local, but in St. Paul they have very extensive cold storage and the whole of the Western trade is handled from that point. The shipments westward are very extensive and are made as far as the Pacific Coast. Mr. B. S. Dodge and Mr. W. M. Marvin are the managers in this city.

M. GANNON, Dealer in Staple and Fancy Groceries, Provisions, Etc., 27 First Street South— The business of which Mr. Gannon is now the proprietor was established in 1879. Mr. Gannon has been here one year, and has already made his presence felt, as the business is making rapid strides toward the large volume which ere long it is bound, under his care and guidance, to attain. Having always on hand a large stock, which is purchased with great judgment, he is able to meet all demands, and every one who deals with him is sure to continue with him, as he guarantees satisfaction in all his transactions. He has two traveling men who are kept busy taking orders, and he also employs four experienced hands in-doors. There are two wagons for delivering the retail orders in the city and suburbs. The sales already have reached a volume of $100,000 per annum, and are constantly on the increase.

A. E. & C. E. HOLBROOK, Dealers in Inglewood Spring Water and Ice, 6 South Third Street —The water from Inglewood Spring is proved by analysis to be remarkably pure, being almost totally free from organic matter. It is recommended by the highest medical authorities for drinking purposes, and those are fortunate who can avail themselves of this delicious and at the same time inexpensive luxury. Mr. A. E. and Mr. C. E. Holbrook were born in Auburn, Maine. They came here about four years ago and leased the Springs at Inglewood Park. They have now established a very convenient system of supplying the water. Families can have jugs filled with it left at their homes, and stores and offices are supplied in bulk. There are ten hands employed by the concern, and eight wagons, and the demand for the water has so increased that the supply delivered averages about 3,000 gallons daily in the summer season, and about 1,500 gallons daily in the winter. The flow from the springs is practically inexhaustible.

PRATT & CONE, Real Estate, Loans and Insurance, Rooms 434, 435 and 436, Bank of Minneapolis Building—This firm has been doing a real estate and loan business in Minneapolis since 1883. During the years of their business life they have handled large amounts of capital to the profit and entire satisfaction of their clients, and to the benefit of Minneapolis, in the form of buildings and other enterprises for which money is borrowed. They adopt the conservative plan in their business, and have established a fixed rule to themselves never to take a mortgage for more than 50% of the valuation of a piece of property. By doing this they secure absolute safety for the interest and principal of their clients, and neither in form of interest or principal has any one of their clients ever lost one cent. Also, where Minneapolis property is concerned the property generally increases in value during the life of the mortgage, and at its maturity additional incumberances may be put upon it with no diminution of safety. This firm also does a first-class real estate business, chiefly dealing in Eighth Ward property. And it is safe to say that for services in their lines of business no better or more competent men can be found.

E. G. BARNABY & CO., Hatters and Men's Furnishers, 17 Washington and 234 Nicollet Avenues—Messrs. E. G. Barnaby and E. W. Goddard came to Minneapolis from Memphis, Tenn., in March, 1879, Mr. Barnaby having been in the gents' furnishing business in the latter city for eighteen years. They at once embarked in the same business at 17 Washington Avenue South, doing $20,000 worth of business the first year. They have since steadily increased their trade, reputation and stock. In 1888, their business had increased five hundred per cent., they doing a business of about $100,000 during that year. Starting with a single front on Washington Avenue and seventy feet of store, they now have fronts on both Nicollet and Washington Avenues and one hundred and forty feet of store. Employing two men and a boy the first year they now have use for twenty men. Their stock of hats, caps and men's furnishing goods is perhaps the largest and most complete of any stock of the kind west of Chicago. They are sole agents in Minneapolis for the well-known Knox hats of New York. They aim to supply the wants of every class of men. They do a very large trade in the country and small towns about, as well as in the City of Minneapolis itself. They have twice suffered severe loss from fire, but have each time fully and easily recovered.

WEBSTER & CHURCHILL, Druggists, Under Nicollet House—This house keeps a first-class drug store under the Nicollet House, on Washington Avenue South. The firm is composed of Mr. H. G. Webster and Mr. G. S. Churchill, both New Hampshire men. The concern is one of the oldest in the city, having changed hands several times before it came into possession of the present proprietors, who succeeded in 1881 the firm of Cable & Judd. Since they have had the running of the business it has increased three-fold in volume. A full line of drugs, toilet articles and chemicals is kept, the stock being valued at $18,000. They also keep on hand a fine stock of all grades of cigars, and in this line they do a large business. The soda water fountain here is very handsome, and the cold drinks that are constantly being dispensed would almost float a man-of-war, one would think. Mr. Webster is Secretary of the State Board of Pharmacy, which important position he has occupied for more than two years, thus witnessing to his popularity and the high esteem in which he is held by his *confrères*.

GOODYEAR RUBBER CO., John J. Tallmadge, Manager, 201 Nicollet Avenue, 1 to 13 Second Street—This is one of the numerous branch houses of the famous Goodyear Rubber Co., whose headquarters is at 487 Broadway, N. Y., and which, as is well known, is one of the largest manufacturers of and dealers in rubber goods in the world. The store here in Minneapolis has been in operation since 1885, and the stock kept on hand at this point is a very large and extensive one, comprising full lines of everything properly appertaining to their line of trade. It is ably managed by Mr. John J. Tallmadge, to whose energy and efforts much of its success is due, and both a wholesale and retail business is transacted, about a dozen men being employed in connection with the establishment. The other stores of this great company are located at 362 Broadway and 57 Maiden Lane, New York City, and also at Buffalo, N. Y.; Chicago, Ill.; Milwaukee, Wis.; St. Louis, Mo.; San Francisco, Cal.; St. Paul, Minn., and Montreal, Canada.

W. F. TRUFANT & CO., Fine Teas and Coffees, No. 120 Fifth Street South—This is an entirely wholesale business, and Mr. Trufant himself is the sole representative of it. He always carries a considerable stock of teas on hand and also a stock of coffees, but as the latter goods are not improved by keeping, and as they are roasted in Boston and shipped to him about three times a week, he thus keeps constantly on hand a fresh stock. His trade reaches over the whole of the State and parts of Dakota, Wisconsin and Iowa. His city and St. Paul trade is very large, indeed, he has a tendency to cultivate trade close to home. Besides his staff at his warehouse, he employs three traveling men, who make Minneapolis their headquarters.

C. A. SMITH & CO., Manufacturers and Dealers in Lumber, Lath and Shingles, 302 and 303 Lumber Exchange—This is a representative firm, which started eleven years ago, at first at Herman, in Grant County, and moved to Minneapolis in 1884, where it has since carried on an increasing and thriving business. The yards are located at the corner of Eighth Street and Fifth Avenue S. E., and at the corner of Plymouth and Lyndale Avenues, and their name is familiarly known throughout the whole city. C. A. Smith and John S. Pillsbury compose the firm. The business has increased from 12,000,000 to 20,000,000 feet annually, and embraces light and heavy lumber, and every product of pine timber. A large jobbing as well as retail business is done by this firm, and their reputation and trade is co-extensive with the limits of the Northwest lumber trade. Some attention is paid to supplying sash and doors, moulding and inside house finishings. Mr. Smith, upon whom devolves the management of this business, has shown himself to be a competent, careful business man. He has been a resident of this city since 1884.

NORTHWESTERN CONSERVATORY OF MUSIC. 608½ Nicollet Avenue, Charles H. Morse, Director—This institution was established here in 1885, by Prof. Chas. H. Morse, Mus. Bach.

Mr. Morse's career has been a remarkable one. From the age of 15 he has held a public position as a musician and always with credit to himself, and much to the delight of those who have been within his influence. In organ playing his instructors were George E. Whiting and J. K. Paine. In piano, Carlyle Petersilea, J. C. D. Parker, Ernst Perabo and Carl Baermann, successor to Hans Von Bulow as King's professor of piano at the Royal Music School, Munich, pupil of Liszt, and one of the finest living pianists. In harmony, composition, etc., S. A. Emery and Paine. Upon his graduation in 1876 Mr. Morse received from Boston University the degree of Bachelor of Music. At the opening of Wellesley College, he was appointed its professor of music,

HOTEL ST. LOUIS, ON LINE OF C., M. & ST. P. R'Y.

and planned the entire work of the music department, which had at the outset two teachers and eight pianos. In 1884 he resigned his position at Wellesley College, leaving a college of music, thirty-six pianos, two pipe organs and a music hall, entirely for musical work, which cost $30,000, and nine teachers besides himself. At the Conservatory there have been taught in the four years during which it has been organized no less than 1,000 students. The attendance has been from twenty-seven States and Territories, including (the N. E. and Middle States) Massachusetts, British Columbia, Manitoba, Missouri, Nebraska and New Mexico. Minneapolis is to be congratulated upon having a gentleman of such eminence at the head of her musical affairs.

GEO. R. NEWELL & CO., Wholesale Grocers, 101, 103, 105, 107, 109 and 111 Third Street North, and 300, 302, 304, 306, 308 and 310 First Avenue North—This is one of the largest concerns of its kind in the whole Northwest, and, carried on by one of the best known men in the Northwest trade, Geo. R. Newell, everything is conducted on a gigantic scale, the stock, the staff of busy helpers, the staff of clerks, the traveling salesmen, and the system which can make such a concern work smoothly must be admirable. The building in which their business is carried on is a beautiful red brick structure 124 x 132 feet and six stories high. The territory covered by them is the whole Northwest. No less than fifteen traveling salesmen represent the house through the country, and in their warehouses and office fifty more hands are employed. The scene presented at their place of business on any day is only comparable to a bee-hive, so busy and full of life is it in every department. Mr. C. Emerson, the manager, is the central figure and must needs have a wonderful head for business or he would never be able to stand the strain put upon him. He has to distribute, after examination, the hundreds of letters that pour in from all parts, and every question of importance must needs be referred to him, so that during the whole time he is in his office he is beset by inquiries enough to bewilder any one not possessing the wonderful power of of concentration with which he is endowed.

PATTERSON & DICKINSON, Manufacturers, Importers and Jobbers of Gloves and Mittens, Hats, Caps, Furs and Ladies' Straw Goods, No. 204 Nicollet Avenue and No. 205 Hennepin Avenue— This concern was first established in 1883 by Mr. R. H. Patterson and Mr. James Chesnut. In January, 1886, Mr. Chesnut sold his interest in the concern to Mr. A. C. Dickinson, of Cincinnati, who then moved to this city and took an active part in the business. Both members of the firm are American born and are active men. There are six traveling salesmen employed in the business besides the staff in the warehouses and office. The trade is very large and extends over the whole of the Northwest. A full stock of each line of goods is carried by the firm and is valued at from $50,000 to $75,000, according to the season. The business is steadily increasing, and bids fair to attain to mammoth proportions.

E. A. OLSON, Merchant Tailor, 275 Cedar Avenue—Among the many worthy citizens from the Northern countries may be mentioned Mr. E. A. Olson, who came to this city two years ago from Red Wing, Minn. During the first few months of his residence, Mr. Olson was employed by Mr. J. H. Thompson, the well-known Hennepin Avenue tailor. Mr. Olson first commenced business at 313 Washington Avenue South. He soon after removed to his present location, where he is enjoying success. Mr. Olson is a practical tailor, and employs none but first-class help. He consequently can guarantee satisfaction. Low rents enable him to make clothing at moderate prices. Cleaning and repairing clothing is a feature of the business. Many of the well-dressed citizens of South Minneapolis are living testimonials of the handiwork of this establishment.

THE SECURITY BANK OF MINNESOTA, Corner Third Street and Hennepin Avenue— This great financial institution, with a paid-up capital of $1,000,000, a surplus of $250,000, deposits of nearly $5,000,000, and loan and discount credits of $4,000,000, is in truth what its name suggests, not alone one of the most secure and reliable banks at Minneapolis, but of the State as well. It is a State bank, and was founded in 1878 by T. A. and H. G. Harrison and Joseph Dean, with a capital of $300,-000. The Messrs. Harrison were brothers, and came to the West when Minnesota was in its infancy, and Mr. Dean is also a pioneer of Minneapolis, he having been a member of the first board of county commissioners of Hennepin County from 1856 to 1859, when he was elected County Treasurer. The latter was the first manager of the bank, and was for years its vice-president, until succeeded by the present incumbent of that position, Henry M. Knox. Mr. Knox is also well known in financial circles —in fact, better known than any other man in Minnesota, he having been the public examiner of banks and officials of the State for the ten years preceding 1888. The other officers are H. G. Harrison, President, and F. A. Chamberlain, Cashier, the latter being a banker of life-long experience, whose connection with the bank dates almost from its earliest days, and the directors are, in addition to the officers, J. Shaw, H. M. Carpenter, W. M. Tenney, A. J. Dean and J. H. Thompson. The bank's principal correspondents are the Union Bank, London, Eng.; the Commercial National Bank, Chicago; the National Exchange Bank, Boston, and the Bank of New York, New York City.

MILWAUKEE STORE, Dry Goods and Notions, Mather & Mather, Proprietors—No notice of the business houses of South Minneapolis would be complete without a description of the "Milwaukee Store." This store was established in September, 1888, by Messrs. L. W. Mather and Alonzo Mather, operating as Mather & Mather. Mr. E. M. Everson is the efficient manager. The members of the firm came from Hastings, Minn. The store occupies an area of 44x96; it is equipped with the Lamson cash railway. Eleven clerks are employed. The stock is valued at $20,000 and comprises silks, dress goods, white goods, hosiery, gloves, all kinds of fancy goods—in short, everything to be found in a first-class dry goods store. The store is easily the largest on Cedar Avenue; it is always a busy place and is extensively patronized by the residents of South Minneapolis.

J. B. WHEATLEY, Artistic Gas Fixtures and Table Lamps, Etc., 604 Nicollet Avenue—Mr. Wheatley, the proprietor of this establishment, was born in New York, and came here in the year 1886 when he started his present business. He carries a very fine stock of goods, which is valued at about $30,000. There are gas fixtures of every conceivable from, all designed with the most exquisite taste. Table lamps, brass plaques, tables, mirrors and ornaments, together with the most beautiful art metal work for parlors, etc. The trade extends all over the Northwest and is very extensive. A traveling salesman is kept busy taking orders for the house, and there are eleven hands employed. Minneapolis, for so young a place, is noted for its artistic taste, and an establishment like Mr. Wheatley's is properly appreciated.

R. J. RICKEY, Dealer in Fine Wall Papers and Interior Decorations, 414 Nicollet Avenue—Mr. R. J. Rickey is one of the most successful operators in his line of business in the city. He has only been here for a comparatively short period, having come here from Ohio about six years ago, yet in that short time he has done wonders, commercially speaking—showing beyond a doubt that he possesses the push and energy that are so necessary to secure a good position in the business of this Western country. Although his beginnings were comparatively small, he has now achieved such a standing that he carries a stock of the value of from $10,000 to $20,000, while his business averages $1,000 per week. He has from seventeen to twenty hands constantly employed, most of whom are men of considerable experience in the trade, and his work as an interior decorator is, beyond dispute, of the very best quality and bound to give satisfaction to his numerous patrons, among whom may be found some of Minneapolis' most honored citizens.

WASHBURN MILL COMPANY, Manufacturers of Lumber and Flour, 42 Washington Avenue South—The mills of this company are here and at Anoka. The capital stock of the company is $500,000. About three hundred hands are employed. The capacity of the mills is, for flour, 2,400 barrels daily, and for lumber, 25,000,000 feet annually. The trade for these products extends over the whole of the United States. The present corporation are successors to W. D. Washburn & Company, and General W. D. Washburn is the President, Major W. D. Hale, Treasurer; and Mr. J. E. Stevens, Jr., is Superintendent of the flour department. All these gentlemen were born in Maine. General Washburn has been prominent not only in milling affairs, but in affairs connected with the government of the State, since he came here in 1857. He served three consecutive terms in Congress. He is largely interested in the principal railroads with which this city is identified. He is president and principal stockholder in the Anoka National Bank. He owns the steamer City of St. Louis; owns a large stock farm in this State, where he is engaged in the breeding of fine grades of cattle. He is largely interested in the Standard Coal Company of Iowa, and is connected with many other commercial and social enterprises too numerous to mention. He is at the same time always ready to assist any undertaking for the benefit of the city. Mr. M. P. Hopkins, his secretary, is prompt in attending to these matters for him. Major W. D. Hale, manages the business of the company. He has been a resident of Minneapolis for some twenty years and has been connected with General Washburn in business ever since he came here. He served in the army for four years. Mr. J. E. Stevens, Jr., attends to all the details of wheat purchasing and the manufacture and sale of flour. He has been here for about fifteen years, during which time he has been connected with the milling business.

LACKEY & LACKEY. Real Estate, Loans and Insurance, 1500 East Franklin Avenue —Worthy of mention among the leading firms of South Minneapolis may be mentioned the enterprising real estate firm of Lackey & Lackey.
The members of the firm are young men who came here from Wisconsin. Mr. W. H. Lackey, the senior member of the firm, established the business in 1885, but in 1887 the business had grown to such proportions that he associated his brother with him. They are always busy. Mr. W. H. Lackey is a notary public, a position that is of great advantage to him. They have a large list of

WESTWARD HO! C., St. P., M. & O. R'Y.

residence and business property for rent, and also a long list of realty for sale, a conspicuous feature of their business is selling farm property. This list includes a large number of farms in Iowa, Minnesota, Wisconsin and Dakota. They are also agents for the following fire insurance companies : "Peoples" of Pittsburg, "Detroit Fire and Marine," "Fireman's" of Newark, "Boatmen's" of Pittsburg, "Rockford" of Rockford, Ill. Another feature of their business is the negotiation of loans. They are thorough believers in the future of South Minneapolis, and are prepared at all times to show to people seeking desirable homes advantageous property.

JOHN H. WINGATE & CO., Dealers in Dry Goods and Clothing, 230 232 Twentieth Avenue North, Branches at 1009 Main Street N. E. and W. Superior, Wis. This firm is composed of John H. and Chas. H. Wingate, of Minneapolis, and S. W. Lightbody, of West Superior, Wisconsin. Mr. Wingate enjoys the distinction of being the pioneer dry goods merchant of North Minneapolis. He first established himself in 1880, at 1229 Washington Avenue North, but removed to his present commodious establishment in 1886. Here the ground floor and basement of above numbers are well stocked with dry and fancy goods, clothing, hats and caps, and men's furnishing goods. It is the largest store of its kind in North Minneapolis, and the presence of such a store is a great convenience to the residents of this part of the city. They carry good goods, such as are demanded by buyers in that part of the city. The rapid growth of their business led to the establishment of a branch in N. E.

Minneapolis in 1885. In January, 1886, the store at West Superior, Wis., was established. In the three stores a stock valued at $45,000 is carried, and the annual sales exceed $100,000. Nine clerks, besides the proprietors, are required to attend to the wants of the business. For many years he was engaged in business in Janesville, Wis., but recognizing the value of Minneapolis as a trade center wisely decided to cast his fortunes with the progress of the Flour City.

C. J. REEVES, Meat Market, Shops, 731 Tenth Street South and 732 Fourteenth Street East—This cosy market was opened some years ago, and purchased by the present owner in 1887. Under this gentleman's management it has been greatly improved. Mr. Reeves runs a market that is the delight of the housewife. Here is to be found a well-selected stock of all kinds of meats, fish, poultry and oysters, in their season. He also has fresh eggs, milk and butter, and is now adding a complete stock of pickled and canned goods. Mr. Reeves has been in this business all his life, having commenced eighteen years ago in Fulton, N. Y., where he ran a market until he went to Michigan. From that State he came to Minneapolis in 1883, and until he went into business was employed by H. A. Gerrist. Mr. Reeves' market is an essentially family one. He personally selects his own stock, and being thoroughly familiar with the business, he knows what and how to buy. He makes all the sausage used by his trade. Two men and two teams are employed to attend to the wants of the patrons.

UNION PACIFIC TEA CO., Importers, Coffee Roasters, and Dealers in Teas and Coffees, 421 Cedar Avenue—It would require a volume to describe the magnitude of the business done by this firm, it being the largest of the kind in the city. A brief summary may convey some idea of the extent of its business. The main houses are located at 79 Water and 80 Front Streets, New York City. There are over two hundred branch stores throughout the United States. The motto of the firm, "We lead! Let those who can, follow," is an appropriate one. Mr. R. P. McBride, of New York, is the proprietor of this vast business. The Minneapolis branch was established in 1885. Mr. C. L. Harrod is the present manager, having assumed this position in December, '87. The store occupied covers an area of 25 x 80 feet. Three men and one team are given employment. This concern is a direct importer, and handling goods in such quantities are enabled to quote the lowest prices. They give presents when a customer's purchases have reached a certain figure. Their stock of presents embraces china in all styles, glassware in endless variety, castors, knives and forks, hanging lamps, and thousands of other articles both useful and ornamental. Since the establishment of the Minneapolis branch the business has shown a rapid increase and has extended to the remotest sections of the city.

STEWART & JOHNSON. Practical Plumbers and Gas-fitters, 1217 East Franklin Avenue—This enterprising plumbing firm of South Minneapolis was established three and a half years ago. Commencing in a small way their business has rapidly increased, until now eighteen men and one team are employed. Both members of the firm are practical men, and to this fact may be attributed much of their success. They carry a full line of plumbers' supplies, and are consequently enabled to fill contracts at short notice. Their specialty is plumbing and gas-fitting in residences; also, they have virtually a monopoly of the plumbing business on the South Side. Their business aggregates upwards of $15,000 per year. Mr. Stewart has been a resident of this city for seven years, coming here from Chicago, his native city. Mr. Johnson has lived here nine years. He learned his trade in Norway, of which country he is a native.

O. MOE & CO., Dealers in Furniture, Wall Paper, Carpets, Pictures, Frames, Window Shades, Etc., 1331 East Franklin Avenue—This popular house was established in 1886 by O. Moe and J. O. Braa, operating as O. Moe & Co. From 1880 to 1886 Mr. Moe had charge of the gilding and framing department of Wales & Co., of this city. Mr. Moe is a native of Norway, and learned his trade in that country. Mr. Braa is also a native of Norway, and, until he entered into business, he also worked for Wales & Co. Both members of the firm are practical men, and this has had much to do with their success. Their business has constantly increased, so that now they have the largest and best appointed store of the kind on Franklin Avenue. They occupy two floors of a building 22x90 feet. They carry a stock of the value of $7,000, and their sales aggregate $20,000 annually. Their stock comprises furniture, wall paper, carpets, pictures, window shades, etc. Their specialty is making picture frames to order. They buy direct from Eastern manufactories, and discount all bills, consequently they can quote the lowest prices. During the winter three men are usually employed, which number is increased to ten in summer. This increase in summer is largely due to the extensive business that they do in paper hanging.

OLANDER & CO., Dealers in Fancy and Staple Groceries, Crockery, Glassware, Etc., 1201 East Franklin Avenue—This grocery is a first-class establishment in every respect. It is one of the oldest in South Minneapolis. The present proprietors acquired its control in January, 1887. Both members are young men, and were fitted for the business while in the employ of other firms. They carry a complete stock of flour, canned goods, coffees, teas, spices, bakery products, cigars, etc. Their display of vegetables and fruits is especially worthy of attention, and is an attractive feature of their store. They employ two clerks and two teams. Their trade is rapidly increasing, and they are now doing a business of $2,500 per month. Both members of the firm are natives of Sweden and have lived in Minneapolis for some years.

ROOD & ERICKSON, Merchant Tailors, and Proprietors of the Castle One Price Clothing Store, 412 and 414 Cedar Avenue—These gentlemen came to this city in 1886 and established this business in the block just south of their present location. Both gentlemen, before coming here, were engaged in business in Wisconsin. The store occupied by them is very commodious, and occupies a prominent location on Cedar Avenue. This store is 33x100 feet. The stock is a well-selected one. They carry all kinds of clothing for men's and boys' wear. They also have departments devoted to hats and gents' furnishing goods. A merchant tailoring establishment is also conducted in connection with this establishment. Three men are given employment in this department. In the ready-made clothing department three men are employed. Both members of the firm are natives of Norway. Mr. Rood has been in this country for fourteen years and Mr. Erickson for twenty years.

TILBURY & McCUNE, Dealers in all Kinds of Fresh and Cured Meats, Poultry, Game, Sausage, Etc., 1209 East Franklin Avenue—One of the long established markets on Franklin Avenue is that of Tilbury & McCune. This firm are the successors of C. A. Tilbury, Mr. McCune having purchased an interest January 1st, 1889. Both gentlemen have lived here some years, and are, therefore, thoroughly familiar with the wants of the people of South Minneapolis. Their market is neat and well arranged, occupying the first floor and basement. Here are to be found all kinds of meat, fish, canned meats, oysters and game in season. All kinds of sausage are made, and the lard used by their trade is rendered by them. They call for and deliver all orders promptly. Three men and two teams are required to attend to the wants of the business, and their trade is rapidly increasing because of prompt and courteous attention to the wants of customers. Before coming here, Mr. McCune lived for some years in Austin, Minn. He is a native of Ohio. Mr. Tilbury is a native of England, and has been a resident of this city for eleven years.

J. A. HALL, Dealer in Fine Boots and Shoes, 1333 Franklin Avenue—No notice of the business houses of Franklin Avenue would be complete without a sketch of the popular boot and shoe store of J. A. Hall. This store was established in 1884 by Mr. J. L. Johnson. February 15th of this year, Mr. J. A. Hall purchased the business. Before coming here, Mr. Hall was engaged in the boot and shoe business in Red Wing. He was born in Sweden, where he learned the trade of shoe-making. He came to this country eleven years ago, and immediately located at Red Wing, where for three years he carried on a shoe shop. He then opened a boot and shoe store, which he carried on with success until coming to this city. He carries a well-selected stock, which is valued at $2,000. This comprises all grades of men's, women's and children's foot-wear. The sales will run upwards of $10,000 per year. In addition to the shoe store he maintains a shop, where two men are employed. Here orders can be given for custom work and foot-wear left for repairs. Mr. Hall buys in St. Paul, Minneapolis and the East.

SCANDIA FURNITURE STORE, 405 and 407 Cedar Avenue, N. L., Enger, Proprietor— Mr. Enger first began business in 1885, at 1805 Riverside Avenue. The development of his business necessitating larger quarters, he removed to his elegant new store at 405 and 407 Cedar Avenue May 1st, 1888. This store is 32 x 75 feet, and in addition to the first floor he occupies two basements. The stock, purchased direct from manufacturers, comprises all kinds of furniture, carpets, pictures, etc. It is tastily arranged, and all goods are displayed in an attractive manner. Picture frames are also made to order, and repairing of furniture is a specialty. Nine months after the establishing of the furniture business the undertaking branch was started. This is located at 407 Cedar Avenue. The firm name of this department is Enger & Ellingsen. The office is open day and night. They are prepared to take entire charge of funerals, furnishing hacks, a hearse, etc. Mr. Enger is a native of Norway. He came to this country in 1879 and to Minneapolis in 1881.

TURNQUIST BROS., Merchant Tailors, 26 Sixth Street South—This enterprising firm was established in 1878 by John A. and Frank G. Turnquist, trading as Turnquist Bros. Their first location was at 623 Washington Avenue South. They removed, in 1888, to their elegant new store at 26 Sixth Street South. This elegant four-story structure, 44x100 feet, was built by them on their own ground at a cost of $25,000. Their business is one of the fixtures of Minneapolis, and they have amply displayed their confidence in its future by the construction of this elegant building. This building is equipped with all modern conveniences, and their store is especially attractive. They carry a stock of $7,500, and give employment to from ten to thirteen hands. Their sales in 1888 aggregated $22,000 and is steadily increasing. They make all grades of men's clothing, but pay especial attention to good clothing at popular prices. These gentlemen were born in Sweden, but have been residents of Minneapolis since 1873. They learned their trade in Sweden. For six years prior to engaging in business they worked for different firms in the city. The business success of these gentlemen is an evidence of their close attention to customers' wants.

CRAIG BROS., Wholesale and Retail Dealers in Dry Goods, 509 Nicollet Avenue, Syndicate Block—Mr. John G. Craig came here in 1882 and established this business. His brother, Mr. Daniel Craig, joined him three years later. They were born in Scotland, but have been in this country since 1870 and 1872, respectively. They carry a stock of general dry goods which is valued at from $35,000 to $40,000. They employ a staff of ten or twelve hands, and their annual sales amount to the large sum of $75,000. Their store is a very handsome one and is situated in the very best locality in the city. Their stock is a very fine one, and as they are both energetic young business men they are bound to continue in the enjoyment of the success which has hitherto crowned their business operations.

SWEDISH-AMERICAN BANK, 28 Washington Avenue South—The large patronage which this new bank has received since its organization in June, 1888, is very significant as showing the perfect confidence reposed in its management and officers by the people of Minneapolis. It began business with an authorized capital of $500,000, one-fifth of which was paid up, and its affairs as a whole and in every department have resulted so satisfactorily as to already indicate a secure and prosperous future. Its foreign exchange is a noticeable feature, and in the matter of loans and discounts it has made rapid progress, as may be seen from the fact that the latter exceeded $300,000 before the close of the first year. The officers are O. N. Ostrom, President; C. S. Hulbert, Vice-President, and N. O. Werner, Cashier; all of whom are well-known and prominent here and the directorate contains in addition to the officers the following substantial citizens: John F. Peterson, John Dahquest, H. R. Halvorsen, Hans Mattson, C. A. Smith, Ernest Dean, J. W. Anderson, C. M. Amsden, H. Enstrom, T. B. Janney, Chas. Larson and C. J. Swanson.

T. W. HANLEY, Merchant Tailor, 51 South Fourth Street—This gentleman was born in Minneapolis in 1857, in a house which occupied the present site of the Pillsbury A mills. His parents were among the old pioneers, having come here from New York State. Mr. Hanley is therefore well known by the old residents. He started in business in 1880, and was the senior member of the firm of

LAKE MINNETONKA—ST. P., M. & M. R'Y.

Hanley & Kelley. Since 1883 Mr. Hanley has had no partner. His store is centrally located and opposite the Tribune building. He does a fine class of custom work. He carries a complete and well selected stock of all grades of suitings. His aim is to keep pace with the latest styles and to this end watches closely the Eastern and European styles. All work turned out by his establishment is guaranteed both as to fit and workmanship. Ten men are given employment. He is a thorough believer in the rights of workingmen, and carries this idea out by employing none but union men in his establishment.

CHAS. D. WHITALL, Wholesale and Retail Dealer in Books, School Supplies, 125 Nicollet Avenue—Unlike the greater portion of the business houses of Minneapolis, this establishment lays claim to an antiquity of something like twenty years, its founder having been W. W. Wales. As in the past, the enterprise is very conspicuously in the foremost ranks of the trade. The stock handled is one of the largest and most varied in the Northwest, and the sales and increase in the volume of business are indicative of most progressive and intelligent management.   The employes of the house are fifteen in number, and both a wholesale and retail business is done—this being the only concern in Minneapolis carrying on a jobbing trade in books, stationery and school supplies combined.   Mr. Whitall, the present owner of the business, purchased the stock nine years ago—that numeral also indicating the length of his sojourn in Minnesota. He came here direct from New York City, where he was extensively engaged in manufacturing operations, and he claims New Jersey as his native State.   Since making Minneapolis his permanent home he has identified himself firmly with the commercial and mercantile interests of the place, and is in every way classed among her most deserving citizens.

IRISH-AMERICAN BANK, Corner of Hennepin Avenue and Fourth Street, Kasota Block—There have been German-American banks, Swedish-American banks, Canadian-American banks and banks whose titles connected them with many of the various nationalities represented in this country, but it remained for the people of Minneapolis to establish the first Irish-American Bank in the United States, and it is a pleasing task to be able to chronicle that the enterprise has proven successful beyond the expectations of its sanguine founders.   The bank opened its doors for business last November with a capital of $100,000 and charter rights to increase the same to $500,000, when occasion may require. Its officers are J. S. Coghlin, President; J. E. Gould, Vice-President, and J. C. Scullen, Cashier, and its directors are all old and well-known professional and business men, namely: Martin Ring, M. W. Nash, J. S. Coghlin, Matt Walsh, Dennis Trainor, J. R. Corrigan, Wm. McMullan, Richard Welsh, Hon. J. P. Rea, H. C. Clarke and John Goodnow.

FOLDS, GRIFFITH & COLVER, Wholesale and Retail, Carpets, Rugs and Draperies, Syndicate Block, 505 and 507 Nicollet Avenue—This is one of the largest and highest class carpet and drapery establishments.   The house was originally established in 1865.   Up to the beginning of this year the firm consisted of Mr. W. B. Folds and Mr. C. J. Griffith, when Mr. Colver, of New York, joined the firm, and it is accordingly Folds, Griffith & Colver.   The premises occupied by them in the Syndicate Block are very fine; they consist of a double-front store, 50 x 150 feet, besides which there are four other floors and a basement all used for the purposes of the business.   Their immense stock is unequaled for richness and elegance, and is valued at $75,000; it is a sight worth seeing.   Since the joining of Mr. Colver the business has received a fresh impulse, and his business ability and sound judgment, added to the experience and high commercial qualities of the other two partners, are sure to push the concern rapidly to the front in the trade.

LINDMAN & McIVOR, 75 Sixth Street South—The establishment of Messrs. Lindman & McIvor, 75 Sixth Street South, interior decorators in fresco and dealers in wall papers, is by far the largest of its kind west of Chicago.   Mr. McIvor is a native of this country; he came here from New York State in the year 1884.   Mr. Lindman was born in Sweden, and has been in the firm of Lindman & Locke, which was dissolved two years ago.   He then joined Mr. McIvor, and they have since carried on business in the premises they now occupy.   Their business is decorating, painting and hardwood finishing.   They also carry an immense stock of wall paper, the largest in the Northwest—especially they handle hand-made and imported goods in that line.   Fresco painting is their specialty.   Among the principal works executed by them are the Hennepin Avenue Theatre, the Presbyterian Church, Fourteenth Avenue South; the new Congregational Church on Park Avenue, in public buildings; while in residences are Mr. B. F. Bull's new residence, corner Ninth Avenue and Seventeenth Street; Mr. Wyman Elliott's residence, Ninth Avenue and Fifteenth Street; Mr. Wells' residence, Hennepin Avenue, upon which they have executed $5,000 worth of work.   Their work in other States includes Mountain City Theatre, Pennsylvania, just burnt down; Love's new Opera House, Fremont, Nebraska; Foster

Opera House, Des Moines, Iowa; Lewis Opera House, Ottumwa, Iowa; Leicester Opera House, Newton, Iowa; State Capitol Building, Des Moines, Iowa, and many others. They procure their goods from all the principal American and European factories--in fact, wherever they can obtain anything possessing beauty combined with other desirable qualities. The number of hands employed by the firm is from sixty-five to seventy-five, and they do a business of from $100,000 to $150,000 per annum.

SAFETY DEPOSIT VAULTS OF THE MINNESOTA LOAN AND TRUST CO., Nicollet Avenue—This is a department of the Minnesota Loan and Trust Company. Mr. Samuel Clark and Mr. Alfred W. Lane are the associate managers of the vaults. They are very rarely at rest during the office hours, 9 A. M. to 6 P. M., owing to the number of applicants for access to their safes. The plan of the business is to afford safe keeping to valuables, no matter of what description. The company rent small safes at from $5.00 to $50.00 per annum, and the renter is furnished with a key which is the only one in existence that can open his safe. The manager has a key which enables the renter to use his, the safes having a kind of double lock. A person renting one of these small safes can take it out, with the assistance of the manager, and retire with it to a small room at the back of the vault, where he can lock himself in and examine or deal with its contents at his leisure, and when he has finished again replace it in the vault. The outside vault doors are the Diebold Safe Co.'s, and are guarded by the Yale time lock. These doors weigh about four and a half tons. They have double combinations and are double at each end of the vault. There is also a storage vault for trunks, packages and other valuables, for which receipts are given when they are deposited, but the contents of the small safes are not known to any one except the renter. The system is about as complete as it is possible to make it, and the backing of the Loan and Trust Company renders a deposit here as safe as could be desired.

MINNEAPOLIS DRY GOODS CO., Importers and Dealers in General and Fancy Dry Goods, 501 and 503 Nicollet Avenue—This house is one of the Syndicate Trading Company, who represent a trade of about $22,000,000 a year. The Minneapolis Dry Goods Company are successors to Barnes, Hengerer, Demond & Co., whom they bought out in August, 1888. Mr. C. F. Gordon is the President and Manager of the company and Mr. J. R. Gordon, Treasurer. They are importers and dealers in general and fancy dry goods. The greater part of their trade is retail and largely for cash, but they also do quite a wholesale business. Their stock is complete in every line and is valued at $250,000. They employ from seventy to seventy-five hands and have two delivery wagons and two wagons for hauling in goods. The strongest feature of the concern is their being one of the Syndicate Trading Company. The advantages of this combination are large and far beyond the reach of any one house. As an instance, it may be mentioned that they have offices in Manchester, England; Berlin and Paris, for buying goods, and in New York they have an office for the same purpose, where every department of the business is represented. Union is strength.

J. A. BIXBY & CO., Hardware, Stoves and Ranges, 623 and 625 Nicollet Avenue—Mr. J. A. Bixby is a native of Vermont and came here in the year 1881, when he commenced business. His career has been one of the most remarkable successes in the city. In consequence of the very large increase in his business he moved this spring into the very fine and commodious premises he now occupies. The frontage is 50 feet and the depth 100 feet, and there are three floors and a basement, all devoted to the business. The stock carried varies in value from $30,000 to $50,000, and comprises all the best kinds of hardware, stoves and furnaces. Besides this there is a tin shop, and large quantities of tinware are being turned out. The principal ranges carried are the Highland, Steward heaters and ranges, and the Fuller and Warren furnaces. A very fine display of these goods was made at the Exposition of 1888, and another exhibit at the same time was made by Mr. Bixby of refrigerators. Most of the business is retail, but there is some wholesale done. From fifteen to thirty hands are employed in the establishment. The annual sales amount to about $200,000 and the business is rapidly increasing.

CHAS. C. LYFORD, Veterinary Surgeon, 712 Third Avenue South—Dr. Lyford is an experienced veterinarian, who has made this profession his special study for years. He was fitted for college at the Rockford (Illinois) High School, and graduated from the Illinois State University in 1875. He

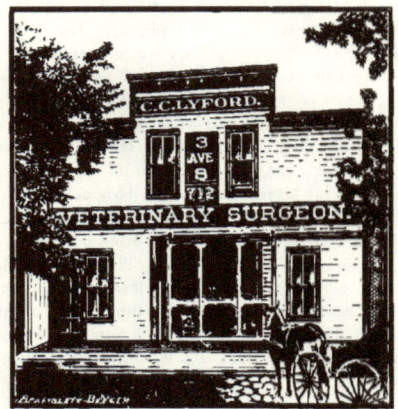

then studied at the famous veterinary college of Montreal, Canada, graduating in 1877, after a course of two years. For the next two years he took a course of practical medicine at the McGill Medical College, graduating in 1879. At the same time he held the position of demonstrator of anatomy at the Veterinary College. The summer of 1879 he passed in study at the Royal Veterinary College in London, after which he studied in Edinburg and Paris. He came to this city in 1880, and located at 300 Second Avenue South. In December, '87, he removed to his present location, where he occupies a stable which was specially built for him. This stable is the most complete of its kind in the city. It covers an area 40x120, and is two stories in height. Here he conducts a regular horse infirmary, presided over by competent men. It is heated throughout by steam. He also has a completely equipped prescription department. Dr. Lyford has accommodations for twenty horses, and receives horses for treatment from all over the West. Dr. Lyford holds the positions of consulting veterinarian of the Minneapolis Board of Health, State Secretary of the American Veterinary Medical Association, and State Veterinarian of the Minnesota State Dairy Commission. He is also President of the Northwestern Veterinary College, an institution incorporated March 14, 1885. Here all students have the benefit of a practical course of instruction. The course of instruction extends over three winters. Each summer a special session is held. The faculty of the college is composed of eight members, who deliver lectures on their special subjects. In connection with the college is a large library, containing works on all subjects pertaining to veterinary practice. The college issues annual catalogues, and the president invites correspondence from men intending pursuing the profession of veterinary surgery.

COL. WEST "2579."

Dr. Lyford is the proprietor of the famous stallion Col. West, with a record of 2:26¼. This stallion is the sire of several 2:30 performers. Mr. Lyford owns Mabel H. 2:26; Blackmont (trial), 2:26¼; Fanny O (wagon), 2:38¼.

JOERNS & COMPANY, Furniture Dealers, 1226 Washington and 223 Plymouth Avenues North—This progressive firm is composed of Fred. Joerns and C. B. Satterthwaite. They first established their business at 406 Plymouth Avenue, but in July of this year they removed to their present elegant quarters, where they occupy three floors. Before coming to this city, they were engaged in the furniture manufacturing business in Chicago. There they acquired a valuable insight in the business which has been conducive to their success. They are easily the leading firm in their line in North Minneapolis. They carry a stock valued at upwards of $6,000 and do a business of from $2,000 to $3,000 per month. Their stock comprises every variety of furniture. Undertaking is a recent venture of their business, and they bid fair to develop this branch into one of importance. They make a great specialty of their time-payment department. This department is a great convenience to many reliable citizens, as it enables them to buy furniture, which they pay for on easy installments. Both members of the firm are yet young men, Mr. Joerns is a native of Wisconsin. He is a prominent member of the Masonic fraternity, and at the present time holds the position of secretary of Plymouth Lodge. This is his second term. Mr. Satterthwaite is a native of Pennsylvania, many of his ancestors bore an important part in the Revolution. His great, great grandmother designed and made the first American flag.

PLYMOUTH BOOT AND SHOE HOUSE, 303 Plymouth Avenue, A. R. Neustrom, Proprietor—Danielson & Neustrom established this popular house in 1883. In 1885 Mr. Danielson sold his interest to Mr. Neustrom, who has since continued the business. On January 1st, 1889, Mr. Neustrom, with Mr. A. E. Talcott, established a store at 217½ Central Avenue, Eastern Division. Mr. Neustrom has been very successful, and has done a constantly increasing business. He carries the largest and best assorted stock of men's, women's and children's foot-wear, in both rubber and leather goods, in North Minneapolis. He is also the special agent for the following makes: Ladies' and gents' shoes of Curtis & Wheeler; the gents' shoes of Lilly, Brackett & Co.; the medium grade goods of Wallace, Elliott & Co., of New York; the medium goods of J. B. Lewis, Boston, and the ladies' shoes of George W. Ludlow & Co. and Elderkin, Taylor & Co. In connection with this establishment a repair shop is carried on. Mr. Neustrom has been a resident of this city for twelve years, coming here from Watertown, Wis. He is a native of Sweden, but came to this country when a mere child.

NICOLLET AVENUE CREAMERY, 1021 Nicollet Avenue—This creamery was established in February, 1888, by Ferris Bros., who sold it in November of the same year to Mr. E. G. Selsemeyer, the present proprietor. Bringing to the business a thorough knowledge of its needs, Mr. Selsemeyer has built up a large and increasing trade. The leading feature of his business is the supply of fresh milk, which is daily received from Northfield and Faribault, Minn. The sales now average one hundred and fifty gallons daily. Two men and two teams are constantly employed in supplying the wants of customers. Mr. Selsemeyer also does a very large business in the sale of cream, cheese, butter and eggs. He has a special brand of cheese, "The Cottage," which he has lately put upon the market. His trade is entirely by retail. Mr. Selsemeyer was born in Fond du Lac, Wis. He came to Minneapolis in 1879. Until he purchased his present business he worked in different city dairies. Three years of the time he was with the old Minneapolis Milk Association. Mr. Selsemeyer has been in the dairy business all his life.

WEST END CASH MEAT MARKET, Fred. A. Armbruster, Proprietor, 3121 Nicollet Avenue—This market was established in October, 1888, and at once took rank with the best markets of the city. Its business is conducted on a strictly cash basis, and to this fact is due its success as a low priced market. None but the best meats are handled, and it easily maintains the reputation of being the leading market in the West End. It is located nearly opposite the Motor Junction depot. Neat-ness and orderly arrangement are conspicuous features. They sell ham and bacon of their own curing and pure lard of their own rendering. One of their leading specialties is their fine grade of pressed corned beef, in which they have a rapidly increasing trade. The building occupied is 22 x 75 feet and they occupy the ground floor and basement. Three men and two teams are given employment. Mr. Armbruster has been a resident of Minneapolis since 1885, coming here from St. Paul. He is a native of Illinois. Before engaging in this business he was for fourteen years a locomotive engineer.

L. K. LOVEJOY & CO., Proprietors of the Nicollet Island Roller Mill—The Nicollet Island Roller Mill is the manufacturer of the famous "Old Gold" corn meal, which has such a wide-spread

PLEASANT VALLEY AND SUGAR LOAF, WINONA, MINN.

reputation all over the Northwest. The mill is also noted as being the first here to introduce the roller process in grinding corn, rye and coarse grains. The traffic is quite large, both locally and in the adjoining country, and some ten hands are employed in connection with the enterprise. Only a wholesale business is done, and the capacity of the mill is constantly taxed to the utmost in supplying the wants of the trade. The firm is composed of L. K. and S. B. Lovejoy, both of whom are practical, enterprising business men, and devote their whole attention to the advancement and care of their thrifty and growing industry. They are true Minnesotians in every sense of the term, loyal adherents to Minneapolis interests and her assured commercial supremacy and future advancement. They are among the largest manufacturers and dealers in rye and graham flours and corn meals doing business in this city, and all their productions have a standard and fixed value in the market on account of their uniform excellence, which guarantees a prompt and ready sale for all the manufactured goods their milling facilities are capable of supplying.

NEUMAN & DETWILER, Livery, Sale and Boarding Stable, 211 and 213 Plymouth Avenue This is the oldest stable in North Minneapolis. It was established upwards of fifteen years ago. The stable was run under different management until February, 1889, when Mr. Clem Neuman became the proprietor. On May 1st, Mr. Detwiler became his partner. This firm has made numerous improvements, and have enlarged the stable so that it now covers an area 50x100 feet. They keep twenty horses for their livery trade, and also have a complete stock of vehicles. They also have a large number of boarders. A very important branch of their business is the sale department, in which they are doing an increasing trade. Both members of the firm are practical horsemen. Mr. Detwiler is the veteran of the firm, having been in the horse business twenty-one years. For much of that time he owned a large interest in a stable in Washington, Iowa. He has been in Minneapolis for the past four years. Previous to engaging in this business, Mr. Neuman was engaged in logging. He has lived in Minnesota all his life.

CARPENTER-ADAMS COMPANY, Manufacturers of Sash, Doors, Blinds, Mouldings, and Building Paper, Office 210 Lumber Exchange—This firm established itself here in February, 1883. It is an incorporated company, with a paid up capital and surplus of $100,000. Mr. Geo. W. Curtis is President, Mr. S. J. Carpenter, Vice-President; Mr. E. L. Carpenter, Secretary, Treasurer and Manager. They are connected with Curtis Bros. & Co., of Wausau, Wis., and Clinton, Iowa, running factories at both those places, that at the former having a daily capacity of 1,500 doors and 700 windows, and at the latter 600 doors and 1,000 windows. Their business at inception amounted to about $75,000 and has grown to $500,000 annually. They make a specialty of southern yellow pine from Mississippi, which makes the harder, clearer and cheaper flooring. They give employment in Minneapolis to about thirty men. Their lumber yard is at Harrison Street and Broadway S. E., and warehouse at Fifth Street and Eighteenth Avenue S. E. Their business is exclusively wholesale, extending over Minnesota, Dakota, Montana, Washington Territory, Wyoming and Illinois, in the hands of three traveling salesmen. Mr. Carpenter is a resident of Minneapolis since 1887.

OYS BROS., Dealers in Fresh and Cured Meat, Ham, Bacon, Poultry, Game, Etc., 1503 Hennepin Avenue—Mr. John Oys established this market in 1886. Six months later he admitted his brother, Mr. August Oys, to the business. The success of their business has been marked. Both members are practical meat men and have been engaged in it nearly all their lives. They learned their trade in Germany. In 1881 they came to this country, and in 1882 they located in Minneapolis. Their business is increasing rapidly. They cater entirely to family trade. They deal in fresh and cured meats, poultry, fish, game, etc. Two men and one team are required in the business. They call for and deliver any orders desired. This firm is deserving of success, being composed of live and energetic men, who thoroughly understand the wants of their customers.

NORTHWESTERN NATIONAL BANK.—Beginning business in 1872, with a capital of $200,000, this bank presents a record of progressive growth and solid and material advancement seldom met with and rarely surpassed by any similar institution in the country. In 1880 the capital was increased to $500,000, and two years later the latter amount had to be again doubled in order to keep abreast of the demands made on its resources. Its officers are S. A. Harris, President; T. B. Casey, Vice-President, and James B. Forgan, Cashier, and the Directors are composed of the cream of the Flour City's business and professional men and capitalists, namely: H. T. Welles, Winthrop Young, Woodbury Fisk, Wm. H. Dunwoody, Thos. Lowry, S. A. Harris, T. B. Casey, Wm. S. Culbertson, Geo. A. Pillsbury, C. H. Prior, O. C. Merriman, Anthony Kelly, W. H. Hinkle, M. B. Koon, W. H. Vanderburgh, Jas. B. Forgan.

DR. N. R. HURD, Dentist, 422 Nicollet Avenue—Dr. Hurd is a gentleman whose position to-day is the outcome of a long and varied practice. He studied dentistry under Dr. Carlton, in New Hampshire, and was also a pupil of Dr. Robinson, at Great Falls. He practiced in Wisconsin in

1862-3-4; two years in Northfield, three in Hastings, and twelve in Faribault, in this State. He came here in 1883, and has been practicing in the city since that time. His long experience in the profession has ripened his knowledge in an eminent degree. He is one who is not satisfied with a little superficial information gained years ago, but he has kept pace with the times in all the scientific discoveries that have been made since he commenced his career, and may now be said to occupy a foremost rank in his profession. He has a very good practice, which is principally kept up by those who have known him the longest, and the scenes of his early labors still contribute to swell the bulk of that practice. It is an old saying that a rolling stone gathers no moss, but in Dr. Hurd's case the principle does not apply, for, although he has traveled a good deal, each move has resulted in his carrying away a good deal of the practice, and always the good will which he had secured. He is in this respect more like a snowball which increases in substance as it travels onward.

RED WING-SHEBOYGAN LIME CO., Manufacturers of Red Wing Brown Lime, Office 205 First Avenue South—This is a recent but none the less important venture in this city. Mr. Linne,

who was born in Sweden and is now the president of the undertaking, has been manufacturing lime in Red Wing in this State, since 1881. This spring (1889), he consolidated with Mr. Braesch, and the company was duly incorporated under its present title. Besides the Red Wing brown lime, of which they are manufacturers, they are sole agents for Sheboygan white lime, Pittsburg lime, Pittsburg mortar colors, and are special agents for Louisville, Milwaukee and Portland cements; New York, Michigan and Iowa plaster, hair, fire clay and brick, sewer pipe, common and pressed brick, etc. Their yards are situated at 1125 Fourth Street South and 1501 First Street

RED WING-SHEBOYGAN LIME CO.'S WORKS.

North. They always have on hand a large stock of lime and cements. Both the gentlemen connected with this concern are practical men of long experience in the business, and as the goods in which they deal are in universal request they are bound, beyond a shadow of doubt, to make the concern a grand success.

E. REESLUND, Merchant Tailor, 709 Hennepin Avenue—This gentleman has been in the tailoring business for twenty-six years, many of which were devoted to the business in Sweden. In 1887 he followed the example of the many thousands of his countrymen and came to America. He came direct to Minneapolis. In the fall of 1888 he established himself in the tailoring business. He has been very successful in his venture. His trade is increasing rapidly, and he contemplates an early addition to his force. His stock of suitings in woolens, cassimeres, etc., is very complete, and shows a marked good taste. He also does all kinds of repairing and cleaning of clothing. His location is very central and only a short distance from the Holmes and West hotels.

CASCADE STEAM LAUNDRY, 316 Second Avenue South—Mr. J. R. Purchase, the proprietor of this laundry, was born in Flushing, Long Island. He has been in this city about sixteen years. His laundry is not excelled this side of Chicago. The premises, which are the property of Mr. Purchase, are in a handsome, four-story pressed brick and stone building, 26 x 120 feet, with a basement. Four floors are occupied for laundry purposes. In addition to this large building Mr. Purchase has branches of his laundry at the four points of the compass, namely, on the East Side, 120½ Central Avenue; West End, corner Twenty-sixth Street and Nicollet Avenue; North Side, 1305 North Washington Avenue; South Side, 1526 Franklin Avenue. Each of these branches has the exclusive handling of the business for their respective portions of the city. Everything is done to make the work turned out by them sustain the very high reputation which the Cascade Laundry has secured. About one hundred hands are employed, and the amount of work turned out by the concern is simply prodigious. A great deal of this is shipped by mail and express to towns in this State, Dakota, Wisconsin, Iowa, Montana and some places in Idaho. In fact, there is more business outside of the State than inside, barring Minneapolis. The annual business amounts to about $70,000. Mr. Purchase is still in the prime of vigorous manhood, and is an exemplary man of business. No better proof of this could be adduced than the business which he has built up and still carries on so successfully.

DR. SUTHERLAND, Dentist, 427 and 429 Nicollet Avenue—Dr. Sutherland studied dentistry at the University of Michigan, Ann Arbor. He came here about three years ago, but prior to that he had been practicing at Duluth for about two years. He makes a specialty of gold, crown and bridge work or teeth without plates, and uses the painless method of extracting teeth by the administration of nitrous oxide. His practice is very large and continues to increase, so that he and his two assistants have all they can do in meeting the demands upon them. Dr. Sutherland keeps himself well posted in all the new discoveries and improvements that have been and are being made in dentistry.

CARLSON BROTHERS, Livery, Sale and Boarding Stable, 102 First Street North—This firm was established in 1881, and is now operating as Carlson Bros. They do a large sale business, and buy, sell and exchange horses, carriages, buggies and harness. They keep in their business twenty-five to thirty horses, and also have accommodations for some boarders. This stable is commodious, and is 27½ x 160 feet, and three stories. They are also proprietors of the N. W. Scavenger Co., which was established with their stable. This is the largest concern of the kind in the city. They do the most of the city scavenger work. They take contracts for any kind of excavating, and their long experience, combined with heavy teams and competent men, enable them to do their work promptly and to satisfaction. In cleaning vaults and cesspools they use Dewey Bros.' odorless tanks. They also have teams to do any kind of heavy hauling. These gentlemen have been located in the city for many years, and have built up a large and increasing business.

JONES BROTHERS, Granite and Marble Monuments, 325 First Avenue South—The members of this firm are Mr. B. P. and Mr. A. P. Jones. The Jones Brothers came here about ten years ago, and it was then that they first established their business. It was, of course, very much smaller at the start, but the Jones Brothers are men of business, and they quickly made their energy and ability felt. They have now a large business extending all over the Northwest, and which is still increasing. It amounts already to something over $30,000 annually. A fine line of marble and granite monuments are to be seen in the warerooms of the firm. They generally have about $5,000 worth of stock on hand. Among others the following fine memorials have been designed and superintended by Mr. B. P. Jones: Masonic, Geo. W. Hale, Dr. Springgate, J. H. Giddings. Lauderdale, Woodbury Fisk, Nimocks, E. B. Ames, sarcophagus; S. J. H. Camp, set at St. Paul; B. S. Bull, cottage style; The Dudley sarcophagus; Dr. Wright, of Oshkosh, sarcophagus, and many later works.

WOODBURN FARM FENCE CO., Manufacturers of Combination Wood and Steel Fence, Office 323 Hennepin Avenue—This company was incorporated in 1886. H. L. Woodburn is the President, and F. R. Hubacheck Secretary and Treasurer. They are both Americans, and have been in Minneapolis for some years. They manufacture every kind of fence, but make a specialty of the Woodburn Farm Fence, a neat combination of wood and steel wire-work. It is cheap, light, and very neat in appearance, and is most effective in turning all kinds of stock, hogs, sheep, poultry, etc. In fact, it is the cheapest and most practical fence made. It is manufactured by steam power machines. The works are at No. 415 Sixth Avenue South. There are about fifteen hands employed in the manufacture. The plant is worth over ten thousand dollars and is very fine, and, of course, well suited to the work done. Some of the Woodburn Farm Fence was in use at the Exposition last year and attracted a good deal of attention. The trade of the company extends all over the Northwest, and has already reached to something over $25,000 annually, with a decided upward tendency.

RYAN & CO., Livery Stable, 20 Second Street North, E. D.—This stable enjoys the distinction of being the oldest established stable on the East Side, having been built in 1875. Mr. John Ryan became the proprietor in 1887, and in September, 1888, Mr. T. A. Bowen purchased a half interest. This stable is very commodious, is built of brick, is 44 x 100 feet, and is two stories in height, with basement. The demands of the business require thirty horses. A large number of horses are also boarded. The stock of carriages is well selected and includes hacks, phaetons and coupes. They also have a line of elegant hearses. Six men are given employment. At the corner of Adams and Spring Streets N. E. they run a branch stable, which is two stories high and 30 x 60. Here three men are employed. This stable is well equipped. The present proprietors purchased the stable in 1888. Mr. Ryan is a native of Indiana, and has been a resident since 1881. Mr. Bowen was born in Minneapolis.

SCHOOL OF LANGUAGES, Syndicate Block, Madame Courdate, Proprietor—This is one of the most useful institutions in the city. In a population so mixed as that of Minneapolis the need of a school of languages has been long felt; and Madame Courdate has come here with a method of teaching and facilities for acquiring modern foreign langages which will go far to supply what has hitherto been lacking in this respect. Madame Courdate teaches orally, according to Dr. James H. Worman's Chautauqua method. What has been called the natural way of teaching foreign languages is defective in that the matter of grammar is generally omitted. Dr. Worman's system keeps this defect in view, and may be called the natural way of teaching with the study of grammar superadded. Madame Courdate teaches both in classes and privately, either at her schools or at the pupils' own home, if preferred. The languages taught are French, German and Italian. Madame Courdate undertakes the French herself, and native German and Italian professors give instruction in those two languages respectively. Persons are thus enabled to acquire a knowledge of these three languages in the shortest possible time, and the terms are reasonable.

GEORGE FRENET, Dealer in Choice Groceries and Provisions, corner Plymouth and Sixth Street North—This is one of the most attractive grocery stores in North Minneapolis. Mr. Frenet established the business three years ago. His stock is attractive, well arranged and first-class in every respect. It consists of staple and fancy family groceries, coffees, teas, spices, canned goods, provisions, and fruit in season. His trade is increasing rapidly. Mr. Frenet came to Minneapolis in 1864, from Michigan. He is a native of Canada. After his arrival here he was employed for eleven years by the Joseph Dean Lumber Company. He then served eight years on the police force of this city. Mr. Frenet also owns considerable inside real estate, which has enhanced greatly in value.

C, MARCHESSAULT, Machinist, Trip Hammer and Machine Forgings. Shop: Nicollet Island Power Building—With a practical experience of thirty years as a machinist, Mr. Marchessault possesses many advantages in this special line of craft which entitle him to distinctive notice in a review of the character of this publication. Born in New York he early became a resident of the neighboring State of Vermont, where he acquired his technical mechanical skill, and was soon promoted to the position of foreman in the machinest department of the most extensive railroad shops in that State, serving in the latter capacity until he came to Minneapolis nine years ago, to engage in business for himself. He began operations here on a somewhat limited scale, requiring at first little assistance besides his own labor to perform such work as he could procure, but he has succeeded so well in developing the business that he now employs a dozen or more men to handle his contracts. All kinds of heavy forging and fancy and ornamental wrought iron work is done, somewhat of a specialty being made of architectural and building designs and finishings, in which lines a vast amount of first class custom is controlled. His machine shop, in the Power Building on Nicollet Island, is one of the best equipped in the city, being supplied with every convenience and facility necessary to the prompt and efficient dispatch of even the most intricate and difficult work.

H. O. PETERSON, Dealer in Carpets, Dry Goods, Clothing, Upholstering Goods, Etc., 1225, 1227 and 1229 Washington Avenue South—Mr. Peterson established this business in July, 1882, at 1229 Washington Avenue South. His business so increased that in 1884 he took in 1227, and one year later 1225, so that he now occupies the basement and three floors of above numbers. He now carries a stock of $60,000, and requires the services of twenty-two clerks constantly, with an increased force at certain seasons of the year. His sales aggregated in 1888 $100,000, but will probably exceed $125,000 for 1889. Mr. Peterson's store is arranged into different departments. In 1225 he carries his stock of gents' furnishing goods, hats and caps; in 1227 his ladies' furnishings, hosiery, gloves, underwear, fancy goods, etc., and in 1229 the stock of dress goods, notions, etc. In the basement are carried the stocks of carpets and upholstered goods, table linens and domestics. Mr. Peterson is a liberal advertiser and as a result he enjoys a very large mail order business. He also does some wholesaleing, but his main attention, is devoted to the retail portion of his business. Mr. Peterson is a native of Norway and came to this country in 1869. He first worked in a sash and door factory, then was engaged in the grocery business. Mr. Peterson is a prominent member of several of the best secret orders. He is now filling his third term as Grand Master of the Exchequer in the Knights of Pythias. He is a colonel of the first regiment of the A. O. U. W.; captain of the Uniformed Rank in

Knights of Pythias, and has taken the thirty-second degree in the Order of Free Masons. Mr. Peterson's record is a most creditable one and he is one of the most prominent of his race in the city.

ALEX. J. FOURNIER, Artist; Studio, Tribune Building—Mr. Fournier is the son of an old settler of St. Paul, where he was born. He came here in 1881 from Milwaukee, where he had been sojourning for some years. A few years ago he went to Chicago to study a particular branch of his art, and, with the exception of that time, has been here continuously ever since he first arrived. He is a young artist of far greater talent than the usual run of his contemporaries. Some of his landscapes are works of exceptional merit, as are also his still-life studies. He had a fine collection of local scenes at the Exposition last year and one equally as fine this year. In his studio at the present time there are some studies from river scenes in the neighborhood, and other scenes of country life that would be ornaments in any art gallery. Mr. Fournier is not without his admirers and patrons in this city and St. Paul. Among them may be mentioned Mr. J. J. Hill, who has one of his pictures of St. Anthony Falls, the family of Mr. Welch, Mr. Conklin, Mr. J. S. Pillsbury and Mr. F. A. Campbell; but we cannot but think that his talents merit a warmer appreciation than would seem to be accorded them by the people at large. That he would receive that warmer appreciation in an older part of the country is certain, if his inclination should take him from Minneapolis.

N. G. NELSON, Merchant Tailor, 30 Fifth Street South—This gentleman established himself in business in February, 1889. Mr. Nelson is a practical tailor, having been in the business all his life. He possesses a wide acquaintance in Minneapolis, having been here since 1871. He is a native of Sweden, and came to this country in 1869. Mr. Nelson gives employment to ten men. He occupies a store 16x60 feet. His stock is well selected, and his long experience in the tailoring business in this city, familiarizing him with the tastes of Minneapolis men, has enabled him to select a stock calculated to please the most fastidious dresser. He does a general line of custom work. His trade, since he started, has been good, and is exceeding his expectations. He personally superintends the making of every suit turned out by his establishment.

FULTON MARKET, James Chant, Proprietor, 713 Third Avenue South—This market was established by Mr. L. R. Gorham at 500 Fourth Avenue South, in 1879. Mr. Chant purchased it in 1885. Two years later he removed to his present location and the wisdom of this removal has been proven by a greatly increased trade. He has been in the meat business since 1879, when he first came to Minneapolis. His business caters principally to the family trade. It gives employment to five men and three teams. Catering to a first-class trade entirely, Mr. Chant handles none but first-class meats. His stock is complete in every respect. Mr. Chant is a native of England. He came to Clay County, Minn., in 1873, and was engaged in farming for six years. During a portion of the time, he held the position of overseer of one of the Minnesota granges. Before coming to this country, Mr. Chant followed the sea for nineteen years, entering the service when a boy as an apprentice. He was successively promoted to positions of able seaman, second-mate, chief-mate, until in 1864, he became master of the bark Cora Linn. He held this position for seven years, when he left it to take position of captain of a steamer. He was engaged principally in the India-China trade, although he went on voyages to nearly every quarter of the world. Mr. Chant takes great pride in the recommendations received from his employers during a long and honorable service.

ADAM ROESEL, Manufacturer of and Dealer in Fine and Heavy Harness, Horse Furnishing Goods, Saddles, Collars, Etc., 1211 Washington Avenue North—Mr. Roesel became the proprietor of this business in April of this year, purchasing it from Adolph G. Schleiner, who established it in 1882. Before engaging in business for himself Mr. Roesel worked at the trade of harness making in this shop, and also for Louis Laramee. Mr. Roesel carries a large and well selected stock of whips, blankets, harnesses and saddles, in short, everything necessary to a well-stocked harness shop can be found here. He also manufactures all kinds of harnesses, but makes a specialty of the finer grade of harnesses. His location is the best of any house of the kind in North Minneapolis. Mr. Roesel is a native of Germany, but has been a resident of this State since 1870.

MINNEAPOLIS OMNIBUS TRANSFER LINE, S. B. Mattison, Proprietor, 13 Nicollet House Block and 619 Second Avenue North—A business that is a striking evidence of the progress of Minneapolis, is that afforded by the Minneapolis Omnibus Transfer Line. In 1870, when Mr. Mattison became proprietor, the business required but eight horses; now fifty or more are required. At that time there was no free suspension bridge, and his buses went to St. Anthony Junction to meet trains. The business was started by Mr. Mattison's brother during the war. Trips were then made to Fort

Snelling to connect with the river steamers. At 617 and 619 Second Avenue North he has a large stable, 60x110 feet, and three stories high. His business gives employment to twenty-five men. His stock of vehicles includes omnibuses, hacks, band-wagons, coupes, phaetons, hansom cabs, etc. Mr. Mattison is also the proprietor of the Minneapolis Cab Line. Mr. J. A. Mattison is the superintendent. These cabs are all furnished with careful drivers and can be called at any hour, day or night. Mr. Mattison has omnibuses and hacks at all trains. His agents board all trains and sell conveyance tickets and check baggage to any part of the city. His drivers call every hour at all the principal hotels to drive guests to trains. This gentleman was born in Vermont and has been a resident of Minneapolis since 1870.

W. H. HARRIS, Livery, Boarding and Sale Stables, 314, 316 and 318 Third Street South—This gentleman has been in the livery and sale business in this city for six years. He has had twenty-five years of experience among horses, and in various parts of the country, principally at Boston, Mass., and Lewiston, Me. Seven months ago he opened

his large, well-ventilated stables at 314, 316 and 318 Third Street South. Mr. Harris is a man who evidently knows his business, and his stables are probably among the finest west of Chicago. They cover one-quarter of an acre of ground and are as clean as a New England parlor. The ventilation is perfect, and the many smells which usually hover around a stable are almost totally banished. In case of fire, the arrangements are such that the horses could be quickly taken out through a number of exits on all sides of the building. Connected with the stable, but entirely secluded from it, is an elegantly furnished ladies' waiting room, so arranged that ladies may enter and leave it without coming in contact with the rest of the stable, and communicating with the proprietor's office by means of an electric bell. Mr. Harris has at present forty boarders, and in stock for sale a variety of horses for teams, for family, carriage or buggy use, for riding, etc. He handles these horses himself, trusting no other hands with such important work. Any one visiting these stables will be struck by the general air of comfort and cleanliness prevailing, and nowhere can the buyer find a better lot from which to make a choice.

MAYHEW BROTHERS, Wall Papers and Decorations, 129 Sixth Street South, corner Second Avenue—This concern was originally started by Mr. George S. Mayhew and Joseph Mayhew, in 1883, who were afterwards joined by their brother, Mr. David Mayhew. Mr. George Mayhew subsequently retired from the firm, but still retains the management of the business. They use the whole of the ground floor and basement of the premises for salesrooms and storerooms for their stock of wall paper, the largest in the city, and valued at from $15,000 to $20,000. The business was formerly retail only, but they have lately added a wholesale department to the concern. Their trade is not by any means confined to the city, as they fill orders all over the country as far as Washington Territory. They have had very large experience in interior decoration, so that they are able to tell at once what effects may be produced to harmonize with any given surroundings, and those who wish to beautify their homes will do well to consult their taste in this respect. As they have always on hand the materials that would be required for decoration under any conceivable circumstances, they are able to show in a few moments the combinations most suitable for each case, and thus save their patrons from possible disappointment and trouble. They employ about forty experienced men. A specialty of this house is the furnishing of samples as well as complete combinations of walls, ceilings, and decorations to parties at a distance, who are not able to find as large an assortment of goods and colorings with their local dealers as they wish, thus giving them as good selections as they could have if they were in the city.

C. H. BLICHFELDT, Wholesale and Retail Grocer, 415 Cedar Avenue—Mr. Blichfeldt may very properly be said to have spent his lifetime in the grocery business, having been engaged in that occupation the past twenty-three years. The field of his operations have been Green Bay and other points in Wisconsin, from which State he came to this city in April, 1885, and at once established himself in his present location. His stock of groceries is the finest kept by any dealer on Cedar Avenue, and he does both a wholesale and retail business, the latter, however, being the principal trade. The class of retail custom controlled by this dealer is a very large and steadily increasing one, and the volume of his sales shows a gross business of several thousand dollars each month. Personally, Mr. Blichfeldt is a man of good business ability and tact. He is a native of Norway, but came to this country early in life, and is yet a man under middle age.

H. WESTIN, Merchant Tailor, 619 Nicollet Avenue—Mr. Westin was cutter for Rothschild's for a period of thirteen years, and has not long been in business for himself. He finds his business progressing favorably, and in fact all he could desire. He has a fine, clean stock of imported and domestic goods, from which any one should be able to select what they want for wear, whether coat, vest or pantaloons. He employs none but the very best workmen, and as he has had such a long and so important an experience as a cutter, and now does all his own cutting, he is able confidently to guarantee first-class work in every respect. Mr. Westin has had some insight into the rise in value of real estate. Though born in Sweden he has been in America for twenty-one years, and in Minneapolis for seventeen. In 1872 he could have bought lots on Nicollet Avenue for $1,500, for which two thousand dollars a foot is now refused. He has seen men who were then working for low daily wages rise up to be worth their hundreds of thousands.

EBEL & HUSSER, Wholesale and Retail Dealers in Hardware, Stoves and Tinware, 1301 Washington Avenue North—This is the largest hardware establishment in North Minneapolis, as well as one of the oldest. Messrs. Ebel & Husser purchased the business. Mr. Ebel was previously a contractor in plastering. Mr. Husser came here from Big Stone City, Dakota, where he conducted a large general merchandise store. The location of this store is very prominent, being located on the corner of the two leading streets of North Minneapolis. Their store is a substantial brick and occupies an area of 30 x 75 feet. In the rear is the shop, size 20 x 30. Here all the repairing and manufacture of tin and iron work is done. A stock of upwards of $10,000 is carried. This embraces stoves, tinware, shelf-ware, shovels, spades, carpenters' tools, paints and oils. The firm are also the special agents for h?fin?i? ?ii? ri?j?i. They also handle the Garland stove ranges. A force of competent clerks is employed, and two teams are required to deliver goods. Mr. Ebel is a native of Pennsylvania, and has lived in Minnesota for twenty-five years. Mr. Husser was born in Germany, but came to this country in 1855.

HENNEPIN AVENUE MEAT MARKET, E. V. Koessel, Proprietor, 413 Hennepin Avenue—A feast for the eye is a visit to this popular market. Here is to be found tastely arranged every variety of meat, poultry, fish, oysters, etc. Mr. Koessel thoroughly understands the business, and when he became proprietor of this market, December 20, 1888, he brought to the business a long record of success in other markets. For twelve years he was foreman of the "Our Brand" market—an evidence of his capability. He has built up a very large family trade, which is rapidly increasing. He also has a large trade among the best hotels and restaurants. Having been a resident of Minneapolis since 1874, he has a very wide acquaintance in the city. His references in business are his customers. Five men and four teams are now required to take care of wants of customers. He contemplates larger quarters soon, and is now putting in a complete equipment for the manufacture of all kinds of sausage. All smoked meats used by his trade are cured in his establishment. Mr. Koessel was born in Germany. He served with gallantry in the cavalry of the Eleventh Army Corps, during the entire Franco-German war. He was twice wounded. Soon after the termination of the war he came to Minneapolis, where he married. He is also a prominent member of the I. O. O. F., and is at present holding the position of Deputy Grand Patriarch for District Number Five, Schiller Encampment.

OLE ANDERSON, Groceries, 1801 Second Street North—This gentleman established this business March 8, 1889. He occupies a substantial two-story brick building, 22x66. This building he owns and it was built expressly for his business. Mr. Anderson has received much encouragement in his enterprise, and his efforts are being rewarded by rapidly increasing trade. He carries a complete stock of groceries, provisions, flour, crockery, fruits and vegetables. He also has a fine stock of canned goods, coffees and spices. Mr. Anderson has been a resident of this city since June 20, 1869, coming here direct from Norway. Previous to entering into the grocery business he was on the police force. Mr. Anderson is justly proud of his record while on the force.

WM. HOCHSTÆTTER & CO., Upholstery and Furniture, Steam Feather Renovator, 620 Nicollet Avenue—This standard house has a good business in this line, which they are steadily pushing to something above the ordinary run of such concerns. Mr. Hochstætter is a native of Germany, but has been here since 1871, and may therefore be classed among the pioneers of the place. He commenced his present business in 1875, and has now always on hand a nice, neat stock of furniture, well selected and purchased at the right price. This business occupies the space of two entire floors, where it is conveniently arranged for inspection. His trade has already reached the sum of $20,000 annually, and, as has been stated above, is steadily increasing. Another industry connected with this establishment is a steam feather renovator, which turns out some excellent work and is much in request. Mr. Hochstætter also possesses exceptionally good facilities for repairing and packing furniture.

E. H. BASS, Real Estate and Rentals, 323 Hennepin Avenue—Mr. Bass was born at Shakopee, his birth being remarkable, as he was the first white child who made its appearance there. He conducts a general real estate business. A great deal of the property which he handles is his own, but besides this he has a very extensive commission business, his list including some of the best residence property in the place. He is principally interested in Eighth Ward property, and makes a specialty of modern residences. He also conducts a collecting agency, collecting rents, taxes, etc., and taking care of property for non-residents and parties who do not wish for any reason to look after their own. In addition to this he does some loaning, principally for Eastern parties. He has control over property to the value of $130,900, the greater part of which belongs to himself. He has now been here about seven years, and has met with the success to which his energy and business ability entitle him. Correspondence solicited and references furnished.

W. C. LEBER, Dealer in Watches, Clocks and Jewelry—Mr. W. C. Leber, of No. 208 Hennepin Avenue, jeweler, is one of the most remarkable instances of the success which attends those who have the ability and courage to persevere through bad times and good times to make their fortunes. He came here in 1875 from Sheboygan, Wisconsin, and commenced business on Nicollet Avenue. About seven years ago he purchased the building, No. 208 Hennepin Avenue, where he now conducts his business. He is not ashamed to say that he commenced without any money; and is it not an honor to any man to be able to say, I have achieved something by careful attention to business, personal supervision and good work? If it be so, surely Mr. Leber deserves credit for what he has achieved. In addition to the fine building on Hennepin Avenue he is the owner of a beautiful residence and a farm of three hundred and ten acres near the city, well stocked and largely improved, for which he could get at least $125 per acre. For his residence he has already been offered $10,000; add to this his stock of jewelry, valued at $11,000, and there is a sum total of nearly sixty thousand dollars, all made in business since he has been here. This is without reckoning his large business, which, of course, is very valuable. He is the only jeweler in the city who constantly employs three watchmakers to repair watches and clocks. He has besides these two other assistants. Besides dealing in jewelry he is a manufacturer of jewelry of all kinds, and is agent for Rockford watches.

STANDARD STEAM LAUNDRY, Office and Laundry 104 and 106 Third Street North.—Mr. A. J. Humphrey is the proprietor of this laundry. He established the business in 1879. Mr. Humphrey was born in Ohio, but has been in Minneapolis for seventeen years. He is one of the 'wise men who

believe in the importance of looking after their business themselves and he accordingly takes an active part in the operations going on in his laundry. All the work is done by steam power, and better and more uniform and cheaper than by hand ; and he would give machinery the preference for this

MISSISSIPPI RIVER, BELOW RED WING, ON LINE OF C., M. & ST. P. R'Y.

reason, if there were no other, but he recognizes the impossibility of turning out anything like the same amount of work by hand at a given cost as could be accomplished by steam, and therein, of course, lies the great advantage. His laundry is fitted up with all the best modern appliances, and notwithstanding the enormous cost of first productions. His latest acquisitions consists of the famous Hagen & Myers' body ironers, used to iron the bodies of shirts, of which he has secured two; also his improved system for ironing collars and cuffs, including ladies' cape collars for which laundrymen have striven hard to secure, owing to the destructive element connected with the old system; altogether he aims to make the Standard in the future what it has been in the past, the most perfectly equipped steam Laundry in the city. It is a well-known fact that the work from this laundry has a certain softness and pliability which is never seen in the work of other establishments.

G. W. CRANE, 900 South Fourth Street, Engines and Boilers, Horse Powers, Etc—Mr. Crane was born in Ohio. In 1882 he came here and started this business. He deals in engines and boilers, both stationary and portable, horse-powers, extras for horse-powers, link-belting, drive-chain, sprocket-wheels, attachments and supplies, for saw mills and grain elevators, shafting, pulleys, couplings, boxes and hangers, mill and elevator buckets, elevator bolts, iron and wood boots; also rubber, leather and cotton belting, spiral conveyors, etc., steam pumps and Chicago standard scales. Mr. Crane has been associated with other parties in this business for a number of years prior to his commencing on his own account in 1887, and has a great amount of experience. Short as his time here has been he has secured a trade through this State, Dakota and the whole Northwest and Canada and Central Iowa, which is all the time steadily on the increase. He usually employs from thirty to thirty-five hands. His premises are very conveniently located and are quite extensive, being sixty-five feet on one street and 150 on the other. Mr. Crane is quite a young man and is making a brilliant success of his undertaking.

A. L. SUMP'S Lake Superior Meat Market, 117 First Street North—This is one of the best known markets in the city, as well as one of the oldest. It is the only long-established market in Minneapolis that has never changed its location. It was established in 1867 by the present proprietor. Mr. Sump has had a long and marked success. He owns the building which he occupies and which is fitted up with modern appliances. Probable there is no owner of a meat market in Minneapolis who is better posted on the wants of the people or who understands the business better than Mr. Sump. His trade is large among the families, hotels and restaurants. Mr. Sump personally supervises his business, and to this fact is due his reputation of carrying one of the finest stocks of meat in the city. His hams and bacon are cured in his establishment. There is also a complete sausage equipment, and all kinds of sausage are manufactured. Mr. Sump was born in Germany, but has been a resident of this country since 1852.

KENNEDY BROS., Mill Stuffs, Flour, Feed, Oil Meal, Baled Hay and Straw, 507 Plymouth Avenue—This firm was established in 1888. Their success has been marked and their trade is increasing rapidly from month to month. They are extensively engaged in other lines of business, also among which may be mentioned logging. This year they cut 1,000,000 feet and next winter they are expecting to cut not less than 5,000,000 feet. They also do considerable teaming about the city, and for that purpose employ twelve horses. They are proprietors of the valuable Kennedy farm, which is situated one-half mile west of the city limits. This farm was pre-empted by their father in 1854. Its increase in value is a marked evidence of the great increase in value of Hennepin County realty. The two oldest brothers were born in Aroostook County, Maine, but came here when children. Wm. Kennedy, the junior member of firm, was born in Minneapolis.

CHICAGO BAKERY, R. C. Miller, Proprietor, 253 First Avenue South—Mr. Miller, of the Chicago Bakery, is one of the happiest instances of business ability that the city affords. Mr. Miller was born in Burlington, Iowa. About five years ago he established the bakery and carried it on very successfully until about a year ago. He then sold out, but circumstances induced him to return to his old stand, and he found that the business was run down almost to extinction. One may judge of the extent to which this running down had gone, when it is stated that upon his resuming business, the first day's receipts only amounted to $1.80. He has had the place handsomely re-fitted and re-furnished, and the takings range from $50 to $70 a day, with increasing tendency. Twelve hands are employed, and there are turned out daily from 400 to 500 loaves, 60 to 100 pies, besides a host of crackers, cookies and other small fry, two men being constantly employed in cake-baking. Mr. Miller makes a specialty of German rye bread, his bakings being deservedly much liked. All his business is retail, and the strangest part of it is that it is all done in the store, no delivery wagon being employed except for the ice cream, of which Mr. Miller makes a large quantity in season. There is a nice, clean restaurant attached to the establishment, which is well patronized.

NEW ENGLAND MUTUAL LIFE INSURANCE CO., of Boston, Massachusetts, Richard H. Flagg, Gen'l Agent, 310, 311 National Bank of Commerce Building—An agency for this company

has been established in St. Paul for several years. It has now been divided so as to leave St. Paul the south half of the State, and Minneapolis the north half. The company itself is a very old one, and one that has deservedly gained the entire confidence of the public. It was established so far back as 1835. The peculiar features of the company are that they give on all their Life and Endowment Policies cash values, after two payments have been made, as well as paid up values, which are larger than those given by any other company, making the policy more desirable as insurance and collateral. There is absolutely no speculation in the system in vogue with this company, each year all the surplus is divided up among the policy-holders. The following is a sample of the cash and paid-up values, guaranteed by the company and laws of Massachusetts, and are written in the policy. Compare these values with any company:

AGE OF ISSUE, 33.—AGE OF MATURITY, 75.—AMOUNT, $10,000.—PREMIUM, $248.00.

Year	Cash-Surr Value.	Paid-up Insurance	Year.	Cash-Surr. Value.	Paid-up Insurance.	Year.	Cash-Surr. Value.	Paid-up Insurance.
2d	$ 90.90	$ 270	16th	$2,289.60	$4,590	30th	$5,437.70	$7,730
3d	222.00	610	17th	2,481.90	4,850	31st	5,710.30	7,920
4th	351.60	950	18th	2,678.60	5,110	32d	5,092.80	8,100
5th	485.40	1,270	19th	2,879.60	5,360	33d	6,286.70	8,290
6th	624.10	1,600	20th	3,085.50	5,600	34th	6,593.80	8,480
7th	767.70	1,930	21st	3,295.70	5,840	35th	6,916.00	8,660
8th	916.70	2,240	22d	3,510.00	6,070	36th	7,257.00	8,840
9th	1,070.90	2,560	23d	3,731.20	6,290	37th	7,620.50	9,020
10th	1,230.60	2,870	24th	3,950.50	6,510	38th	8,011.30	9,210
11th	1,395.50	3,170	25th	4,187.50	6,720	39th	8,435.60	9,400
12th	1,565.10	3,470	26th	4,424.30	6,930	40th	8,901.20	9,600
13th	1,739.60	3,760	27th	4,667.30	7,140	41st	9,418.40	9,800
14th	1,918.90	4,040	28th	4,916.90	7,340	42d	10,000.00	10,000
15th	2,102.10	4,320	29th	5,173.40	7,540			

WEST HOTEL LIVERY, BOARDING AND SALE STABLES, W. H. McCague, Proprietor, 24 Fifth Street North—One of the largest livery, boarding and sale stables in Minneapolis is that of Mr. W. H. McCague. This stable is located at 24 Fifth Street North, and occupies two floors of a building 100 x 165 feet. This stable has accommodations for 128 horses. So heavy is the patronage that the stables are nearly always filled. For his regular livery business, he ordinarily has from thirty-five to forty horses. His stock of carriages includes coupes, hacks, phaetons, buggies, English carts, etc. He makes a specialty of saddle horses, and, perhaps, leads any stable in the city in this line. The location of this stable gives it a popularity among horse owners, and as a result Mr. McCague does the largest business in boarding horses of any stable in the city. Sixteen men are constantly employed. The location is especially favorable to the guests of the West Hotel, being located directly opposite, so that teams are very quickly summoned. An order stand is maintained at the hotel. This stable was established in 1882. Mr. McCague became part owner in 1885. January 1, 1889 he bought out his partner's interest and is now the sole proprietor. He is a native of Illinois. He came to Minneapolis in 1884. For many years he devoted his exclusive time to the operation of a large stock farm that he owns in Clear Lake, Minn. He now owns 900 acres there, and raises horses and cattle in large numbers.

ENTERPRISE MACHINE CO., 423 and 425 Fourth Street South—The members of this company are Mr. G. D. Sampson, Mr. Wm. Kampff and Mr. C. H. Sampson. It was established in 1884 and Mr. Kampff joined in 1887. Both the Messrs. Sampson were born in the East and came here at the time they established this business. They do all kinds of repairing and manufacturing of special machinery. They employ about twenty hands, and their business is more on the outside than inside the city. The value of their plant is about $10,000. They have very commodious premises, 100x200 feet, and have a good solid business, which is increasing rapidly. In addition to his connection with the Enterprise Machine Company, Mr. C. H. Sampson, is interested with Mr. P. J. Wright, in the same city, in the manufacture of the Wright Valve File and Re-seating Tool. This impliment will in a few minutes repair the seat of globe and angle valves, both flat and taper, without removal from the pipe. When the seat of a valve has become imperfect it is such a waste of steam that the cheapest plan has hitherto been to discard it at once and substitute a new one for it. Now by this machine a perfect seat may be made, and if the brass disc does not work satisfactorily the firm furnish a new vulcanized rubber disc and brass disc holder which can be placed on the old stem, and all this can be done at a trifling cost. It will probably not be long before every engineer in the land will be provided with one of these machines, and they will be almost as commonly used as a monkey wrench.

GOETZENBERGER & WANGSNES, Dealers in Stoves and Hardware, House Furnishing Goods, Oils, Paints and Glass, 605 Cedar Avenue—One of the distinctions enjoyed by this house is that it is the oldest establishment of its class to be found on Cedar Avenue; but it must not be inferred from this the place is otherwise lacking in importance for the very opposite is the truth. The store is well stocked with goods in its line, including stoves, ranges, and house furnishing goods, general and builders' hardware, mechanics' tools and cutlery, paints, oils, glass, nails, putty, painters' and glaziers' supplies, etc. Tin and sheet iron work and jobbing is also done, and a general line of household tinware manufactured. J. J. Goetzenberger and O. S. Wangsnes compose the firm, and they are both young men who went into business immediately on their arrival here six years ago. The first is a native Minnesotian and the second claims Wisconsin as his birth-place. The number of men employed in their establishment is an average of five.

DORAN & LAMBERT, Dealers in Groceries and Provisions, Glass and Crockery Ware, 529 Cedar Avenue—Established so lately as 1885, this grocery house has already grown to be one of the best patronized and most important trade emporiums in this section of the city. The proprietors of the store, Messrs. J. W. Doran and O. M. Lambert, devote their whole time and attention to the business, are both practical and experienced grocers and well acquainted in the city, the first having resided here the past sixteen years and the latter since 1882. They are both comparatively young men, active, enterprising and energetic, and they carry a line of choice, select groceries, delicacies and table luxuries, teas, coffees and spices, crockery and glassware, equal to every demand of their customers, and of such superior quality as to be unexcelled. The firm was at first Doran & McDermott, which condition prevailed until last year, when Mr. Lambert succeeded to the interests of the junior member of the original partnership. Mr. Doran is an Ohioan by birth, and Mr. Lambert was born on alien soil, the Dominion of Canada being the place of his nativity.

JAMES ELWIN, Cigar Manufacturer, 418 Hennepin Avenue—The accompanying cut represents one of Minneapolis' most prosperous young business men, James Elwin, the manufacturer of the celebrated "All Stock and No Style" cigars, and wholesale dealer in tobaccos at 418 Hennepin Avenue.

Mr. Elwin has been a resident of Minneapolis about seven years, coming here from Broooklyn, N. Y. When a mere boy he embarked in the cigar business, beginning at the foot of the ladder. By perseverance and strict attention to business he has steadily worked his way up until he has now one of the largest factories in the city, and in the State about the third or fourth largest. By doing a strictly cash business he is enabled to make a clear Havana-filled cigar that can be sold for five cents, and his returns to the government show his business to have increased during the past year fully 100 per cent. His most popular cigars are "All Stock and No Style" for five cents, warranted a clear Havana filler, and his "Elwin's Best," a 10-cent cigar, made of the finest and most expensive Havana tobacco that can be bought. His store, at 418 Hennepin Avenue, also shows him to be one of the largest jobbers of tobacco in the city. He keeps two wagons in the city and one in St. Paul to attend to his many customers, besides his force of employes under the management of Philip Duttenhoefer, an able and courteous gentleman. Mr. Elwin will have an exhibit at the Exposition this year, showing his whole force of manufacturers at work making his famous brands of cigars, just how they are manipulated, the grade of stock used, and all about the production of a first-class cigar.

MINNEAPOLIS PAPER BOX CO., Frank Heywood & Co., Proprietors, 121 and 123 Washington Avenue North—This is the only paper box factory in Minneapolis, and it is no exaggeration to say that it is a most deserving and popular institution. It was founded April, 1882, by the present owners, and the head of the firm, Mr. Frank Heywood, became one year later a member of the partnership of Fisher & Heywood, who opened a similar factory in St. Paul, the location of which is now corner East Fifth and Robert Streets. About twenty-five hands are employed in the factory here, and nearly as many in the one at St. Paul. All kinds of paper boxes are made, and the best and most perfect machinery and equipment for the successful turning out of such articles is to be found in the factories. The floor-space occupied in Minneapolis alone is 12,000 square feet. The members of this firm are Massachusetts men and have only lived in Minnesota since they went into business here.

WILSON & SULLIVAN, Livery, Sale and Boarding Stable, 20 Second Street North—No city in the country has more, if as many, beautiful drives as Minneapolis. As a result, the livery business is of enormous proportions. This firm does probably the largest business of any stable in the city. It has reached such proportions that they have recently established a branch at 80 Ninth Street South.

They keep one hundred or more horses constantly. Their stables are very commodious, the main stable being 50x210, two stories, and the branch 40x125. Their stock of carriages embraces coupes, victorias, phaetons, English dog carts, etc. They have recently purchased five new hacks. They make a specialty of family trade, and their stock embraces trusty family and saddle horses. The deserved success of their business has been the result of careful attention and thorough knowledge of the livery business. They employ twelve men in their two stables. They also do a very large boarding business, and their stables are the home of many of the horses of our professional and business men. In addition to the livery business they carry on a large sale business. They supply by contract all the street railways of Minneapolis, St. Paul and Duluth. About two thousand head of horses are annually handled. Mr. M. D. Wilson established this business in 1879. He is a native of La Porte, Ind., and has been in the livery business nearly all his life. Mr. E. E. Sullivan is also a native Indianian, and became a partner November 1st, 1888, coming here from Cokeville, Wyoming.

KINNE & BOYD TRANSFER COMPANY, 47 Washington Avenue South—In any branch of business reliability and honesty are prime requisites in building up a business and becoming

established in a city as desirable citizens. Messrs. Kinne and Boyd here built up their large transfer business on this principle in a year and a half, and have proved its truth. They own first-class teams and outfits and employ none but reliable men, who must come recommended for honesty and carefulness, and by so doing they make their patrons feel that an order left with them will be attended to

RESIDENCE, BARNS AND WOOD YARD OF KINNE & BOYD.

properly and as ordered. The business has increased from one team to sixteen horses, and more will be added soon. They attend to all kinds of transferring, making a specialty of moving household goods. They manage a wood yard at 3136 First Avenue South, where are located their barns for the accommodation of their teams and wagons. By running regular trips twice daily they can carry parcels cheaper than regular rates. Their office, with telephone connection, is at 47 Washington Avenue South, where they will attend to all business entrusted them.

HARRISON'S Variety Store, 111 Nicollet Avenue and 2605-2607 Stevens Avenue—This representative house was established by Mr. Harrison, the present proprietor, in 1884. The original house was opened at 2605 and 2607 Stevens Avenue, where he still continues, and where the headquarters are still located. The branch, at 111 Nicollet Avenue, was opened only last June, but is already receiving a good patronage. A stock of goods is carried in the three stores aggregating $26,000 in value, and the annual amount of trade is very large, extending throughout the city generally. An ample force of people is employed in the various branches of the business, and is now looked upon as one of the most thriving concerns in the Flour City. Mr. Harrison sells his goods for cash at bottom prices, and sells both on the installment plan and for cash, and can always offer bargains in crockery, glassware, hardware, stoves, ranges, furniture and carpets, besides an endless variety of goods in the five and ten-cent line, for which branch he has special counters. Mr. Harrison in a native of Clarke County,

Illinois, and has now been a resident of Minneapolis for some years, and has the utmost faith in the future of the city and the Northwest generally. All in all, this is a standard house and one well worthy of the large patronage it is receiving.

THE GRAND OPERA HOUSE. J. F. Conklin, Manager—This very fine building was erected by a syndicate of wealthy Minneapolis gentlemen. The interior of the house is handsomely decorated

and it is one of the most beautiful and at the same time most comfortable houses in the country. This is especially true since its elaborate redecorating and remodeling during the present summer by Mr. J. S. Bradstreet, whose taste in this instance marks him a master-hand at his work, and old patrons of the house will hardly recognize the place. It is certainly now one of the most beautiful interiors west of New York. The seating capacity is 1,400. Mr. Oscar Cobb was the architect and the building in every respect does him credit. The public, and particularly the lovers of the drama, are much indebted to the very able manager, Mr. J. F. Conklin, for the manner in which he has conducted the business entrusted to to him. In inducing him to take the office upon himself the syndicate displayed much sound judgment, for verily he is the right man in the right place. No paltry performance has ever been allowed to lower the reputation of this house. The highest class of entertainment is what Mr. Conklin will ever permit to be given there, and the fact that a play is going to be represented at the Grand is sufficient recommendation of its quality and merits. Mr. Conklin was formerly assistant manager of the Academy of Music, and having exquisite taste as a musician would allow only the best class of performance. He has adopted the same plan since he has had the management of the Grand

Opera House and with the happiest results, as already indicated. He also manages the affairs of the whole Syndicate Block. Mr. Charles Parker fills the onerous position of treasurer of the house and in that capacity has distinguished himself by the admirable manner in which he has conducted the duties of his office.

NORTHWESTERN MARBLE WORKS, J. M. Donlin & Co., 110 Fourth Street South—This is a standard business in this line, and was established by Edward Donlin, the firm as now composed being a successor to him. It is one of the oldest establishments in its line in the city, and they now do one of the best trades in the line of marble monuments, gravestones and other memorial work. The firm make a specialty of monumental work, and many specimens of their taste in this line can be seen in their rooms and through our finest cemeteries. The prices of J. M. Donlin & Co., for good work, are as low as can be quoted, and they have done much fine work for some of the most prominent people in Minneapolis and throughout the Northwest.

WARREN HILL, Manufacturing Chemist and Perfumer, 609 First Avenue South—That Mr. Hill is a skillful chemist in this department no one will question, after a visit to his establishment and a trial of his exquisite goods. He has ample and very complete facilities for the manufacture of handkerchief extracts, toilet waters, sachet powders, and in fact every thing in his special line. One of the most popular and pleasing odors made by Mr. Hill is the famous Nile Lily, which now has an immense sale, as also the Nile Lily toilet soap, which is without an equal for purity and delicacy of perfume. Beside the Nile Lily Mr. Hill also makes a full line of all the standard and popular odors, and is the only manufacturer of the kind in the Northwest. Dealers can rely on getting as fine goods, and at as low prices here, as from any manufacturer in the United States. These perfumes now have an extensive sale from this point to the Pacific Coast, besides in a large radius both North and South, and are considered by dealers as among the very best on the market. Mr. Hill has been in the business since 1882, and was originally from the East, coming here from Boston, Mass. A price list for any goods in his line will be cheerfully furnished on application.

S. OVERMIRE, Real Estate and Loans, 255 Temple Court—Mr. Overmire is a long-experienced operator in real estate, having been in the business for upwards of fifteen years. He was formerly in Decatur, Ill. He came to this city in 1882, and carried on business with a partner, Mr. Pearson, under the firm name of Pearson & Overmire for about three years; since then Mr. Overmire has been conducting the business alone. He handles all kinds of business property, suburban and acre lots and farm property in this State and Dakota, also Lake Minnehaha property. The firm platted two additions in the city—Nicollet and Illinois additions. Mr. Overmire handles his own property and also the property of others on commission. He has always done a general real estate business from the start. He also does loaning on real estate security to some extent. Mr. Overmire now has an extensive list of properties of all kinds, and his long experience in the business and fair dealing have secured him the confidence of a large circle of friends.

C. R. DICKENS, Dealer in Horses, 417 and 419 First Avenue North—This gentleman came to Minneapolis in 1881, and established the West House Stables. In 1887 he sold out his interest, and in 1888 he built his present commodious stable, and entered extensively into the sale business. In this venture he has been successful. Since coming to Minneapolis he has sold upwards of 4,500 horses. He handles all classes of horses and mules, and makes a specialty of fine stock. He has obtained a high reputation for honorable dealings, and his references comprise the leading business men of Minneapolis. He guarantees every animal sold as represented. His capital is ample, and he is enabled, when necessary, to advance money on stock. He boards also many horses. He also has the contract to convey all the mails to and from the post-office of this city. He is a native of Edgar County, Ill He has been engaged in the horse business for over twenty years.

P. G. HANSON, Dealer in Staple and Fancy Groceries, Meat Market 404, Grocery 406, Second Avenue South—The business success of this gentleman is a most striking example of what energy and strict attention to business will accomplish. Commencing business in 1877 with a capital of but $30, and a high reputation for honesty, Mr. Hanson so availed himself of circumstances that he is now doing a business of $100,000 annually. His business gives employment to from fourteen to seventeen hands. Sixteen are required to attend to the large order business. He has been in his present location for three years. For nine years he was at 1304 Fifth Street South. Here he occupied a small store, and at the outset of business, he and his brother with no teams, comprised the entire force. At his present location he occupies the first floor and basement of a building 44x80. One-half the building is devoted to his grocery business, where he carries a very complete stock of staple and fancy groceries, dairy products, fruits and confectionery. To make his establishment even more complete he, in 1887, purchased the meat market adjoining his grocery establishment. Here is to be found one of the most complete markets in the city. All kinds of meat, fish, oysters, game in season, are sold. Mr. Hanson's trade is of a permanent character. He believes in the Golden Rule in business as well as in other walks of life. Mr. Hanson was born in New York City, but his boyhood was passed on a farm in the "Nutmeg" State. He has been a resident of Minneapolis since 1877. His brother grocers honored him in 1888, by electing him President of the Retail Grocers' Association for that year.

NORTHWESTERN MEAT MARKET, Wm. H. Wittey, Proprietor, 214 Fifteenth Street South—This popular market is conducted by a man who thoroughly understands the meat business. Mr. Wittey established this market in 1883, coming here from Chicago, where he had been engaged in the same business. Mr. Wittey is a veteran in the business and has been in it twenty-nine years. His success in Minneapolis has been marked, and he is now doing nearly $2,000 per month business. This spring numerous improvements have been made, and there is not now a neater or more orderly market in the city. Three men and three teams are given employment. Mr. Wittey caters entirely to family trade and carries only the better grades of meat, such as his trade requires. He carries in stock fish, ham, bacon, sausage, game and poultry in season.

SIMPSON & HENDERSON, Men's Furnishing Goods, 309 Nicollet Avenue—The firm of Simpson & Henderson, dealers in men's furnishing goods, now located at 309 Nicollet Avenue, next door to the Loan and Trust Building, is the oldest firm in the Northwest, and, perhaps, the best known in the State of Minnesota. They started in business seventeen years ago under the name of Fuller & Simpson. They carried on the business until the year 1881, when R. R. Henderson purchased the interest of Mr. C. A. Fuller. The style of the firm since has been Simpson & Henderson. Their business has grown as the city has developed, and no establishment anywhere has a better record. They have the best wishes and patronage of this community, and their word is as good as their bond. Messrs. R. Dunlap & Co., the famous hat manufacturers, selected Simpson & Henderson as their sole agents to sell and control their hats in this city. They handle the finest grades of all goods in their line. Fisk, Clark & Flagg's neckwear, gloves, suspenders, and Holroyd's underwear, besides a large line manufactured in this and foreign countries. They are the only manufacturers of chamois underwear and men's chest protectors in the Northwest, and it is said by importers of chamois skins that they are the largest manufacturers west of the Alleghany Mountains. Their goods in this line are known from Maine to California, as they ship to all the leading cities in the Union. Besides their men's furnishing business, they are the proprietors of one of the largest and best laundries in the city. They do good work, and their wagons, collecting laundry work, go to every street and number in the city. They take great pride in their business, and as citizens and manufacturers Simpson & Henderson are known as pushing, progressive men, and take a great interest in and give a hand to every project that develops the city in which they have lived so long.

BOWEN'S Livery and Boarding Stable, No. 7 Royalston Avenue—This stable has been conducted for some years. Mr. F. R. Winston was proprietor for two years. June 1st Mr. A. J. Bowen, of Jamestown, N.Y., and his son, Mr. G. C. Bowen, leased this stable. Mr. A. J. Bowen was for many years engaged in carriage making in the city of Jamestown. His son has been in the livery business all of his life and thoroughly understands all departments of it. Their stable is one of the neatest and most commodious in the city. The main stable is two stories high and 24x146 feet. The L. is sixty feet long and two stories high. The equipment is entirely new and first-class throughout. Their stock of carriages includes hacks, phaetons, single and double rigs. Including boarders, they now care for thirty three horses and are prepared to take more. To owners of horses they invite inspection of their stable and guarantee first-class treatment of horses and carriages. A competent force of men are employed. They also do horse-clipping by power.

LAKE FLOMME DRIVE ST. P., M. & M. R'Y.

Their intention is to have the best stable in their part of the city, and judging from the present appearance of their stable, their expectations will be fulfilled.

MIDDLEMIST & EARLE, Dealers in Furnaces, Stoves, Ranges, Etc., 100 Nicollet Avenue— This old land-mark among the business houses of the Flower City is one of the very oldest in the city, having been established so far back in the history of Minneapolis as 1856. Its originator was Charles F. Lucas. In 1866 it became Lucas Bros., in 1877 it changed to John T. Lucas, and in 1888 became Middlemist & Earle, this firm purchasing the business at that time. Mr. Middlemist was connected with the house for eighteen years prior to the time of becoming one of the proprietors of present firm, as foreman in charge of the manufacturing department of the house. Fifteen people are employed.

A stock of $16,000 to $18,000 is carried, and a yearly trade done aggregating from $75,000 to $80,000, which extends all over the city and the Northwest generally. A specialty is made of hot air furnaces, steel ranges and mill work. Boynton's celebrated furnaces are carried, and also Gold Coin and Born's steel plate French ranges, and they are also extensive manufacturers of sheet iron and tin work. Mr. Middlemist is a native of Michigan and Mr. Earle of Massachusetts, the former coming there in 1871 and the latter about 1877.

BADGER & SAWTELLE, Real Estate and Loan. 535 Temple Court—We take pleasure in calling the attention of the reader to one of our oldest and most reliable real estate firms, that of

Badger & Sawtelle (Walter L. Badger and J. P. Sawtelle), who are located at 535 Temple Court. Mr. Badger is an old resident and has been in the real estate business since 1882. Mr. Sawtelle came here from New York City about four years ago and engaged in the real estate business. His large acquaintance throughout the East among capitalists, with Mr. Badger's large acquaintance in the city as well as in the West, enables them to handle real estate to the advantage of all parties, either buying or selling. They buy or sell on commission or joint accounts. They are exclusive agents for several hundred thousand dollars worth of choice city property, besides other property throughout Minnesota and Dakota. They invite correspondence and will send list of references upon application.

THOMPSON & NORBY, Cash Grocers, 265 Cedar Avenue South—This retail grocery house was founded in 1881 by T. J. Anderson, the stock and business becoming the property of the present proprietors the past fall, when they bought Mr. Anderson out. They are both young, active business men, and natives of Norway, and have lived in Minneapolis about eight years. Personally, they are known as T. Thompson and John A. Norby, and the latter has been connected with the house almost from its earliest opening. The stock kept by the firm is a very good and strictly first-class one in every way, and they sell at reasonable and current prices—facts which account in a great measure for the rapid advancement of the trade of the house since its management and control passed into their enterprising hands.

F R WINSTON, Proprietor Oak Lake Livery and Boarding Stable, 18 Royalston Avenue— This gentleman has been identified with the livery interests of this city for about three years. For two and a half years he was located at No. 7 Royalston Avenue. His present stable is three stories high 50 x 100 feet in area. His stock is first-class; including boarders, he has now thirty-five horses. His equipment is first-class and comprises three hacks and a complete stock of single and double rigs. He caters to family trade, and at all times is ready to furnish family driving horses. He also makes a specialty of saddlers. Mr. Winston has done a constantly increasing trade, and now does easily the largest business in his part of the city. Three men are given constant employment. Mr. Winston came here twenty-two years ago from Illinois, his native state. His long residence here has built up for him an enviable reputation and he is justly proud of his business success.

M. H. CRITTENDEN, Manufacturer of Ornamental Sheet Metal Work for Buildings, 704-706 South Fifth Street. Mr. Crittenden is a native of Michigan, and has been in this business for upwards of twenty-five years. He manufactures all kinds of roofing in pitch and gravel, tin, iron, metal, shingle, slate and bodine; also every description of ornamental metal work for buildings. His specialty is ornamental copper work. He has lately manufactured a copper figure of Justice, twelve feet high, for the Court House at Mankato, which is a very excellent piece of workmanship in every respect. His trade extends all over the whole Northwest and is steadily on the increase. His workshops cover nearly the whole of a quarter-acre of ground and are fitted with the best plant in the Northwest. He employs from forty to sixty-five hands, nearly all of whom are the very best skilled mechanics. Mr. Crittenden gives his work the benefit of a personal supervision and that no doubt reflects a benefit upon himself by securing the confidence of all who have occasion to employ his talent.

THE BIJOU OPERA HOUSE. This popular house, formerly known as the People's Theatre, has been auspiciously opened under its new management, under a new name.   The whole of the interior

MISSISSIPPI RIVER BELOW WINONA, ON LINE OF C., M. & ST. P. R'Y.

of the theatre has been renovated and cleaned during the summer. The hangings and draperies have been changed, and the theatre looks as fresh and new as though it had just been opened for the first time. The lobby has been entirely refitted and is practically new. The finishings are in the Queen Anne style, while the floor has been freshly tiled and the walls prettily decorated with pictures appropriate to the Thespian art. The Bijou, under its former management, has always been one of the favorite resorts in the city, and the opening now was a good omen for its continued popularity. Heretofore it has been run as a stock company theater at popular prices, but from now on nothing but traveling attractions will be placed upon the boards, the company changing every week, and the prices remaining at the same figures as they always have been. The new lessee and manager is Jacob Litt, the well-known theatrical man of Milwaukee. Frank L. Bixby will be the local business manager and Theo. L. Hays, the son of the proprietor of the house, treasurer. This house has a seating capacity of about 2,000, and is one of the most comfortable and safest houses in the Northwest. Popular prices reign here and the highest class of opera, tragedy and comedy are placed before the people at prices enabling the masses to see the popular plays of the day. Jacob Litt, the lessee, is too well known to need comment, and Frank L. Bixby is about equally well known in his line as a peculiarly successful man at the helm, while Theo. L. Hays comes in for his full share in the success of the house.

EDSTEN & FOSS, Real Estate, Insurance, Loans and Steamship Line Agency, 408 Cedar Avenue—The senior member of this firm is an old citizen of Minneapolis, having come here twenty-two years ago from Chicago. In the fall of 1888 he associated with himself Adolph Edsten (his son) and Christian Foss, and established the firm of Edsten & Foss. This firm carry on an extensive business. They operate heavily in real estate in South Minneapolis, and have land for sale in Wisconsin, Minnesota, Dakota and Iowa. They buy and sell on commission. They are prepared to make loans at all times on real estate. They collect rents and attend to any kind of real estate sales. Mr. Adolph Edsten is a notary public. Among insurance companies they represent the "Syndicate," "Hekla" and "North British and Mercantile" companies. They sell tickets to and from Europe on all first class lines. Mr. A. H. Edsten is a prominent citizen of South Minneapolis, and at one time was alderman from the Tenth Ward. The members of the firm are all natives of Norway.

ALEX. MURRIE.
See page 60.

INDEX.

ILLUSTRATIONS.

CHEAP FUEL.

The Great Fuel Problem Solved at Last.

PETROLE, the wonderful invention, enables the manufacturer of the Northwest to successfully compete with the heretofore more fortunate resident of the East. Numerous tests of this fuel, made under every possible condition, have demonstrated to the entire satisfaction of scientific and practical men the superiority and economy of Petrole fuel over any known fuel; its advantages over coal are very important, because *complete combustion* is obtained and much less storage space is required. It also renders unnecessary most of the labor in handling coal and ashes. We utilize, as fuel, materials which heretofore have been treated as a useless waste, such as coal screenings, sawdust, lignite, peat, straw. etc., etc. These can be used with our Petrole Compound wherever any known fuel is burned for heating and manufacturing purposes, and can be profitably made in every county in America, with a remarkably small investment for machinery, etc.

This enterprise has commended itself to the leading capitalists wherever introduced, the interests of the company in the State of Minnesota being controlled and managed by well-known and representative citizens of Minneapolis, St. Paul and Duluth, who are now erecting extensive factories for its immediate production in their respective cities, and are now prepared to negotiate for the formation of local organizations throughout this State for its manufacture.

The cost of a complete outfit of machinery, exclusive of power, with a capacity of from 75 to 100 tons per day, is but $3,000. A plant with capacity of 50 tons daily will cost but $2,000.

Simple and inexpensive machinery will be furnished, enabling farmers and manufacturers to produce Petrole fuel for private use.

The Fuel Patents Co. has secured the sole rights of all the patents and machinery for Minnesota, and guarantees the validity of all the patents and processes.

The fuel can be produced and sold at a net profit of fully $1.50 per ton, giving the consumer the best fuel in the world at a saving of fully 25 per cent. over any known fuel. It has been burned here by thousands, and we have enough orders now on hand to keep the works here, in Duluth and St. Paul busy for months, besides holding many large orders from adjacent States.

We invite you to come here, when we will furnish all information desired; also, giving you an opportunity of seeing the fuel made, being satisfied we can show you the best investment offered in America.

A plant of a 100-tons daily capacity will earn $50,000 a year.

We append statement of tests, made in several cities, showing the value of Petrole fuel as compared with the best bituminous coal, to all of whom we refer.

P. H. KELLY MERCANTILE CO., St. Paul.   HOLMES HOTEL, Minneapolis.   NEWS OFFICE, Duluth.
CHALKER'S STONE WORKS, Minneapolis.   STEAMER "BARKER," Duluth.

Applications are coming in from all parts of the State, so we advise prompt action. Awaiting your pleasure,

We are respectfully yours,   **WALTER J. BALLARD, President.**
MAX NIRDLINGER, Vice-Pres't and Patentee.
HENRY P. LEOPOLD, Manager.

Main Office, 406 Lumber Exchange; Works, Fifth Street and Second Avenue N. E., Minneapolis, Minn.

CLIPPINGS FROM THE PRESS.

THE NEW FUEL.

A Test of Petrole To-Day—How It Is Made.

[From Minneapolis Evening Star May 3, 1889.]

The first public test of the new fuel, Petrole, was made before the Board of Trade members. At the foot of Laurel Avenue this morning, before the test took place, Mr. Nirdlinger explained the fuel and the material from which it is made. It can be manufactured from sawdust, peat, corncobs, straw, tanbark, coal screenings, and, in fact, anything that will absorb oil. The only other ingredients used are oil and petrole. This oil is the waste of the still, and is comparatively odorless and will not explode. Oil and either of the above mentioned absorbents constitute the fuel Petrole. It has been adapted to the wants of the Dakota farmer by using lignite coal as an ingredient. The process of manufacture is comparatively simple. The oil, etc., is first heated and together with the sawdust, or whatever used, is run into a mixing machine, where the two ingredients are thoroughly mixed. The proportion of oil and petrol used is about 25 per cent. After the mixing the material is carried to the floor above by a pocketed belt; it is then put into a chute, where it is deposited into the hopper of the depressing machine. This is a heavy machine, with a horizontal revolving table, in which there are a number of oval-shaped dies. Into these dies the material is dumped and receives an enormous pressure. The block is then pushed out and is ready for the stove. It takes about ten horse power to run this machine, and the capacity is sixty blocks per minute, or seven tons per hour.

These machines can be made of any capacity. The blocks can be shipped like bricks, as no amount of rough handling will break or crumble them. A machine for making this egg-size for boilers will be made.

Many prominent manufacturers were present at to-day's test, including C. A. Pillsbury, and they were well pleased with the test. Another test will take place to-night at the Holmes. This will be what is called an evaporated test, and will be conducted by the National Board of Engineers. Mr. McMillan, the secretary of the board, E. E. Steele, the vice-president, and A. Bement, representative of "The Engineer," of Chicago, will be present. The test will be made under the Holmes' boilers, E. E. Steele, who is a practical engineer, will run his boilers for one hour with thirty pounds of Petrole, which take eighty pounds of coal for the same time.

[From the Minneapolis Tribune May 18, 1882.]

At the Holmes Hotel, in Minneapolis, occurred a practical evaporative test of this wonderful invention. The test was made by several expert engineers, officers of the National Association of Stationary Engineers, and in the presence of gentlemen who reside in Minneapolis, and in adjoining States, who came to Minneapolis to investigate the subject.

The boiler under which the fuel was tested is of the Haxton make, and supplies a sixty horse-power engine. Nine hundred pounds of the Petrole fuel kept the engine in operation five (5) hours, from 7 to 12 P. M. The average consumption of coal during the same period is one ton, or 2,000 pounds, it being the time when the two elevators are busiest, and four hundred (400) incandescent lamps are burning. It burns freely, makes an intense heat, is clean and compact to handle, and burns without leaving clinkers or other objectionable refuse.

A GOOD TEST.

[From Duluth Tribune May 15, 1882.]

The following is the statement of the engineer and master of the Steamer Barker in regard to their test of the Petrole fuel yesterday forenoon:

H. F. Leopold, Manager Petrole Fuel Company—We desire to state that we have made a test of your Petrole fuel on the Steamer S. B. Barker, on May 14, 1889, a run on Lake Superior, with the following results: An engine 16½ by 18 and boiler of about 60 horse-power. We used 300 pounds of Petrole fuel in one hour and thirty minutes, giving from 50 to 70 pounds of steam. We ordinarily use 900 pounds of soft coal per hour. While this showing is a great saving of fuel, we could have obtained better results from your fuel with a slight alteration of the fire-box. We find that it gave a minimum amount of smoke, and there was a great saving in handling of the fuel, with almost no ash.

EDWARD MOUNIER, *Engineer.*
C. O. FLYNN, *Master Steamer Barker.*

Witnesses:
DR. L. S. WALBANK.
F. H. HANNARD.
R. E. PATTERSON, *Engineer Board of Trade.*

www.ingramcontent.com/pod-product-compliance
Lightning Source LLC
Chambersburg PA
CBHW032006010726
47493CB00007B/2297